Praise for
The Secret Papers of Madame Olivetti

"I thoroughly enjoyed this wise, witty, sensuous exploration of a woman looking back over her rich and complex life."

—Lisa Tucker, National Bestselling Author
of *Once Upon a Day* and *The Cure for Modern Life*

The Secret Papers
of Madame Olivetti

Annie Vanderbilt

NAL
ACCENT

New American Library
Published by New American Library, a division of
Penguin Group (USA) Inc., 375 Hudson Street,
New York, New York 10014, USA
Penguin Group (Canada), 90 Eglinton Avenue East, Suite 700, Toronto,
Ontario M4P 2Y3, Canada (a division of Pearson Penguin Canada Inc.)
Penguin Books Ltd., 80 Strand, London WC2R 0RL, England
Penguin Ireland, 25 St. Stephen's Green, Dublin 2,
Ireland (a division of Penguin Books Ltd.)
Penguin Group (Australia), 250 Camberwell Road, Camberwell, Victoria 3124,
Australia (a division of Pearson Australia Group Pty. Ltd.)
Penguin Books India Pvt. Ltd., 11 Community Centre, Panchsheel Park,
New Delhi - 110 017, India
Penguin Group (NZ), 67 Apollo Drive, Rosedale, North Shore 0632,
New Zealand (a division of Pearson New Zealand Ltd.)
Penguin Books (South Africa) (Pty.) Ltd., 24 Sturdee Avenue,
Rosebank, Johannesburg 2196, South Africa

Penguin Books Ltd., Registered Offices:
80 Strand, London WC2R 0RL, England

First published by New American Library,
a division of Penguin Group (USA) Inc.

First Printing, October 2008
10   9   8   7   6   5   4   3   2   1

ACCENT   REGISTERED TRADEMARK—MARCA REGISTRADA

LIBRARY OF CONGRESS CATALOGING-IN-PUBLICATION DATA:

Vanderbilt, Annie.
    The secret papers of Madame Olivetti/Annie Vanderbilt.
        p. cm.
    ISBN 978-0-451-22527-6
    1. Americans—France, Southern—Fiction. 2. Psychological fiction. I. Title.
    PS3622.A592S43 2008
    813'6—dc22   2008005203

Set in Bembo
Designed by Alissa Amell

Printed in the United States of America

For Bill

Acknowledgments

This book was not written alone in an ivory tower. My love and appreciation to those who kept me company.

Colleen Daly, who taught me how to write, wielding a sharp, gentle, loving, critically astute and supportive red pen with which she marked up the many drafts of this manuscript.

Mary Alice Kier and Anna Cottle, my tigress agents at Cine/Lit, who believed in me with a ferocity and joy that all writers should be so lucky to experience.

Sunny Chen, who, never having met me, kept the flame of Madame Olivetti flickering.

Leslie Maksik, who metamorphosed from a good friend into a tenacious terrier committed to seeing this novel published.

Maria Chocolate and Pedro El Tigre, who provided unwavering love and support.

Elsie Aidinoff, Andy Newburg, and Olinka Hauser, who introduced me to old stone farmhouses on the Côte d'Azur.

Flo's Girls, who lovingly kept track of my mother's bobby pins, Kahlúa truffles, and Metamucil while I was typing away in the basement.

All my dear patient friends, who, never having read the manuscript, still supported me through the highs and lows of the creative process.

Ellen Edwards, who, as my inspired editor at NAL, had the brilliant thought that Madame Olivetti, not Lily Crisp, was the keeper of the secret papers.

Bill, who for forty years has kept perspective and balance alive in my life and still storms the ivory tower on a regular basis to maintain his, and my, sanity. *Abrazos y besos.*

Love, all alike, no season knows, nor clime,
Nor hours, days, months, which are the rags of time.

—John Donne, "The Sun Rising"

Prologue

He comes to her in the evenings, after work. They make love and then talk, she in English, he in French, while beyond the open windows and doors of her bedroom the sky turns a lively pink, not unlike the color that flushes her cheeks.

"What will your mother be making you for dessert tonight? Chocolate pots de crème?" she wonders. "Or something less sweet . . . Perhaps a tart of quince and sour lemons?"

He grins, uncomprehending, a simple man who asks for nothing more than the generosity of her body and the lazy postcoital murmur of her voice speaking to him in a language he does not understand.

"I am feeding you my life," she tells him. "In heaping spoonfuls."

He groans, aroused and hungry, as if her words are a feast of exotic dishes she has set before him.

Below them, in the village, in a neat stone house that overlooks the sea, his mother is preparing dinner. She suspects that Yves is up the hill with the American widow, but she cares only enough to punish him in small ways: a bitter smile when he compliments her on the tarte au poire she has made for his dessert; a hostile arm's length between them when she kisses the air, not his cheeks, to wish him good night.

It is seven p.m. when Yves turns his truck up the rutted gold-dust road to Lily's house. It is eight thirty when he rumbles past the news vendor's shop, headed for home. The villagers watch but say nothing, for Yves is one of their own. So, too, is Lily, and it is no one else's business. This is nothing new. There have been plenty of sexual goings-on in La Pierre Rouge, the house of the red stone, over the past century.

"You'll be late," Lily warns, this time in French.

"*I don't care.*"

She reminds him gently, "*She is your mother. You live in her house. You must think of her dignity.*"

"*I think of this.*" He caresses her breast and the smooth inward slope of her thigh. Sex for them is a healing unguent, liberally applied but short term and, thus, light on the soul.

"*Quickly then . . . ,*" she says.

Twenty minutes later, rattling through town in his old Deux Chevaux truck, Yves waves at the news vendor's wife. Frowning, she points at her watch. It is almost nine o'clock. For the first time in years he will be late for dinner. The thought flits through Yves's mind: the grumpiness of Madame Bibot must sour the flavor of her husband's dinner. He toots his horn to try to cheer her up, but he is thinking of Lily. He is wondering what is the story of her life, unaware that he has heard every word of it.

She has fed it to him, in English, in heaping spoonfuls.

One

*L*ily Crisp was aware of the whispers that heralded her arrival in the village, the eyes peeping out from behind half-closed shutters and starched lace curtains. She trusted that the whispers carried only kind feelings toward her and her family, although, as she drove through the center of town, she noticed the news vendor and his scowling wife locking up their shop for the evening. Now there was a woman who shunned goodwill, Lily thought. Madame Bibot was probably remarking that Madame Crisp looked unreasonably vibrant and healthy for a widow. Monsieur Bibot, who had a wandering eye, though he tended toward women more buxom and Germanic than Lily, would doubtlessly have said something to enflame his wife, some nonsense about Lily's skin glistening with the sheen of sorrow, which adds luster to a woman's complexion. Or how Lily and her husband had made a fine couple and, with their two children, such a happy family. The fairy tale of familial happiness no longer charmed Madame Bibot. In fact, glancing in the rearview mirror, Lily saw that the news vendor's wife was glaring at her husband. Monsieur Bibot was gesturing boldly, perhaps attempting to calm the waters by suggesting that grief had certainly aged Lily Crisp. She must be ... what? On the near side of fifty?

"On the far side," Madame would be replying tartly, and Lily smiled because she knew that Madame's assessment of Lily's age, and Lily's assessment of Madame's response, were both on target.

Lily had visited the village most summers over the past twenty years. At first she had come with her husband, Paul, and her son, Pierre. Paul had seldom stayed more than a week—he was busy with his cows, gainful employment of which the villagers approved. This was something they could understand: livestock, hard work, and commitments. His concern for his herd of cows in a land called Idaho, reportedly filled with snakes and dried bushes, balanced the polite awe in which they had always held him, for he was a wealthy man, had inherited money, unlike his mother, who had been born in the village, not a penny to her name; but with that saucy beauty, who needed a fortune? She had married one.

Lily remembered those early visits, spending a month at the house that Paul had inherited, reading to Pierre under a plane tree or walking down the hill to the beach with his hand clasped in hers, building sand castles, splashing in the sea, setting up an umbrella to protect her son's fair skin from the burning rays, then dragging their weary, salt-sticky bodies back up the hill to shower in a dribble of rust-colored water. Pierre had been in his teens when Lily had presented him with a baby sister. The next summer there had been no shortage of raised eyebrows and knowing smiles—sixteen years and Paul Crisp, still busy between the sheets, and potent!—when this beautiful child, with her startling blue eyes and corn-silk hair, had turned up in the village.

Was it only two years ago, Lily mused, when the four of them had been sitting on the beach in folding chairs and Justine, aged seven then, had asked her father, "What's the name of the water out there, Daddy? What do you call it?"

"Lily's Lily Pond," he had told her.

"Lily's Lily Pond," she had chimed in with him, and, crawling onto his lap, had squirmed into position with her back against his chest, straddling his knees. He had wrapped her up in his arms and set his chin on the top of her silky blond head, and the two of them—one dark-haired, one light—had gazed at the sea, limpid and pale, bleached to the blue of the faded blue sky.

Justine had asked, "Is that because Mom floats her dreams on it?"

"Absolutely. On blow-up hippos and walruses."

"And dragons?"

"And elephants."

"Do the dreams ever fall off—like little girls?" she had said, in a hushed voice.

"Never ever," her father had assured her.

Lily had put down the book she was reading, smiled over at them, and asked, "Shall we run down to the sea and float with my dreams?"

"Oh, yes, Daddy, can we?" Justine had cried, and he had scooped her up and carried her, squealing with delight, across the sand, to where he sailed her back and forth, belly down and arms extended, over the water. Justine had whooped and yelled for her brother, Pierre, to come and see her, she was flying, she was flying like an angel. . . .

Squinting through the windshield, Lily returned her thoughts to her driving and swore softly as her rental car, its engine grinding, lurched up the gold-dust road to her house. Midway up the hill, the car stopped with a judder, then charged ahead in a great jump and shuddered. "Don't die on me," she threatened, calling down the wrath of the gods on this cursed Peugeot the color of a turnip. It jolted forward, up and over a ledge that scraped the oil pan. "Think light," she urged as the vehicle swerved into the driveway and halted abruptly. She cut the engine.

Relief washed over her, and, in the silence that followed, she could almost hear the ebb and swirl of the profound exhaustion that engulfed her limbs. Here at last she could sleep. Here at last she could sort through her memories and write them down, let in air and light and tidy the clutter of a scattered life.

Somewhere nearby a dog was barking. She glanced around her. It was growing late, the sky's mauve glow having faded into blackness. Yet, the sun's warmth lingered. Heat enfolded her body as if she had been wrapped up in moist leaves and shunted into an oven. The air trembled, garnering each whiff of moisture that trailed up from the resting sea. She fanned her skin, cooling the sweat that had rolled down her thighs, her shoulders, and dampened her armpits. Not surprisingly, her temples throbbed. She had drunk a full bottle of wine with dinner; it had gone down like water, in great cooling gulps that, afterward, had made her head spin and her mouth grow sticky.

Nighttime was when the sadness assailed her. The pall of loss spread over her then, like a cloth dipped in ashes and smoothed across her skin. She had felt smothered at first, as though if she struggled the sorrow might do greater damage than slow the beating of her heart or interrupt her dreams. But drinking with grief as one's sole companion was not a pastime she intended to pursue; although it blunted the sadness, it brought down an early curtain on the evenings, and there would be thirty-eight evenings until her children's visit. Self-imposed, she might add. *Her* choice to come here, to the south of France, to La Pierre Rouge, the old stone house on a hill above the sea that would be her refuge.

For one moment, before hefting her luggage from the back-seat of the car and carrying it to the house, Lily closed her eyes, thought about Paul, and let the fragrant air of the Côte d'Azur drift through her.

All night long the dog barked, fretful barks followed by a precarious silence in which she heard the wind, its soft breath hot as a lover's kiss on the plane tree leaves beyond her window. Hours after midnight, when she opened her eyes and the darkness that embraced her was more sensuous even than the weight of sleep, she remembered creeping into the shelter of Paul's arms.

She had never had far to creep, for he had liked to feel her near him. Their bed was a narrow double, and Paul's leg, thrust out to the side, often pinned her ankles. She would nudge his thigh, and, at her touch, he would sigh as if a forest maiden had entered his dreams and laid a hand where he most wished she would. His body would sometimes respond with a quick, hard thrust into the mattress and she would laugh aloud. She laughed now at the memory, so alive and tactile that she could almost feel the mattress jiggle and the cozy, bearish heat of him.

Paul had died in Idaho, quickly, and with their son, Pierre, unhurt beside him. Lily pictured the two men sitting quietly in Paul's truck, tired, driving back to the ranch in the cold November rain and listening to the radio. Men at ease in each other's company. Men with dark, curling, unkempt hair and thick black eyebrows that met in the middle over strong French noses. There were five ducks in the cooler behind the seat, "three greenheads and a couple of teal," she remembered the officer had said. They had shot five ducks, only five, and were driving home to shower, shave, and meet her for lunch. They were to celebrate her fifty-first birthday.

Justine, almost eight then, was perched on the countertop beside her in the kitchen. She was cutting out cookie-dough figures, punching silver balls into the turkeys' eyes and the pilgrims' bellies. Lily was opening the letter that had been lying on the kitchen table since the mail had been delivered earlier that morning. She had been saving it—savoring the opening, the reading, the learning about Monsieur Dupré's wonderful stay in the old stone house on the French Riviera. Another glorious September, she supposed. Another glamorous, unknown, unmentioned companion whose dark perfume would linger in the sheets, and whose black silk panties would lie forgotten under the red couch or in a clump of lavender, leading her to speculate, once again, about their renter. What books had he read this past September, and which one would she find—had he left for her—on the long wooden table? Which wines—red or white? from Burgundy? Bordeaux?—had he drunk with his meals, and how many bottles would there be—his gift—when she peeked next summer into the stone-dark *cave*? Six, no doubt. Punctilious and dependable, he always left six. Just as every July for the past eight years he had sent a check in advance of his stay. Just as every November he had written a thank-you note couched in superlatives.

Monsieur Dupré was their only renter.

She had just extracted his letter from the envelope when the doorbell rang. "I'll go, Mom," Justine had said brightly as she jumped down from the counter, where her gamin's legs, in shorts in November, had been swinging. The announcement of death had come just that swiftly: Justine's legs swinging and her swinging blond hair as she hurried to the door, opened it, and was asked by the officer, who would later mention the ducks in the cooler, if her mother was in.

"Just a minute," Justine had replied, her smile widening. "She's right behind me, and Daddy'll be home soon. Did you come for Mom's birthday party?"

The policeman had taken off his hat and held it awkwardly in both hands. "No, I didn't," he'd said.

Lily had come up behind her daughter and run her hand over Justine's silky hair, so pale it appeared white in an unexpected shaft of sunlight that lanced through the open door. "Can I help you?" she'd said, and then reading the discomfort in the man's eyes, had put her hands softly on her daughter's shoulders and urged her around. "Why don't you run upstairs to my bedroom and bring me my shawl?" she said. "It's getting chilly."

But Justine had crumpled, with the shake of a muffled sob, against Lily's stomach, and Lily, who had begun to shiver, looked into the policeman's eyes and mouthed Paul's name over Justine's head. The man nodded.

"My son?" she said out loud.

"He's fine."

She had bitten into her lower lip to stop its trembling and held her daughter close, and her face had turned into a steely mask and her eyes had seemed sheeted in some black throbbing substance that slowly closed out the light. Something between a groan and a wail tore through her body, ripping her heart to pieces without making a sound. She had stared at the officer and Justine had snuffled, "Mom, what's wrong? When's Daddy coming home?" And Lily had lifted her daughter's delicate chin, tilted it upward, and looked down into her sparkling blue, tear-filled eyes. "Everything's going to be all right," she'd said. "Everything's going to be all right, Justine. Everything's going to be all right."

Lily crushed her knees against her chest and held on tight. This was pointless, all this suffering. Why revisit that moment? This was not why she had come here. This was not the story she intended to write, how her husband of twenty-six years had died after a modestly successful duck hunt, died instantly, at least she had that, and in peace beside their son. Or how Pierre had grabbed the wheel, grabbed it too late, and Paul, whose heart had already stopped beating, had died a second death, his neck broken, the truck smashed on the lava while the ducks in the cooler, dead as Paul, had sustained no injury. As if dying once were enough.

Impatient for sleep, for the night to end and the day to begin, Lily closed her eyes. As always he was there, behind her eyelids, a smudge of recollection more heat and shimmer than an actual man. She breathed in his chin, his mouth, his nose—*le nez*—Paul's heroic, proud, improbable, quintessentially French proboscis, and she smiled.

As she fell into sleep, the dog barked again.

Two

Seated at her desk, Lily shoved back the old portable Olivetti typewriter she had brought with her from Idaho. A few days had passed since the dog had kept her awake with its barking. Where was it now? Muzzled? Banished to the garage? Locked in a closet? Or—as she preferred to believe—tucked cozily under its owners' duvet?

Her writing had gone smoothly. The sea was her confidante. It smiled as the dawn raised a blush to its skin, a glass-calm surface that suddenly, between the moment Lily looked down at the page where she had been working and then up, sported a series of wrinkles. How quickly the wind came up in the mornings, as if pulled on a leash by the sun.

With more ease than she had expected, a routine was emerging. She wrote for an hour before it grew light, drank a small cup of coffee, then jogged down the hill through the village and along the beach, until she turned back to swim. There were few people about so early in the morning: an old man sweeping the streets; a merchant, yawning, bringing in boxes of peaches and courgettes; lights glowing in the baker's window; birds chitchatting above the sidewalks, before the tourists and the heat drove them into the oak woods and the oleander hedges. This was her favorite time of day; she fetched warm croissants and a baguette as she swung back through town, then trudged up the hill, ate a leisurely breakfast, and continued to write.

From time to time she lost her concentration. The sea changed its moods and coloration as often as a French coquette: now the sun slapped its cheeks with a brassy, gold-flecked rouge; now scudding clouds lay melancholy bands across its forehead. The ravishing sight of water and sky, so vibrant a blue against orange tiled roofs and dusky green hillsides, offered her solace, pushed her to forget. She was easily distracted, enthralled by the view.

"Madame!" A man's voice bellowing up at Lily startled her out of her reverie. "Madame—"

"Je suis ici." I'm here, she called out. "Up here. I'm coming right down." She glanced quickly in the mirror, trying to pat her billows of red hair into shape—had she even bothered to comb it that morning? When the writing and memories took hold of her, she forgot to drink and eat, or brush her teeth. The day before she had bundled her hair on top of her head and jabbed a chopstick through it. That had worked nicely—but now she saw that she had dribbled coffee down the front of her shirt. What an image of middle-aged disarray and neglect she presented!

Hurrying onto the porch and leaning over the railing, she caught sight of a large, rough-looking man wearing bright blue work pants and a blue jacket. He smiled up at her from the terrace. "Madame Crisp?" he said.

"You must be Yves Lebrun. You have come to fix the roof over the kitchen," she replied in French, for she had been forewarned that beyond the standard classroom phrases—good morning, good-bye, and what is your name?—he had mastered no English. Moderating her pace to appear less harried, she descended the staircase. *"Monsieur Lebrun . . . Enchantée de faire votre connaissance."* Delighted to make your acquaintance, she said, extending her hand.

Yves shook it. *"Enchanté, Madame."* Then, when he had let go of her hand, he asked, "You are called Lily Crisp?"

"Yes, that is true."

"Crisp. This is a name I have not heard before. It is different, isn't it?"

"It's British. My husband's great-grandfather came from England. It's an old name."

"Then you must have much history," he said.

Oh, yes, Lily thought, I have too much history. That is precisely the problem. That is why I have come here. But she said to Yves, "Don't we all have history . . . ?"

He gave a small laugh, shrugged, and indicated the roof. "It is time to begin my work," he admitted, "before your kitchen floats down to the sea when it rains. *If* it rains. I wonder . . . the dryness, it is not good for the trees and the hills. And now"—he pointed at a distant hillside thick with its dusky canopy of cork oaks—"they will build a golf course on the mountainside. Over there. Can you believe it? How will they keep the golf balls from rolling into the sea? And where will they find enough water for the grass?" Shaking his head and muttering to himself, he turned and walked briskly—not in the comfortable shamble Lily had expected from so hefty and loquacious a handyman— to his truck to fetch his tools and a ladder.

She called out, "I'll be upstairs in my room, writing, if you have any questions." She saw him raise his hand—he had heard her; and so she climbed back up the stairs, smiling inwardly as she seated herself at the old chestnut table with cabriole legs that she used as her desk. She reviewed their conversation. What was it Yves had said? "Crisp—it is different, isn't it?"

Lily chuckled, recalling Esther, her outspoken older sister. "For God's sake, Lil, why did you marry Paul without telling anybody? You barely know him! And why change your name? Lily Fern is a great name. Lily Crisp sounds like the star of a pornographic movie. Or a cookie."

—

Lily's neighbors were in residence. This she knew from the music that wafted up from the pink house with the lime green shutters. She enjoyed the Telemann and the Mozart in the mornings when she wrote, although not late at night when she had gone to bed and the Belgian couple had just sat down to dinner. The house was young and enchanting, as were its owners. From her hillside perch, she could peer down upon them: the woman listened to Debussy while reading in her garden; the man grew tomatoes and aubergines, and had planted lemon, plum, and fig trees on the sun-drenched slope between Lily's house and his.... Lily's house. La Pierre Rouge. *Her* house. Not Paul's. Not his mother's or his grandfather's, but Lily's. By a twist of fate, which the villagers doubtlessly found amusing, this house that was French down to the cold stone core of its bones now belonged to an American, to a Midwesterner.

La Pierre Rouge was set high on a hillside, quite alone, up a steep and narrow, winding dirt road that was deeply rutted. During his lifetime Paul's grandfather must have kept the road open manually with a pickax and shovel, filling the potholes and ruts with gravel and chipping away at the crystalline bedrock that projected into the broken track. Around the final bend, from the forest of cork oaks and pines, the house rose up squarely, age-scarred and handsome, built of rough-chiseled blocks of local stone quarried from the hillsides. Shiny, black-painted shutters flanked windows and doors that opened wide to let in the heady fragrance of early-summer blooms and the delicate southern light. Inside, the patina of dark wood set against the brilliant colors of patterned cloth warmed the cold stone-walled interior. There were huge wooden beams overhead, red tiled floors with threadbare Persian carpets, and a crush of comfortably uphol-stered peasant furniture, some of which, like the house itself, was over a century old.

According to family legend, Georges Lafond had brought his young Italian wife in a wooden cart, pulled by a plump and frisky pony, to this rocky plot of ground, where he had built her a house. She had carried with her in the cart a massive, squared-off chunk of red limestone from the village in the Dolomites where she had been born and had lived until reaching puberty. A bride of two weeks, she was fourteen years old and still sore between her legs. Her husband, smitten with the ripeness of her young buttocks and peach-scented breasts, had vowed to set the block of red stone plumb over the center of the main doorway, but she had said no, and had refused as well its symmetrical placement over or under a window, or midway across the rugged, golden gray wall that faced the sea. "No marriage is perfect, nor do I seek perfection," she had told him, remembering the muscular but by no means satisfying tussle in their conjugal bed the first night of their union. The red stone must be mortared willy-nilly into the wall so as not to show pride before the eyes of God. Georges had obeyed her wish, and in the course of a long and satisfactory marriage she had borne him nine children, five of whom had survived into adulthood. The oldest, Gérard, a stonemason like his father, when he died at the age of ninety-one, had bequeathed the house of the red stone—La Pierre Rouge—to Justine Lafond, his surviving child and only daughter.

Upon Justine's death, the house had passed to her son, Paul.

And now it was Lily's, and as the dawn grew brighter and Hayden's trumpets tooted a fanfare of joyous greeting—*bonjour* to the birds and the cork oaks and the flotilla of clouds draped softly, like jellyfish trailing streamers, and to Lily arrested in her writing and reflecting on the proud-nosed clan who had built this house—she blessed her deceased mother-in-law, who had never coveted jewels or fancy clothes but had believed in land. The summer after her father died, Justine Lafond had returned to France, having sailed away over forty years earlier. She had ordered new plumbing, tile baths, a washing machine, double-wide French doors opening onto the terrace, fans for the upstairs ceilings, and a new firm mattress in the master bedroom.

(The old one, which had folded together in the middle like a fallen soufflé, she had given to the woman who beat the Persian carpets and swept the floor.) She had also bought up the entire hillside above, on either side of, and below La Pierre Rouge, down to the narrow strip of rocky earth where the Belgian couple would later plant their orchard. It was this buffer of land that now provided Lily with the solitude and the setting, if not the consummate silence, she required for her writing.

Three

Monsieur Léon's campground at the foot of the hill, below the Belgians' house and across the road where the rutted gold dirt turned to pavement, had filled with tourists. *"Les Hollandais . . . ,"* Adèle Simoni announced with a hiss. "They have returned in their caravans, with all their food, even suntan lotion. The Dutch . . ." She spit out the words, then ground them under her shiny pumps into the tiles of the Hotel de la Plage terrace.

Lily waited, never disappointed by her friend Adèle.

". . . and the Germans," the Frenchwoman added, with limitless disdain.

Lily stood below her in the sand, in the clean morning light. According to Adèle, the hotel had changed little over the years. The terrace had grown wider. The tiles were now a deep clay red, not the rough gray flagstones that Justine Lafond used to swill with water and sweep on mornings such as this, before she met Freddy, her lanky Idahoan—her future husband—and experienced a fateful melting of the legs.

Adèle was eight years older than Lily and far more chic. Even now, at half past seven in the morning, as she swept the clay tiles of the hotel terrace and mourned the return of the Dutch and the Germans, she was dressed in a tight challis skirt, a paisley silk blouse, and a cashmere sweater. Copper eyebrows penciled on in elegant arches over soft hazel eyes matched her copper-colored hair. She wore lipstick and heels to sweep the terrace. Conscious of her own wrinkled T-shirt, unwashed shorts, scuffed running shoes, unpainted lips, and uncoiffed hair, Lily remembered how she had felt when Adèle, whom she had known for over twenty years, had first said, *"Bonjour, Lillie,"* instead of *"Bonjour, Madame."* Realizing that a breakthrough had just been made and that it was now *her* turn to greet the proprietress of the Hotel de la Plage as more than a casual acquaintance, Lily had kissed Adèle on both cheeks, then, feeling gauchely American and overly demonstrative even as she'd pulled the petite Frenchwoman to her, she had given her a hug. But this morning, so many years after that awkward leap into informality, Lily said with ease, *"Bonjour, Adèle,"* and her friend replied with affection, *"Bonjour, Lillie."* The breeze ruffled Lily's hair, although not Adèle's, which was sprayed in place. As they chatted in French, the sun beat down on their shoulders.

"You are here for the summer?" Adèle asked, squinting into the sun.

Lily answered with a nod. "Until the first of September. Then Monsieur Dupré will have the house. I am planning to stay here after my children leave so that I can finally meet my mysterious renter. This is nonsense, isn't it? Ten years and we have never met."

"Ah, but I have seen him," Adèle said. "It was in September of last year."

"You have seen him?" Lily asked in surprise. "How did he look? My daughter will be very excited. She has drawn a picture of him. He is small and sporty, with a marvelous black mustache and pointed shoes . . . and a little belly because he enjoys his croissants and his pastries."

Adèle frowned, a wrinkle appearing like a tiny crevasse at the top of her nose. "He had no mustache, *chérie.* In fact, I believe he is German."

"But he is French, Adèle. He is a banker in Paris."

"So you have told me. But I have glimpsed him, you see, walking on your road."

"On the road to my house?"

"Yes. Blond. Tall. Such legs."

"But you are mistaken," Lily protested. "You have seen another man. Dupré—this is a French name, isn't it?"

Adèle replied with a certain indulgence, as if explaining to a child incapable of logic or leaps of intuition, "Even so, his mother could be German or Dutch, the unfortunate woman"— she trilled a little laugh while applying her broom in vivacious sweeps to one corner of the terrace—"or Czech or Hungarian. She could have married a Frenchman who calls himself Dupré. Is this not possible?"

"Yes, of course, this is possible, but . . ."

"Everything is all right up there?" Adèle asked, sounding concerned. "It is not too cold in the old fortress? La Pierre Rouge—it is a house that sucks in the cold like death into the bones, isn't this true? You are too much alone, Lily."

"But it is hot, very hot. I sleep without covers," she assured her friend while wondering, who was this tall blond man with his memorable legs who had climbed up her road? "Excuse me, Adèle, if I seem disconcerted. Many people walk on my road. There are paths into the hills. This man whom you have seen . . . he could be anyone at all. Is Monsieur Dupré such a recluse? Doesn't he go shopping? Doesn't he eat in the hotel's restaurant?"

"I think that I know who he is, you see"—Adèle flung her hands into the air and broke into an impish grin—"and then someone else appears!" She seemed pleased with the level of confusion. "This man with blond hair—he could be anyone, you are right. There are paths. I was mistaken. With a name like Dupré, how can he be German? Ah, well, he has left you a present? Six bottles, as always?"

"A white Bordeaux, very dry. I cannot remember the name but it tastes like . . . how do you say . . . like grass?"

Adèle laughed, pleased with the image. "Pierre will enjoy this wine, your son, with his herd of cows. . . ."

"But no, what I mean"—and Lily sat down on the low stone wall that surrounded the terrace—"it tastes clean and crisp. Delicious. You remember a few years back when Monsieur Dupré left as a gift *The Red and the Black* by Stendhal? I wrote to him that Justine called it *The Yellow and the Green* because those were the colors I turned when I searched for words in the dictionary. I meant this as a joke, of course, but this year his gift is a book by Simenon, the stories of Inspector Maigret. They are written in a French I can read to Justine. She will enjoy it."

"He is a kind man, your renter," Adèle mused, leaning gracefully on her broom. She had removed her cardigan and draped it over the back of a chair; the day was warming, the quiet morning hours when the air fell soft as powder on a woman's skin quickly drawing to an end. "You will come for an apéritif this evening?"

"Perhaps tomorrow, or the next day," Lily said.

"Of course, *chérie*. You must telephone when it is convenient. Your daughter, she arrives when? The lovely Justine, like her grandmother."

"The first of August. I cannot wait for the moment—and Pierre is coming, too."

"Your son, he has married?"

"No," Lily told her. "He has just turned twenty-six. He is still a bachelor."

Adèle nodded gravely. "He has need of joy, your Pierre. He is a serious young man, but very kind."

"Yes, he is kind."

"We missed you last summer," Adèle said, "but of course we understood. What a tragedy! Your husband's death. . . . It was his heart, of course. He had the heart of his father, whom I never met. Paul was young and very vigorous, no?"

"He had sixty-five years," Lily replied.

Laughter escaped Adèle's lips in a dainty burst. "I will have sixty years this summer, you see? This is not so many. My mother tells me if I live long enough, every age I have been will seem young. She has eighty-five years and calls me a girl."

"Well, then, until tomorrow or the day after," Lily said as she turned toward the beach, but Adèle had not finished.

"I see that Yves Lebrun has been up to your house to fix the roof," she said.

Lily tossed back over her shoulder, "Yes. Rain leaked into the kitchen last winter. A few of the tiles are broken."

"This is good that you have hired him. He is a man who mends more than broken roof tiles," Adèle called merrily after her.

Four

*L*ily trotted down the beach along a narrow, breathtakingly beautiful sweep of white sand. A short way along she stopped, stripped down to her black one-piece swimsuit, and ran splashing into the water.

She had the sea to herself, the warm salty sea where one morning in June, Justine Lafond had met Freddy Crisp for a swim—just like this, before breakfast. As the story went, oft repeated in the family, Freddy was a sober American not given to frolicking in water or on land, so he lay on his back, buoyed by the salt, still wearing his glasses, considering the soft, romantic Mediterranean sky. Justine, who was by no means a sober woman, came up under him and tipped him onto his toes. He was tall enough that his feet touched bottom and his glasses stayed dry, but Justine, like a silvery minnow, darted around and down and between his legs. On the second floor of the Hotel de la Plage, Mrs. Crisp, dressed in a peignoir, strolled onto the balcony with her feckless dachshund, Fritzy, squirming in her arms. Justine closed her legs at the same moment as Freddy lost his footing and, catching sight of his mother, went under. Mrs. Crisp, on shore, held her breath, as did her son underwater, though he was not, as she supposed, searching for his glasses.

It was later the same day, after lunch, that Freddy had announced his intention to marry, and Mrs. Crisp had observed, "It's about time."

Lily loved to remember. Here, in France, in the village where Paul's mother had grown up and met her Freddy and sailed off to the New World, to a ranch in Idaho, Lily felt the past strongly—her own wayward history as well as the incestuously flavored past of the French Lafonds. Memories and rumors shadowed her in the mornings as she trotted down the hill to the beach, as she stood on the terrace of the Hotel de la Plage and chatted with Adèle, as she slid into the sea and felt its limpid grip, its slow caress. As she stroked and kicked in a sudden, energetic burst toward shore.

How different this was from the landscape of her youth, the small wooded lake and varnished, yellowing pine log cabin her parents had owned in northern Wisconsin. As children, she and her two sisters had spent their summers there, swimming to the canvas-covered raft anchored off the end of the dock, climbing up the ladder and then plunging again into the water, snorkeling over the fish beds behind their mother in her leopard-print swimsuit, on the lookout for Mr. Renquist's remains. Mrs. Renquist had scattered her husband's ashes on the lake and Oscar Fern had teased his daughters, "If you find something that resembles a shell, it may be Mr. Renquist." Lily's older sister, Esther, had collected what she claimed were traces of their deceased neighbor in a peanut butter jar that she kept on a shelf above the couch, between a tinfoil-wrapped copy of *Lady Chatterley's Lover* and a shiny black rock.

Lily would awaken in the living room on those chill summer mornings, tucked under two Hudson Bay blankets on the rollaway bed, her sisters yawning on the foldout couch while their mother tiptoed past them to light the fire. When the flames were crackling and heat poured out of the wide stone chimney, their father would shout through the flimsy pine walls, "Hey, little pumpkins, is it warm in there yet?" And the three girls would throw off their covers and fly in their flannel pajamas across the kitchen, bursting through the army blanket hung over the doorway and leaping onto his bed. . . .

So much trust, so much love in those young girls' hearts.

Their mother would stand in the bedroom doorway, wrapped in an oversized terry-cloth robe, and click her tongue against the back of her teeth. "A wash before breakfast?" she'd ask.

"It's too cold," Lily and her sisters would squeal in protest, their cries swiftly turning to giggles as their father herded them with slaps on their bottoms out of his bed. Their mother would reach for her leopard-print bathing suit, which dangled from a hook beside the dresser, and swing back into the kitchen to change her clothes. Her daughters would join her there, their suits cold and clammy from a swim the night before. Then the four of them would run together down the hill through the birches to the lake and sit on the dock, on the peeling white paint; Lily's mother would grumble a bit because Oscar hadn't done what he said he would—again!—and the wind had blown branches and dead leaves onto the clean white sand of the lake bottom. And all the while she would be tucking her long chest-nut hair into a bathing cap and pulling down the elastic leg openings of her suit to shield her buttocks when she stood up. The girls, of course, would do the same, those firm little globes modestly covered.

Then their mother would hand them each a small bar of soap and say, "Grease up," and they would bathe in the pristine, unpolluted, clear-water lake (back then they even shampooed in it!) and wade in deeper, up to Lily's waist, until her mother would shout, "Dive!" She would call out commands like a drill sergeant. Lily loved it: the ritual, the excitement. Then they would dive in and kick like hell. The water felt chilly, as if it had been kept in the refrigerator overnight.

When they climbed out, clean and refreshed, and sped up the hill, they would meet their father striding out of the cabin, letting the screen door bang behind him so that their mother winced. Wrapped at the waist in a beach towel, he was naked underneath. He bathed in the nude. Lily was shocked and thrilled. She suggested to her mother that they do the same, take off their clothes and run splashing, screaming, into the water, like men. Her mother rumpled Lily's hair and smiled sweetly, as if privy to a secret her daughter was too young to share.

But once, on a dare from Esther, Lily had ripped off her bathing suit and bounded down the pathway after her father. Philomena, the youngest, left behind with their mother, had shrieked something about how only bad girls showed their fannies in public, but Lily was already speeding past her father and leaping off the end of the dock. Lily heard him shout, "No! Get back here!" as she splashed into the water and stroked toward the fish beds, entering the English Channel, her nine-year-old body greased and muscular, swimming toward France—or was it the Cliffs of Dover?—her feet kicking up a tremendous wake and her powerfully stroking arms propelling her forward to world acclaim as a champion swimmer. . . .

"Okay, little miss. Up to the cottage now." Her mother had been standing above her on the dock, her pearly white legs leading up to that leopard-print swimsuit that Oscar had bought her. "Hurry it up there, girl. Put your clothes on, pronto. Your dad has something to say to you."

Lily knew she had been an impossible child, and her mother, Gladys Fern, had been certain that *she* knew the reason. "Lily's just different because she wasn't born a boy," Gladys was often heard defending her daughter, usually against Oscar.

After Esther's birth, Lily's father had predicted that the next young Fern would be a son. They would call him Hamlin, Hamlin Fern, a name that pleased Oscar—an assertive, male, intelligent-sounding name for a boy who might one day end up a lawyer or a doctor, or CEO of his father's elevator manufacturing company. To Oscar's undisguised disappointment, his

second child had not been a boy but a sweet-faced, red-haired
Hamlin Lillian.

When Lily's mother suggested to her husband, "I think Lily
is a bit . . . different because you—we—named her Hamlin. It's
a boy's name, after all. . . ." Oscar almost threw a plate of pork
chops at her. Gladys loved to tell the story. She'd seen the mean
look in his eyes as he raised the plate of chops, then paused to
reconsider: the meat might hit its mark, but the gravy would
surely spatter the wallpaper. Reluctantly, Oscar had set the plat-
ter down.

The birth of a third daughter, Philomena, had cleared up the
question of a tainted heritage that Lily, with her corkscrewing
clouds of red hair and golden skin, had raised. Phila was solidly
Swedish-Swiss-German. Her eyes were the summery green of
a high alpine meadow, her complexion was milky, and sunlight
wove through the hanks of chestnut hair that Gladys coiled and
pinned like seashells over her daughter's ears.

"That last one's a beauty," Mrs. Renquist had said of Philomena the same day as Lily had plunged naked into the lake. Mrs.
Renquist (of the scattered ashes) had been invited to Sunday
supper with the family. Esther and her mother were putting
slices of Colby cheese on Ritz crackers in the kitchen, Grandma
Fern was sitting in front of the fire, knitting a sweater for one of
the girls, and Philomena, dewy-eyed with admiration, was following Lily around the cabin as if her older sister were a movie
star and she, Phila, was hoping for more than a bit part in Lily's
next production. Lily's father had poured himself and Mrs. Renquist a second round of vodka martinis.

As Lily approached their dinner guest with a tray of cheese
crackers, the tall, pleasant-faced woman ruffled Lily's curls.
Lily cringed slightly, while Mrs. Renquist, having popped two
cheese crackers, one after the other, into her mouth, beamed

over at Oscar. "Your young Lily, here, must have a splash of the Irish in her somewhere, don't you think? With that hair?"

Lily watched with delight as Grandma Fern dropped her knitting into her lap, reddened in the face, and grew visibly larger, more swollen in the ankles and the elbows, and the great jutting presence of her well-braced bosom. She avowed, sharply, "There's not a drop of Irish blood in that girl from either the Fern or the Brunner side of the family, I can promise you that, Mrs. Renquist. Of course I cannot speak for Gladys's heritage. . . ."

More disturbing was Lily's burnished skin. Her father recalled at the top of his voice, when a third martini had washed away his better judgment, that his grandparents had employed an Indian servant, a golden-skinned man. Quiet and graceful. Slim-hipped. "When was that, Mother, when what's-his-name worked for Grandma Brunner?"

Grandma Fern, so livid and puffed that her skin seemed primed to burst like an overripe fruit, heaved herself to her feet, turned around, and with all her gathered dignity and inflated size, through tightly knotted lips, hissed, "Gupta was his name. Ram Gupta. He dusted the furniture and he served my parents sherry. When he made the bed—contrary to what you have suggested, Oscar—my mother was *not* in it." She spun about and sailed through the kitchen doorway.

The next morning at breakfast, when Grandma Fern called across the room, "Oh, Hamlin, would you bring me my spectacles?" Lily had complied with a scowl. She picked up her grandmother's glasses case from the table where it lay beside the coffeepot, transported it to the old lady's lap, dropped it in, and stepped aside.

"Do not," Lily warned her, "ever again call me Hamlin."

"What rudeness is this?" cried the displeased woman.

"Did Grandma Brunner say Ram Gupta smelled good, like a papaya? Do you know?"

"You scamp! You little devil! Gladys!" But Lily's mother had gone out, and the old woman glowered at the unrepentant child, who did not run away or squirm or apologize—or cry. "We will pretend you never said such a thing. We will pretend you are a nice little girl whose red hair does not indicate a rebellious temperament."

"Do you think Ram Gupta liked to travel, Grandma Fern? Do you think he paddled a canoe all the way from India? Do you think if he was here now he'd take me with him?" Lily had whispered, her eyes sparkling with the adventure of foreign lands as she climbed onto her grandmother's lap, on top of her grandmother's glasses, and hugged her.

———

The morning parade of bathers had begun. Their bodies came in all shapes and sizes, in varying shades of black, brown, golden, pink, or a frightening red. Lily toweled off in the sun and crossed the street to the news vendor's swim shop, where she picked up the *International Herald Tribune* that Madame Bibot had grudgingly saved for her. Then she stopped by the bakery to buy croissants, strolled past the post office and the hairdresser's shop, and walked up the boulevard lined with eucalyptus trees and oleanders to the base of the hill, where Monsieur Léon's campground was located. He had built a cement sanitary block lined with sinks and toilets in an old lemon orchard not far below the Belgians' house. A few backpacking tents and larger, more elaborate canvas structures, which were tall enough to stand up in and broad enough to serve dinner for ten, dotted the grass. There were caravans and Volkswagen buses parked among them. Two blond-haired women, muscular as wrestlers, stood at the outdoor sinks, washing their breakfast dishes, while other campers sat on folding chairs, drinking coffee in the sunshine. Lily gave them a quick wave, turned left onto the dirt, and began to climb.

Her Belgian neighbors, he in gardening shorts, she in a bikini, with a large gray cat curled across her stomach, were stretched out on chaises longues on their terrace. The lime green shutters, freshly painted, looked splendid with pink in the filtered morning light. Baguettes and Brahms for breakfast, Lily noted.

"*Bonjour, Madame,*" they called out.

"*Bonjour, Monsieur. Bonjour, Madame. Bon appétit.* What is the name of your pretty cat?"

"Alonso," the woman cried. "But you must call me Christine, and my husband is Jacques."

Lily smiled. "Then you must call me Lily."

"Such a pretty name. *Lillie. Lillie.*" Christine trilled the words as if they were the two bright notes of a song. "But Alonso—he is not a pretty cat. Last night he dined on one of Monsieur Léon's pet canaries and that horrid man has threatened to call the police. The police! Can you imagine? He is a cat, not a criminal."

"What a shame," Lily said. "Even so, he is a handsome cat."

Christine beamed. "How you are kind. You have heard this, Alonso?" She picked up the gray cat, whose plump body drooped like a furry handbag, and waved one of his dangling paws. "Say thank you to Lily, you silly cat."

Alonso squirmed and, with an unmanly peep, broke loose and bolted for the garden.

Jacques cried out, "*Attention!* The peppers . . . !"

"*Au revoir, Christine. Au revoir, Jacques.*" Lily waved and, with a nod of her head, set off again up the hill. Upon reaching the house and emptying the contents of her string bag onto the kitchen counter, she put the two croissants, butter and strawberry jam, yogurt and muesli on the massive tile table Paul's mother had ordered and never lived to see. While the coffee brewed, she cut half a banana and a fresh peach dripping juice into a green glazed bowl and topped the fruit with raspberries.

At last, when the coffee was ready, she filled a mug, and, taking her seat at the head of the table, leaned back against the tile bench, her hands warmed by the mug of coffee, her eyes resting on the breadth of blue sea where she imagined her thoughts set adrift in the sunlight and aimlessly wandering, until the gentle tug of an offshore current or breeze swept them from view.

It was already after one o'clock and close to lunchtime when the companionable clatter of Yves working on the roof died suddenly. Lily strolled out to the porch to check on his progress and saw him straddling the ridgeline, smiling up at the sky. He appeared to be singing, although so quietly that she couldn't hear him. He was gesturing with his right hand, flourishing an invisible baton, waving it in dramatic sweeps and figure eights. "What are they playing?" Lily shouted. "Your orchestra."

"Beethoven's Fifth. It's marvelous. It's triumphant!"

"A great job of conducting," she called back with a friendly wave. She had been annoyed at first when she had discovered the broken tiles on the kitchen roof. She knew she would have to find someone to repair them, and then there would be the bother of a workman's presence, unwanted conversation, awkward cross-cultural moments—should she offer him lunch?— the clinking and thunking of tiles being replaced, the thud of feet going up and down a ladder. But Yves had a cheerful way about him. He had a gentle face and soft, dark, sensitive eyes. He chatted—but then he got down to business. There was a certain cozy feel to his male presence on the roof, and his phantom orchestra. Clearly, he remembered that she had said she would be writing, a pursuit that required concentration and reflection. He had not wanted to disturb her.

But her stomach had no such compunctions. It growled. She was hungry. Yves must be, too, she thought, and against her better judgment, but not wanting to be impolite, she ran down the stairs and called up to him, "You've been working hard, you must be starved. Can I offer you some lunch? Nothing fancy, some bread and cheese, and some wonderful ripe tomatoes."

He stood up, hands braced on his knees. His tall, broad body loomed above her. "This is a kind offer," he said. "I would be pleased to accept it, but my mother, she prepares for me . . ." He cast his eyes toward the sky, as if searching for today's menu in the puffy white clouds that hovered like soft meringues above them. He continued, "She makes desserts as sweet and tempting as the heavens."

Lily gave a sigh. "That sounds a lot tastier than a square of chocolate and a slice of apple."

"No, no. I would actually prefer it. The apple," he confessed as he descended the ladder, unhitched his tool belt, and patted his waistline in a gesture that shot Lily back across the years to the first time she had met Paul at a lecture on the French Impressionists. He had been carrying a few unwanted pounds around his middle and had tapped his belly just as ruefully.

"Maman and I, we have this little . . ." Yves paused, taking a deep breath and then blowing it out in a gust of laughter as he explained how she made him desserts that in her eyes, at least, held him to her. Her concoctions were light and tender, or so dark and richly decadent that he devoured them slowly, in a state of languor. He grew red in the face after admitting this to Lily. "I am talking too much. But you understand, now, why I cannot join you for lunch," he said gruffly, no doubt to cover the confusion his appraisal of his mother's culinary practices had brought upon him. "She will be waiting with a potage of leeks and mushrooms, tender points of beef with a purée of garlic potatoes, *fromage*, and for dessert"—he grinned, his eyes dancing over Lily's face and shoulders—"this is often a secret."

"Good food is one of life's great pleasures," she answered agreeably, surprised at how sorry she was that he wouldn't be eating with her. She enjoyed these snippets of conversation.

They forced a break in her routine and her isolation; they carried her out of herself and what could easily become—and she dreaded this—a useless contemplation of her own navel.

For God's sake, she thought as Yves trundled off toward his truck, tossing a wave over his shoulder. He was only the handyman! It was only lunch! Or was she regretting less the absence of his convivial chatter across the table than his soapy clean smell, his flirtatious eyes, and his wide romancer's mouth?

And if she was, what of it?

Five

*A*n unexpected dose of frivolity—was this how she expected to achieve equanimity? As much as she had looked forward to her time in France, she had also dreaded it, fearing the potential for emotional carnage. Instead, swept along on a spate of delightful childhood memories, she had taken to flirting with the carpenter! Perhaps sexual froth was a function of this house. She had not slept well the night before, as if the walls themselves were respiring, as if ghosts were sighing, weeping . . . and why not? There was Justine Lafond, like a minnow softly nipping at Freddy's legs while his mother and Fritzy looked on from the balcony. There was Justine's brother thrusting his serviceable member into the village sweethearts. There was Justine's mother strapped into a complimentary, top-of-the-line bra and girdle, and her father, wild-eyed and heaving like a wounded bull. And there was Justine's aunt, Giselle Godard, her dark hair pulled like a veil over the knotted rope. These walls held stories that made Lily's detours from the path of virtue seem like children's mischief.

Obviously she had never believed, while still daring to hope, that equanimity was a product one could deftly manufacture on a typewriter. She knew damn well that, no matter how many pages she typed, at the end of the day the so-called broader picture would result not only from delving into her own uneven past but from gazing outward. At her friend Adèle, for instance, who viewed life's adversities as one more proof of God's inexplicable quirkiness. Or at her bulky handyman, whose buoyant step mirrored to perfection his buoyant outlook. Or at her mother-in-law, whose gumption and spark had plumped up her spirit and made her invincible.

Justine Lafond—how Lily had loved and admired that woman. In Lily's bedroom in La Pierre Rouge there was a photograph of Paul's mother, looking ravishing and resolute in a tight-fitting dress that buried her breasts in bouquets of marigolds and wrapped her hips in poppies. Lily ran up the stairs to the chest of drawers beside her writing desk and picked up a wide silver frame from among the other framed photographs of Paul and her children. Justine Lafond, aged seventeen, gazed brazenly back at her.

She was standing in front of the old stone house, the brilliant sea behind her. She wore a man's fedora with a sprig of lilac tucked into an alligator hatband a pen pal had sent her from Florida. Her dark hair had come undone; the right side swept up under the brim of her hat while the left curled in saucy waves over her shoulder. She was wearing heels. She had once told Lily they were high and red as a hooker's heels. They belonged to her aunt, Giselle, who was not in the picture.

But Justine's brother, Paul, was. Strange, Lily thought, how Paul's mother had named her son after a brother who had tried to rape her. But then love and hate were so closely allied, and there was the blood—that lurid, tempestuous connection. In the photograph, Justine's brother lounged to her left, a burly young man of twenty as ravishing in his musculature and the vitality of his sex as his sister beside him. His hand rested on her shoulder alongside the truant hair, a dark cloud beside his dark fingers as if he had torn it loose. With a firm grip on the shirred fabric that clung to her shoulder, he pulled her toward him while she pulled away.

According to Justine, she had been wearing her flowered dress the evening Freddy Crisp checked into the Hotel de la Plage. The tall, strong-limbed American had been accompanied by his widowed mother and her little sausage dog. Justine had been seated behind the polished oak counter reading a book while the setting sun, enmeshed in a violent tangle of golds and reds, lit the marigolds that wreathed her breasts. Freddy, who was almost thirty and had thus far shown more interest in cow and calf operations than in women, had barely been able to see her face for the fiery mingling of flesh, flowers, and sun. But when he approached, shielding the thick lenses of his glasses from the sunset blaze, and saw her eyes beneath the brim of a man's fedora, beneath an alligator hatband, he had lost his heart.

Lily once asked her mother-in-law, when they had both overdone on the cognac, "Was your brother, Paul, ever—abusive, Maman?"

"Pffft! That scoundrel with his unzipped trousers? You are talking nonsense!" Justine had exclaimed, flaring her nostrils as if catching a whiff of weak coffee or overcooked lamb. "You Americans lack two things: the nose and the tact. Have you never heard of *le tact*? All the civilized world treads with little tender toes, but you come at me, my darling, like a *bouledogue*—a bulldog, *non*?—with this question that cannot be decently put to a mother-in-law."

Later, just before Maman died, she had confided in Lily, in that full-throated voice thick with the French accent she never discarded, "Violence, we all agree, *chérie*, is an evil tool, but it has its uses. You once asked if my brother had abused me, and I tell you now, I met violence with violence and remained a virgin. But the history begins with my mother, you see. I was fifteen years old when she ran off with a lingerie salesman. My father was left to cope with me, his prize peach of a daughter, and a cocksman of a son who had harvested the rest of the fruit in the village. . . ." At this deliciously ripe image, Justine gave a husky chuckle and her dark eyes shone with the devilment of a woman adept both in sexual matters and self-promotion.

"One night," she continued, "my brother came into my room. He'd been drinking; he didn't say a word. He just stumbled over to the bed and wrenched up my nightdress. I could smell the stink of liquor on his breath and shot a gob of spittle up into his face. He was seventeen and handsome. *Mon Dieu*, he was handsome, and strong! But I was a fighter. I scratched at his eyes and clawed his neck and I kicked him down here, *ici*. . . ." Justine gestured downward dramatically. "How is it you young people say . . . ? In his unit? As if my brother's genitals were something you could plug into the wall to make coffee in the morning!"

She sniffed and went on, "It is absurd, *non*? But this is *exactly* where Paul was clutching himself when my father charged into the room and ripped him off me. He battered my brother with his stonemason's fists, and all the time he was shouting—my father, Gérard, he could bellow like a bull—'*Voilà, alors!* So, it has come to this! May her soul rot in hell!' My mother, you remember, had run off with an underwear salesman, and Papa was so angry that he blamed it on her, Paul's trying to rape me. Pffft! As if she would have tried to stop her little darling.

"A week later Papa sent to St. Tropez for my mother's younger sister. Giselle was twenty-six and single when she arrived at La Pierre Rouge. She must have been thinking, *This is only a visit, I won't stay long*, for she acted with a dispatch I have always admired . . . or perhaps, on her part, it was a simple lack of worldliness. In less than a week she became the guardian of my virtue and my brother's lover. Two years later, after I married Freddy and moved to Idaho, Giselle stayed on in La Pierre Rouge with those two dark, violent men. It is a bizarre family history, *non*? Paul eventually left the village and was killed in the war, a hero of the Resistance, and Giselle, who must have been forty by then, was still keeping house for my father. When she learned that Paul had died, she walked up to the goat shed and hung herself."

This horrific news tripped off Maman's tongue as lightly as if she had been describing the plateful of braised beef with fresh spring vegetables that Giselle had eaten for dinner. Lily was dumbstruck. Questions jostled for position in her mind: Why did Giselle stay with Monsieur Lafond? Did she love him? Why didn't she run off with her nephew-lover? Did she sleep with both men? Where was the goat shed? Why did she hang herself? What did she look like?

But Lily held her peace, for Justine Lafond was too weary to reply. She took Lily's hand gently in her own and, smiling, closed her eyes. She had cancer, and was dying.

<hr />

"Excuse me, Madame. I have finished repairing the roof over the kitchen. It should not leak anymore."

Yves Lebrun stood with his cap in his hand on the porch outside her bedroom. He had returned to work after lunch, but still absorbed in the story of Justine Lafond and her aunt Giselle, Lily had merely called out a greeting and ignored him.

Seated at her desk, her fingers resting on the keys of her silent typewriter, she had been unaware of Yves climbing the steps and positioning himself at a respectful distance from the open doorway. Upon hearing his voice she started, and pressed the *k* and the *l* keys with such force that she jammed them. "Damn," she muttered in English, and then swung around to face Yves, smiling apologetically. "Not you. I didn't mean you," she said, realizing as she did so that he couldn't understand a word she was saying, so she switched to French. "Sorry. You scared me. Come in," she suggested, but he did not hear the invitation (or pretended not to hear) and turned away, bracing his hands far apart on the grillwork that surrounded the porch. Leaning his weight on the railing, inhaling deeply so that Lily noticed his shoulders lift and his broad back expand under its coarse blue shirt, he took in the view.

Was he embarrassed to enter her bedroom? she wondered. He must be ten years younger than she, somewhere in his early forties. Could the wide bed with its down puff invitingly folded back over white linen sheets be seen as a temptation? Could she? Amused by the notion, Lily pulled out the page she had just inserted in the typewriter and placed an old cashmere shawl over "Madame Olivetti" (as she had christened her trusty machine), to keep the dust off her.

"You're going to France to write your memoirs on that ancient clunker?" Esther had scoffed when, three months earlier, Lily had told her of her plan.

"I'm not writing my memoirs. It's the process that interests me, Es."

"Of typing?"

"No, the process of remembering."

"If you took your laptop you could remember quicker."

"That's why I'm taking my old Olivetti, not my laptop. I can't edit as easily. I can't delete and move things around . . . manipulate. I have to formulate my thoughts ahead of time. They come out less contrived and contradictory."

"And more forgiving," Esther had said and harrumphed.

"If anything, *less* forgiving," Lily reflected, giving Madame Olivetti's square-cut shoulder a fond pat as she rose from her desk, stretched her arms over her head, and locked her fingers, arching her back. Her breasts rose pleasingly. Yves had turned back from his apparent preoccupation with the sea and the sky, or the islands in the distance, and was studying her, smiling to himself with the same wry twist of the mouth she had felt on her own lips moments earlier: the unmistakable awareness of male-female propinquity.

She walked quickly through the doorway and onto the porch, where she motioned for him to take a seat in one of the two lounge chairs that faced the sea.

"I cannot stay," he said.

"Even for a glass of wine? You've worked hard today."

"It's late. Maman is preparing dinner."

"That's a shame," Lily said. Once again, she would have welcomed his company. He was a calming presence around the house, a big man who carried extra flesh on his bones, although none of it was overly soft or unappealing. He had a warm open face, with a large nose that arched in such a way that his look could be mistaken for disapproval or arrogance were it not for his eyes, soft brown as a deer's, and at times as skittish and gentle. His hands were thick and wide-knuckled, yet capable of the most delicate operations; Lily was certain they could wring the neck of a buzzard as easily as they extracted a tiny screw from a delicate piece of woodwork. She watched him set his cap jauntily on his head, on his wavy black hair, and for an instant she had to restrain herself from reaching up and running her fingers through it.

"Oh, by the way," she blurted out awkwardly, "the bedstead in my daughter's room—"

"I noticed a few panes of glass—" They spoke at the same moment and stopped, laughing, to apologize to each other. Lily gestured for him to continue. "Some panes are cracked," he went on, "in the bathroom windows. I could fix them tomorrow. I have some glass in the garage at home. It's easy enough to cut the glass to fit and replace those broken pieces. And the bedstead . . . ?"

"It's broken or warped or . . . certainly something is wrong with it. It pulls apart and the mattress falls on the floor. My daughter sleeps there and she'll be here in August. If you could find the time . . ." She put out her hand. "Thank you, Yves, for all your help."

He took her hand in his strong grip and shook it. "I will return tomorrow," he promised, and bounded down the steps—

again she noticed how lightly he moved for such a large man—and strode along the pathway to the gravel turnaround where he had parked his truck. He slid his ladder and tools into the back and, waving cheerfully, climbed in behind the wheel. Then he set off down the hill toward his mother and his dinner.

But Lily's thoughts were still entwined with his dark hair, the unruly waves that reminded her of Antonio Cassata.

Six

She was twenty-one and newly graduated from college with a degree in languages. She was mowing the lawn of her parents' flower-edged, redbrick bungalow in a northern suburb of Milwaukee, Wisconsin. Even now, thirty-one years later, Lily remembered the clean, fresh smell of the cut grass in the June sunshine. She remembered the satisfying buzz of the lawn mower and the plush nap under the soles of her tennis shoes. She remembered the moisture glistening on her skin from the mounting heat and humidity, as if she had been hit with spray from the sprinklers. She wore Bermuda shorts and a halter top, and when Antonio Cassata roared past on his motorcycle, she knew she looked lovely. A slender body. Shapely legs. Well-formed breasts. Smooth, buttery (not pale like a redhead's) skin. Billowing curls of soft red hair pulled back in a ponytail. Gray-green eyes that were hidden behind a pair of oversized tortoiseshell sunglasses. She caught a glimpse of his black hair slicked back gigolo fashion, a cigarette dangling from his lips, his broad shoulders nicely filling out a black leather jacket that had obviously been around for a while. He gunned the engine and waved. She smiled while maintaining a firm grip on the lawn mower.

Philomena, a college sophomore, pushed open the screen door with her knee and stepped outside. "Who was that guy on the motorcycle?" she yelled at Lily. She wore pedal pushers and a striped oxford shirt with the sleeves rolled up to her creamy elbows. On his second spin around the block, Antonio waved once again as he powered past them. Philomena tossed

back her thick head of chestnut hair in recognition. Lily ignored him.

On Antonio's third swing past the Fern residence, yet another
female had appeared. With long slim legs that led up and up to
unexpectedly full hips, Esther towered over her two younger
sisters, who were now standing together chatting on the doorstep. Miming a swoon at the quantity of bare flesh on display
in so peaceful and homely a setting, Antonio pulled into the
driveway, shut off the engine, kicked out the stand with a heavy
black boot and, lifting his jeans-clad thigh over the gas tank,
sauntered toward them. Pinching off the end of his cigarette and
tossing it behind him onto the grass, he said, "Hey, is this Lilac
Lane? I guess I'm lost." He had a slow smile and mocking eyes
and looked the sisters up and down, settling—he later confided
in Lily—on the one with the honeyed skin and the wild red hair
who'd been pushing the lawn mower.

The bronzed god, they called him. He was twenty-five, had
a master's degree in communications and marketing, and was
assistant manager of his father's sausage factory. He was quickly
drawn into the Fern family. On weeknights he dropped by after
work and drank a few beers with the sisters in the backyard,
while their mother moved the sprinkler from beneath the maple
so it wouldn't spray them on their lawn chairs. On weekends
they were an indolent bunch of princesses and a single prince,
listening to the radio, singing along with the Beatles in "Penny
Lane" and "Strawberry Fields Forever," making lemonade with
plenty of ice cubes and fresh lemons, pulling a weed or two in
their progression around the patio, prone on chaises and slathered with sun lotion, an alarm clock ringing at fifteen-minute
intervals, reminding them to roll over so as to toast their bodies
evenly. Lily and Esther wore bikinis that their mother did not
approve of. Philomena covered her voluptuous midsection with
a paisley-print one-piece suit. Antonio flaunted a European-

style nylon brief that the three sisters discussed at length in bed at night. Rolling their eyes and laughing knowledgeably, they remarked on how often he flipped over on his stomach. "The guy should wear a tent," Esther said. "For all the good that suit does him, he might as well be naked."

One evening when the rest of the family had gone to the movies and Lily was finishing up the dishes in the kitchen, Antonio surprised her at the back door. He peered in through the screen.

"Hey, why not put down that towel and join me?" he suggested.

"I've had better offers," she said.

He smiled easily. "I doubt it."

She pushed open the screen door and walked out onto the stoop, drying her hands on the towel and tossing it aside, and then flipping off her sandals while he lit up and blew a couple of perfect smoke rings into the air. They stood side by side gazing out over the backyard, arms folded and elbows—although neither of them appeared to notice—touching.

He took a long drag on his cigarette and said, "Why do you have to go to Italy?"

She said, "I hate the taste of smoke."

"The taste or the smell?"

"Both."

"Why didn't you say something?"

"I am. Now."

He stubbed out his cigarette on the concrete. "You should have told me."

"I didn't think it would matter. I thought you were interested in Philomena."

"I'm not."

"I know." She stepped down onto the grass.

He followed. "If you want to learn Italian," he offered, "I

can teach you plenty of nouns and verbs. Private lessons are an option."

She shrugged her shoulders. "No one's forcing me to go, Antonio. It's my choice. I'll be living with a family in Cortina, in the Dolomite Mountains. Have you heard of them?"

"I thought they spoke German in the Dolomites. They eat spaetzle and strudel."

"The Dolomites are in Italy. I'm not interested in learning German."

"Why not, if you're such a linguist?"

She gave an aggrieved sigh and explained, somewhat shortly, "After living in Cortina I'll be traveling in Europe, where I can speak my languages."

"That's a little presumptuous, don't you think? *Your* languages? I don't know if I can associate with—"

"Oh, knock it off, Antonio. French, Spanish. What's the big deal? You market bratwurst. I speak languages. With Italian I'll have them all. The Romantics. Then I can go on adventures and get a job overseas."

He said, "You're the romantic."

"No, Antonio. Phila's the romantic one in our family," she told him. And prompted by nothing more than a sense of asymmetry, she leaned over to pluck a strand of dark hair off his shoulder. Reaching up, he caught her hand in his, turned it over, and pressed the back of her wrist to his opened lips. Heat and moisture exploded on her skin, and laughter caught in her throat as he bent his head and kissed her on the cheek and, with his fingers, gently turned her face toward his. Then he kissed her again, deeply, on the mouth. She whispered, with her lips against his and her eyes tightly shut, "Can you teach me some verbs in Italian?"

"My God, you're beautiful," he said, and he pulled her with him down the hill and across the lawn to a bower of fruit trees, where Lily had once spent an entire fall weekend planting daffodil bulbs. He was wearing a loose cotton T-shirt and baggy shorts, both of which offered easy access to her unpracticed hands. He peeled off her blouse and skirt, half-slip, brassiere and cotton panties, then ran his tongue around her ear, tickling the lobe and causing her to giggle while his lips, like fluttering moths against her skin, took liberties she had never imagined. "Does that please you?" he asked.

Surprised by the location of his head vis-à-vis her legs, Lily had inquired anxiously, "Can the neighbors see us?" Then, with a great gasp for air, control, sanity, perspective—and relief that she had not achieved them—she gave herself over to the power of his grip and tongue, the heat and hard-grinding core of his body. They made frantic love beneath a flowering apple tree that dizzied them with its fertile, sweet, intoxicating scent and left them reeling. Then they made love again, more slowly this time, and every night thereafter, until the first of July, when Lily, reluctantly, boarded the plane for Italy.

Never before had she felt such a wrenching of her heart, such a visceral blow of separation from a loved one, such an agony of tactile memory: Antonio's skin that felt as though live coals were smoldering beneath it, his powerful hands stroking her breasts, the silken weight of him resting inside her. She believed she could not live without his lips and his hair and the tips of his fingers, his flashing black eyes boring into hers with an intensity that robbed her of any will to move or speak until he touched her again and told her he loved her, he loved her. It's forever, bambina.

Cortina and her small room in a baker's cramped house, her narrow bed, the single bathroom the whole family shared, the kitchen with its gamy smells—these were a nightmare without him. Her appetite faded. Her skin lost its healthy sheen. The sadness in her eyes and the flesh melting off her bones distressed

Signora Miceli, her Italian mother, who tempted her with luscious risottos and spicy pastas, vine-ripened tomatoes, the smell of which could make a woman swoon, and veal lightly floured and fried, so delicate it demanded to be eaten in tiny mouthfuls, like love nips on Antonio's knuckles or the cords of his neck. Lily was at one moment sick with desire, and at the next coldly researching how to change the date on her ticket and fly home to Wisconsin.

When she missed her period in the middle of July, she chalked it up to stress and the change in food and climate. But by early August all four members of the baker's family, who queued up every morning in the hallway while Lily vomited into the toilet behind the locked bathroom door, had no doubts as to the source of their boarder's flagging appetite and her moodiness. Signora Miceli embraced her one day and delivered a stream of words Lily could not understand, but she was comforted by the strong, flour-dusted arms smelling of thyme, and the expansive bosom like a great feather pillow that cushioned the pain and terror that threatened to burst from her chest . . . *Lacrime*, the signora said to her. Tears. But Lily could not produce them, so the kind woman smoothed her hair and soothed her with beautiful foreign words that acknowledged the fate of all women, brought upon them by the treasure men sought between their thighs. The baker's wife wept when Lily could not.

Then they talked it over.

"I am torn into pieces," Lily said in her burgeoning Italian. "I dream that I will live overseas and be a translator. I want to travel in all kinds of places and see the world. When I was a little girl, I always read books about foreign countries, especially hot places like India and Africa. . . ."

"And Italy?" the signora queried with a teasing twinkle in her eyes, attempting to open Lily up and ease her suffering.

Lily smiled.

"Yes," she said. "And Italy. But you see, I love Antonio, and now I am pregnant and I want this, too. Marriage and a family. But not yet. I wanted—"

"Both?"

"Yes! You understand. Only the timing is imperfect."

"Timing! Timing!" the signora cried in a state of high emotion. "When I was a girl you got your period, you got a boy with a *pene* hard as a week-old *filoncino*, you got married, you got a baby. *That* was timing! You must write to your parents," she urged.

"No," said Lily.

"Then you must write to your lover."

Lily shook her head again and the signora, in frustration, flung her hands into the air and stormed about the kitchen calling on her mother, the Madonna, and Jesus, if any of the three were available for counseling and could talk some sense into this lovely but misdirected and obstinate child.

"I'll fly home at the end of October," Lily conceded quietly. "It's easier in person. I can look into his eyes and make sure that he loves me and wants this baby. Then we'll get married. We can travel afterward. Antonio will need to travel overseas for his business."

The signora beamed. *"Grazie a dio, grazie a dio,"* she said over and over.

The baker, who had spoken not a word, wisely leaving the meat of the discussion to the women, now assured Lily, "Your father will stand by you. We cannot say no to our daughters, who are always, in our minds, our helpless little angels." And Lily felt the knot of anxiety rise up from the dark fold in her stomach where it had lodged, and unwind into the rich yeasty smells of the kitchen as she was crushed to the baker's chest.

What she assumed was to be her last month in Cortina passed happily for Lily as, with escalating flutters of excitement, she imagined herself locked in Antonio's arms, whispering her secret: You're going to be a father, my sweet lover. . . . Did you know? Did you guess? She felt vaguely disquieted when he never wrote back after his initial enthusiastic response to her homecoming. But then, the Italian mails were not to be trusted, a belief loudly espoused by the baker and his wife and borne out by a letter from Esther that arrived weeks after she had sent it.

"Sons of whores and wastrels, may a dog urinate on their buttocks," Signora Miceli apologized to Lily as she handed her the crumpled airmail envelope.

Lily immediately tore it open.

Dear Lil, [Esther wrote]

Philomena and Antonio just ran off and got married. Eloped! Can you believe it? They kept everything a secret. She's pregnant, two months gone. Dad is furious, as you can imagine. Mom keeps trying to calm him down. Phil is pretending to be cowed and repentant but she's absolutely glowing, like some fertility goddess who just popped the king in the cornfield. Don't be mad at her, Lil. I don't think she has a clue.

Last night when the newlyweds came by for a beer, Antonio looked shell-shocked. When we were alone for a second, he asked when you're coming home. You know what I told him? I told him, You bastard.

I'm sorry, Lil. I miss you and love you,
Esther

Even then, Lily could not cry. She hid the blow of Antonio's betrayal in a secret place inside her that wasn't her heart, because hearts not only pump blood but pain. She stored her tears on ice and remained in Cortina with the baker's family.

Lily worked in the bakery, and as the months went by, the

clientele expanded from the usual assortment of schoolgirls, housewives, and widows to the young men of the town. They came to buy loaves of bread and pastries and oftentimes there would be three or four of them lined up at the counter chatting with Lily while the women behind them kept up a running commentary, sotto voce. About what? Lily wondered. The allure of a pregnant woman? Was it a smell she gave off, a perfume of fertility that these lads could not resist? Was it because she was a foreigner and no one in the village had deflowered her; hence, there was no blame or outrage attached as a stigma? Was it because her skin glowed like amber honey that grew smoother and richer in its tones as her belly expanded, or because her cheeks carried an intimate flush that could not but suggest the moment of high passion that had led to her present condition? It seemed as if her stomach was secretly transmitting to each man who walked through the bakery door—I am a sexual being and here is proof, the bulk and warmth of me, this great aproned belly lying inches from the loaf of bread you have purchased and will soon sink your teeth into. And so they came, the young men with smiling faces, like so many adoring brothers and admiring champions with something between reverence and outright lust in their eyes.

The debilitating hurt of betrayal and rejection by a man to whom she had given her body and love wholeheartedly lessened over time; emotions as harmful as anger and vindictiveness seemed unable to sustain themselves in a household so openly loving and supportive. Signora Miceli's hearty and healthy cooking commingled with warmhearted laughter, her husband's fiercely paternal ministrations that mellowed at mealtimes into jovial concern, the nurturing aromas of bread baking and almonds toasting in the ovens, of butter and chocolate melting in pots on the stove counteracted the toxins of humiliation and heartache. At first it was assumed that Lily would keep the child and raise it in Italy, or, more boldly, in her homeland. But as the letters piled up from Philomena, begging forgiveness for "stealing Lily's boyfriend," spilling over with news of her elopement and pregnancy, so naïve and girlish and openhearted in her joy, Lily realized that she could never return to her family with a child who in any way resembled Antonio Cassata.

Signor Miceli had a younger sister, Mariella, who lived in a nearby chalet. She was married to a mountain guide named Guido, who bore an unsettling resemblance to Antonio: dark-eyed and six feet tall, glossy black hair, pale skin, and a muscular build. For five years the couple had been trying to have a child. Gradually, and with a sense of its inevitable rightness, the idea of Mariella and her husband adopting her baby grew in Lily. She knew and liked them, they believed in fresh air, exercise, and a solid education, and there was no doubt that Lily's son or daughter would be loved and well cared for. One day Lily spoke to Signora Miceli, suggesting that Mariella might adopt the baby. "Oh, no! Never!" the good woman cried, sounding as horrified as if Lily had suggested tossing the newborn over a cliff or down a well. "You cannot give up your baby. You will be a fine and loving mother, one can see this in the way you carry your stomach in front of you, like a steady ship on a windy sea. We will not allow such foolish thoughts—" She hesitated for a moment. "But this is a most generous offer. . . ." Her eyes slid off the edge of Lily's cheekbone and skittered across the wall to a painting of the blessed Madonna. She said firmly, as if trying to convince herself, "I will not mention this to Mariella."

But she did.

Mariella said no. Impossible. She could never accept this wonderful, unimaginable gift of a baby . . . unless, of course, Lily *truly* desired it . . . in which case, perhaps, with Lily's urging, she could. And so Lily became the focus not only of a score of young Italians' bedroom dreams but the solicitous counsel of the adoptive parents and grandparents of her unborn child. They monitored her every bodily function as if she carried a rare dynastic seed inside her; any misstep that might jar the princeling, any bite of poorly prepared food that might damage his nascent digestive tract, any whiff of unclean air that might weaken his lungs must at all costs be avoided.

Two months before Philomena Cassata gave birth to a squalling, lustily kicking baby girl in Wisconsin, Lily, in Cortina, was delivered of a stillborn son. For days after the loss of Leo—Lily's name for the boy—tears of a sadness so great that she could barely catch her breath slid down her cheeks and soaked the sheet pulled taut across her chin. She remained in bed for a week and stared dully at the walls while Signora Miceli clucked and tutted and plied her with healing broths and tempted her with pastries. It took a second week for her to gather enough strength and determination to venture out of the house and pay a call on Mariella, who, upon seeing Lily's drawn face, collapsed backward into an armchair in a fit of sobbing. Lily bit her lower lip and patted Mariella on the head, but she felt cold and stiff, her heart a frozen lump in her breast, and she was barely able to tolerate the living warmth of the young woman's hair beneath her fingers. When the moment of emotion had passed, Lily lurched out the door of the pleasant chalet on the outskirts of Cortina.

That night, her last in the baker's house, she hacked off her billows of soft red hair with a nail scissors, then jammed the scissors into her shoulder and dragged it through the flesh of her upper arm for good measure. Signora Miceli, hearing what sounded like gasps of pain, or passion, through the bedroom wall, rushed to Lily's door and, without knocking, flung it open. She screamed when she saw the ragged, shorn hair, the bloody arm, and the comforter drenched in blood. "My child! What have you done to yourself?" she cried. Then quickly, pulling herself staunchly upright, with the age-old authority of Italian womanhood dealing with all manner of suffering and barbarity, she cleaned and bandaged Lily's shoulder.

Meanwhile the baker stood in the doorway in his nightshirt, the skin on his legs pale as whipped egg whites. He shook his head and called down curses on various heavenly beings and mothers' sons—Antonio Cassata foremost among them. Tears stained his cheeks. Lily could not bear their kindness, this heartfelt display of solidarity and compassion. Enfolded in the signora's arms, her face pressed against that great, soft, all-comforting bosom, she broke down and wept once more.

Lily fled to Sweden, attracted by the chilly landscape and the antiseptic nature of the scrubbed pine floors, unembellished white walls, and spare furnishings of the house where she lodged. Her shoulder pained her. Her hair grew brittle. She tutored English and cleaned houses in the summer, and in the winter rode her bicycle through the snow and darkness to a local high school, where her proficiency in French and English was put to use in the language department.

She retained few memories, and even these she would have been happy to release into the strange white light that illumined that period of her life: attending a crayfish feast at a long table, her host skoaling her so many times that she became drunk on aquavit. Gagging on a slab of blood pudding served with a sauce made of lingonberries. Picking mushrooms in a forest spongy with moss and damp shadows. Coupling with a stranger in the eerie incandescence of midsummer's eve when the sun never set and her lover danced through the firs like a blond-haired satyr. There were other men—beautiful, stern, and unmemorable—with whom she slept.

To carry a child almost to term and then lose him . . . who was to say what happened to a woman? Who was to say what a person did after something like that? She had read about people from whom a loved one had been taken. They had coupled right there on the floor, in the dirt, where they had suffered their loss. It was a scream of life. A reaffirmation.

She had given herself time to come to her senses, to wear out the scream.

Then she'd returned to Wisconsin.

Seven

Lily jolted upright. She had fallen asleep on the lounge chair, drifting through a still forest where the spectral figures of young girls bearing bouquets of wildflowers pirouetted around her in the pale half-light. The ringing of the telephone woke her. She opened her eyes, startled, and for a moment caught her breath: a platinum moon poked over the hilltops. On the terrace below her the plane tree shuddered; a ghostly luminescence flowed along its leaves like a milky soup. From behind its stout trunk a smoke-colored cat slunk forward and froze, slunk forward and froze, more a process than a being, stealing ninjalike toward a grove of mimosas.

Uncurling her legs and pushing herself to her feet, she thought, Oh, damn the phone, and, caught up in the soporific spell of the evening, she leaned over the railing, calling softly, "Alonso, Alonso. Come here. *Viens ici.*"

The cat shot an icy glance in her direction, as if to say, "Keep a lid on it, would you? Can't you see I'm hunting? You may be a *flâneuse*, a lazybones, napping on the porch, but I've got a job to do, and it requires silence. Dinner is at stake here, and mice have ears." A pale tongue darted out and flicked across a whiskery upper lip. "Ummm, tasty. Mouse ears."

It had grown cool while she dozed, a change in the weather. Lily shivered as she ran into the bedroom, sweeping the cashmere shawl off Madame Olivetti. "*Je suis desolée, Madame,* but I need it more than you do," she apologized to the typewriter. As she lunged for the receiver, the fringe of her shawl brushed against the stack of typed papers that had been accumulating over the past week and sent the topmost sheets flying. When Lily shot out a hand to catch them, she toppled the rest of the pile. Pages slid across the floor. The telephone continued to ring. With an explosive curse she grabbed the receiver, juggling it in one hand while crouching near the desk to gather up papers with the other. She spoke hurriedly into the mouthpiece. *"Allo? Allo?"*

"Hi, Mom," Justine called out loudly, investing her greeting with all her young love and flinging it across the Atlantic. She was calling from the ranch in Idaho. "What's wrong? Why didn't you answer? You sound out of breath. I let the phone ring forever. Hey, guess what. The siskins are back."

Lily could see her daughter through her voice, childish still, but impudent, clipped. Absentmindedly, she dropped whatever papers she had collected onto the bed and sat down beside them. "Have the finches arrived yet?" she asked.

"Flocks, Mom. We can't keep up with them. They're all so fat, and Apples just sits under the feeders, drooling. Pierre says they'd be great in a pie. Finch pie. He says Aunt Es will make us one, but Mom . . . could you tell him not to shoot them?"

Lily smiled and said, "Your brother would never shoot a finch, I promise."

"He shoots doves."

"He eats the doves."

"Well, what about finch pie? Isn't it filled with dead finches?"

"He's kidding you, honey. Pay him no attention. So what else are you up to?"

"Not much, Mom, but"—her girlish voice rose an octave with suppressed excitement—"you'll never guess who called. Monsieur Dupré. Our renter."

"Monsieur Dupré?" Lily said in surprise, and then fell silent, digesting the news while Justine rushed on breathily:

"He wanted to talk to you, Mom, but I explained how you needed a break and had to go to France for a month to work things out. I told him you were doing a lot of writing and thinking and those kinds of things, because Daddy died. I told him that's why you needed to be alone and get away from the ranch. Because Daddy died and you miss him."

"Thanks, honey, for filling him in," Lily observed drily, thinking, Why not take out an ad in the *Idaho Statesman*? What else had her daughter told him—and in what language? Monsieur Dupré had always written to her in French, never a word in English.

"You discussed all this in French?"

"Of course not. He speaks perfect English. I asked if he had a mustache and ate napoleons for breakfast and he said he *always* eats napoleons for breakfast and yes, he has a mustache, but not a big droopy one with pointy ends. Then he laughed and said you must be very proud to have me for a daughter."

"I *am* proud," Lily said.

"That's what I told him."

"Modesty, honey—"

"I know, Mom. I said it in French so it sounded more modest."

Smiling inwardly at her daughter's wily intelligence, a precocity that often left Lily scrambling for an adequate adult response, she said, "Did he talk to Aunt Es?"

"She wasn't here, so I took care of everything. I told him my schedule, your schedule . . . I said we were flying back to Idaho alone, me and Pierre, because you wanted to be there at La Pierre Rouge to check him out. Is it okay that I told him you were staying, Mom? It wasn't a surprise, was it?"

"Sort of," Lily admitted, aware that events were proceeding out of her control and that Justine had become a font of information dispensed to all who would listen. How did one turn such spontaneity off?

"He said he'd write you in France," Justine offered apologetically.

"I hope he does," Lily replied, but without enthusiasm, trying to shrug off the sudden uneasiness that tugged at the back of her mind. "How's your brother?" she asked to turn the conversation away from their renter and her own misgivings.

"Boring. Cows, cows, and more cows, you know. But Aunt Es is great. She tickles him at the dinner table, he even *laughs* at the dinner table. Can you believe it? She cooked . . . let's see, what was it? Coq au vin. You know that old rooster you thought was ready for the stew pot? Aunt Es chased it through the garden, she knocked down a few peonies—"

"No!"

"They already bloomed, Mom. Don't get all drippy about your peonies. They're pretty boring now, just green without the flowers. Anyway, Aunt Es caught the rooster and wrung its neck. I never thought she'd do it, but she's tough. She dumped it, feathers and all, in boiling water, and then she plucked it, just like you do, and threw it in your big pot with a bunch of herbs and some of Daddy's red wine. . . ."

Lily sensed a hesitation. "What is it, honey?"

"I still miss him. Don't you?"

"Of course I do. I miss him more than you can imagine."

Justine replied huffily, "Well, I *think* I can imagine. I'm nine years old. I'm not a baby anymore."

"Of course not," Lily agreed, careful to hide her amusement. Through the window the sea looked like a blue silk scarf tucked into the lap of the cork oaks. "It's just a little more than a month until you're here. Do you think you can manage?"

"I'll be fine, Mom, but what about you? You sound sort of lonely, and you've only been gone nine days. Do you think *you* can manage?"

"Without you?" There was a silence. "I'm not sure I *can* manage without you and Pierre."

"And Aunt Es," Justine chimed in loudly. "You should have seen her kill that rooster."

"I wish I had," Lily said with a chuckle. Then she added quickly, more to reassure herself than Justine, who seemed delighted with her status as Idaho correspondent for the Crisp ranch report, "July will speed by."

"Don't worry, Mom. You probably needed a vacation from Pierre. He can really crack the whip. He tries it with me, but I'm not a pushover like you are. Aunt Es isn't either."

A pushover?

"I miss you, honey."

"I miss you, too, Mom."

Then gently, as if she were lowering her hand to stroke her daughter's hair, Lily hung up the receiver.

Eight

*P*aul.

Now, this evening, without food in her stomach so that it was aching and grumbling as much as her heart, she would write about Paul.

I still miss him. Don't you?

I told him that was why you needed to be alone . . . because Daddy died. . . .

Paul Crisp. The only child of Justine Lafond and Freddy Crisp. The husband of Melinda Trumble for one year. The husband of Lily Fern for twenty-six years. Idaho rancher. Doting father of a son named Pierre and a daughter named Justine, born sixteen years apart. Dead at sixty-five of a heart attack like his father.

Before Lily met Paul, while she was busily engaged in moving into an apartment with Esther, finding a job, and reacquainting herself with the chatter and demands of family members, she stayed away from Antonio Cassata as much as was possible. She saw him once at her homecoming dinner when the extended Fern clan had gathered to celebrate. He managed no coherent greeting but kissed Lily warmly on her forehead. "You've changed your hairdo," he said.

"So have you," she replied, and stepped away from his hands before she recklessly took them in her own and placed them on her breasts. To keep her fingertips from stroking the high arch of his cheekbones, she tapped them on Philomena's swollen belly, where the second Cassata offspring was six months into production.

"Doesn't he look great?" Philomena asked dreamily, pressing Lily's hand against her stomach while slanting her eyes in her husband's direction. "Tonio's gotten back into motorcycles. Harleys this time around—"

And suddenly, without warning, Lily's vision had blurred. She felt as if she'd been pushed from an airplane into a howling wind. She was hurtling toward earth, and if she smashed into it and crushed what remained of Lily Fern, what small nuggets of fortitude and sanity she held tightly in her fists, so much the better. *Was it possible that she still loved him?* Her stomach lurched. Memory struck her like a blow to the abdomen as she saw herself clutching the toilet bowl and retching into it, her back heaving, the Micelis' voices in the background, through the closed door, animated in debate over what to do, should they send her home? Would her parents in Wisconsin hold them responsible? Of course the poor girl was more than a few weeks pregnant, she had carried this little sugared bun in her belly all the way from America. . . .

And then, miraculously, the air around Lily had cleared and she had heard a voice speaking; her own voice. It was saying breezily, "So tell me, Phila, do you have your own Harley, or do you ride on the back of Antonio's?"

And Philomena replying, paddling her stomach with her hands as if slapping a beach ball, "You have got to be kidding."

A month after returning from Sweden, Lily met Paul at a Saturday lecture on the French Impressionists. After living abroad for almost two years and having grown accustomed to making her own decisions, she was desperate for a day alone. Escape into France, into a previous century and the lives of painters who had fractured whole landscapes into dabs of color, seemed the perfect indulgence. Just before the lecture began an attractive older man slipped into the seat beside her.

"Do you mind?" he said.

Lily shrugged and smiled and hoped he wasn't a talker.

He wasn't. In fact, it was Lily who introduced herself when they broke for lunch. "Lily Fern," she said, and stuck out her hand. "I'm from around here but I can tell you're not, from your getup."

"Paul Crisp," he said. "Originally from Idaho. A transplanted rancher." He wore a pair of scuffed cowboy boots, blue jeans faded from repeated washings, and a brown leather belt with an intricately worked silver buckle. He looked neat in a fresh plaid shirt, lightly starched and expertly pressed. His cheeks were so closely shaven and smooth that they begged touching. Lily caught a pleasant whiff of lime from his aftershave or shampoo.

"So, what's an Idaho rancher doing in Wisconsin? Herding loons?" she asked.

"It's a long story," he said. "You don't want to hear it."

She raised an eyebrow. "You mean you don't want to tell it."

He suggested, "I could give you a few of the less sordid details when I know you better."

"Do you plan to know me better?" she said, and immediately put her hands to her lips and felt the color rush to her cheeks. "I'm sorry—that was rude. I've spent the past year in a very cold country, and I find that as I thaw, I've lost most of the social graces."

Paul grinned. "That makes two of us."

Lily found him appealing in an unconventional way, strong-featured, with a lofty wedge of nose that shaded a small but full-lipped and sensitive mouth. His eyes were a deep, liquid brown, almost black, overshadowed by thick slashes of eyebrows and fringed by long, upward-curling lashes. The distinctly roguish cast to his face was comically offset by a helmet of dark cherub's curls that frothed across the top of his head and cupped his ears. He was taller than Lily and muscular in build, although saddled with a few extra pounds around his middle, which he tapped fondly, if regretfully, when they ate their bag lunches together.

"Why are you interested in the art of France? Are you French?" she asked.

"I'm half French. Can't you tell? My mother was born in a village on the Côte d'Azur. There's no getting around heredity, is there?" And he thrust his nose upward, tapping its end. *"Le nez,"* he said with a grimace (and later, when Lily met his mother, she would recognize this same gesture of feigned dismay overlying a ferocious pride in the family nose). *"Et le ventre."* And the belly.

"And your father?"

"He grew up in Wisconsin, but he bought a ranch in Idaho and never came back here."

"Are those the sordid details you didn't want to tell me?"

Paul managed to wince while smiling. "I was thirty-six when I cut the strings that attached me to my mother, and my wife had already left me."

"You have a wife?"

"Had. She left three years ago," he said thinly. "She's remarried and living in Cincinnati."

"Not much of a life," Lily observed.

"Living on a ranch in Idaho?"

"No," she said. "Living in Cincinnati."

He gave a great percussive belly laugh, startling Lily. "I *would* like to know you better," he said.

"I think you'd be making a big mistake," she warned. "I need time to regroup. I'm a woman transitioning back into her life."

"I've always thought that what you're doing, even if it's a mistake, *is* your life. It's not something you slide in and out of."

"An Idaho rancher herding loons in Wisconsin sounds like slippage to me. Maybe we're both regrouping."

Paul cocked his head sideways and gave her a funny little

smile. "Could I interest you in some poached whitefish for dinner?"

She responded, "Could you broil it?"

He said, "Certainly."

The broiled whitefish dinner took place the following evening at the small apartment Paul kept in the city. He explained that he spent most of his time in his house on a lake near the Michigan border, in northern Wisconsin. Lily said her folks had once owned a cabin there and she would never forget the loons yodeling across the lake, or the silky-soft feel of the water as she slipped into it. They'd sold the cottage when she was fifteen and she'd fumed for a week, refusing to eat, and then gotten over it.

Paul said, "Good. You'll have to come up for a visit."

That first evening they discussed politics, families, and religion, laughed and drank too much wine, and lingered for a leisurely two and a half hours over the meal of broiled fish, roasted potatoes, and Caesar salad that Paul had prepared for her. He'd made a flan for dessert and served it with a dollop of freshly whipped cream. He poured a generous glass of Château d'Yquem for each of them.

"How do you manage?" she said when they were doing the dishes. "An apartment in Milwaukee, a house up north, and a ranch in Idaho. Doesn't it get expensive?"

Paul replied with a shake of his head, sounding slightly discomfited, "My grandfather cut down trees, lots of trees. He made a pile of money in timber."

"So what do you do? Just go to lectures and—"

He cut in quickly, "It's summer vacation at the college where I teach geology."

"I thought you were a rancher."

"I am," he said. "But when I went away to college I figured geology might be a good career for a guy who loves rocks and requires solitude. If I was a teacher, at least I'd have my summers free. So I got my master's degree and taught for a while in Montana, but at heart . . ." He shrugged and tapped the tip of his nose with his index finger, as if *le nez*—the nose—was where his own heart resided. "Maybe I just missed my mother's old-world cooking, brains and kidneys. You can't get them in Missoula. So I moved back to the ranch with my parents."

"But then you left again. I can't keep track."

"My mother owns the ranch," he explained. "The house on the lake belonged to my grandmother, and I rent this apartment just to get some culture from time to time."

She said, "End of interview. I've got it."

He said, "Have you noticed that you ask all the questions and I do all the talking?"

Later, standing beside her car in the cool summer night, he kissed her good night on both cheeks in the French fashion. Then he helped her into her seat, asked if she was okay to drive, and when she nodded—perhaps a little too vehemently—closed the door after her.

In the weeks that followed they went to the movies, where he held her hand, while with their free hands they shared a large carton of buttered popcorn. They went to the art museum; walked along the lakeshore; rode bicycles all the way to Doctor's Park; and took a Sunday drive in the country, stopping for a late-afternoon supper of deep-fried perch, baked potatoes, and coleslaw in a restaurant overlooking Lake Michigan.

As they were lingering over their wedges of key lime pie, Lily told Paul that she had finally found work translating manuscripts from French into English. "It's a stretch," she admitted. "I'm a bit rusty, but at least I can set my own hours."

"Are you receiving a salary commensurate with your talents?" he prodded her with mock formality.

She quipped in return, "Enough to pay my share of the rent and keep me in chocolate."

It was a sunny but breezy afternoon, the waves of Lake Michigan cresting in topknots of foam, brilliant in the sunlight. Sailboats cut through the chop in a jubilant dance of speed and lightness. Lily and Paul smiled at each other and shook their heads at the wonderment of such a day, such clean-washed sunshine and high-spirited water. Even the rocks on the beach, where the waves rushed in and splashed the shore almost playfully, seemed animated, lighthearted.

"So what's today's interview?" Paul asked blithely, caught up in the spirit of the sunny afternoon.

Lily feigned a lack of curiosity, but a question sailed off the tip of her tongue as lightly as the boats riding the frisky waters. "What was your wife like? Do you mind my asking?"

"Melinda? I fell in love with her legs," he answered agreeably, licking a dab of whipped cream from his upper lip and washing it down with a gulp of coffee. "I was living on the ranch at the time. Melinda was a college senior on Christmas break, writing a paper on water in the west. Her aunt was a friend of my mother's. She suggested that Melinda give me a ring and ask me some questions. She had this soft, hesitant voice over the phone so I thought, what the hell—"

"How old were you then?" Lily interrupted, having just wolfed down the last of her pie and covetously eyeing what remained of Paul's. With a wary grin, he cupped his hands around the back of his plate.

"Thirty-four," he said. "Too old for Melinda. But her voice was enough to get me into my car, driving north in a blizzard. She had told me she was actually majoring in Dutch painting, so before the interview could get under way I slipped in a comment about the light at the ranch, how it drifted in through the pantry window. It was cool and clear, like in a painting by Vermeer. I went on about an old cracked pitcher frozen in the pale light and Blanca, the Mexican woman who did the cleaning, lit up like the Holy Virgin. It was snowing like hell out and Melinda's aunt had cranked the heat up so high I wanted nothing more than to strip down to my boxers. That would hurry things along. She was wearing shorts and her legs just didn't end."

"How long before you got married?" she asked.

He was swallowing a bite of pie and mumbled his answer, sounding slightly embarrassed. "As soon as she graduated. She was flattered because I was a rancher and so much older than she was. I think she fell in love with my love for her. I was pretty well gone and I made her feel like an infinitely fascinating woman— which of course I thought she was. My folks made an effort to make her feel like a part of the family since we were all living together under one roof, but she didn't stand a chance. My father was immensely wealthy from all those trees my grandfather cut down, and he didn't say much. Melinda took his silence as a personal slight because she didn't come from a moneyed family. But Dad never put on airs. My mother didn't either, but she was an even more formidable problem for Melinda. My mother is . . . a piece of work. She's shrewd, outspoken, flamboyant, and charming, and she smokes cheroots. All of this was light-years beyond Melinda's experience.

"I tried to convince her that Maman had this terrible bark but she never bit the people she loved. Melinda said that sounded less than reassuring. It wasn't at all clear that Maman loved *her*. That was the beginning of the end. I'd always assumed that after I was married nothing would change. My dad would still get out of bed before daylight to check the fences. My mother would still cook potage for lunch and boiled tripe for dinner. Blanca would still belt out Mexican love songs while cleaning the toilets. Except I'd have a woman in my bed, and she'd love me.

"Then my father died of a heart attack. Some of the neighbor's cattle had come through the fence during the night and Dad was riding out to repair the break. It was before dawn when he knocked on our door. Melinda and I were . . . otherwise occupied, so I told him I'd meet him at the break in fifteen minutes. It took a little longer than that," Paul explained, with a wry smile, "and the next thing I heard was the clatter of hooves on the driveway. I looked out the window and there was the chestnut mare Dad always rode. My mother wept for weeks. Dad was sixty-five."

"What about Melinda?" Lily asked. She had been listening intently, intrigued as she always was by family histories. She had been careful not to interrupt Paul so he wouldn't lose the thread of his narrative.

Paul snorted in reply, "Melinda waited until after the funeral to inform me that she couldn't bear the bawling of the damn cows for one more day, her entire wardrobe smelled like manure, she was fed up with eating organ meats, and I was damn right that my mother only bit the people she didn't love."

He pushed what was left of his pie toward Lily. "Here, you eat it," he said, and chuckled. "All my life I've been lean and fit. I've been a rancher. But after Melinda left, my mother cooked five-course meals to bring me around. And I ate them."

In early August, five weeks after they first met, Lily drove up from the city to visit Paul in his lakeside home. As soon as she stepped out of her car, the mosquitoes attacked every inch of exposed flesh—her feet in sandals, her legs in shorts, her bare arms in a tank top, her throat and the back of her neck, a tear-shaped area of bare skin between her shoulder blades, her cheeks, her chin, and the top of her head. She fled across the driveway and burst into the house, slapping at her limbs, screaming, "Get these damn things off me."

Paul handed her a can of OFF! and said, "Here." And then: "Would an old-fashioned help?" He walked away and began to make one.

Later they took a swim in the lake, showered, dawdled over more drinks and conversation on the screened-in porch, and dined as the sun was setting. Lily felt herself returning to life as the tension and grimness of that interminable year after losing Leo finally receded. The wound inside her had begun to close over, heal, and form a scar that she could touch upon lightly in her mind, checking for tenderness and roughness, just as she ran her fingers over the scar on her shoulder. Her growing friendship with Paul encouraged recovery, a gently assisted reentry into youth, with its innocent gifts and its mundane pleasures.

Over dinner Paul told her his grandmother's story. This was her house, he reminded Lily. His grandmother had willed it to him. His father had married a French girl and brought her with him to his ranch in Idaho. "For the first few years Granny Fi lived with them," Paul explained. "But Dad was so besotted with my mother that he forgot his own mother's birthday, and, even worse, suggested that she might enjoy spending Christmas in Detroit with my uncle. There was an exchange of words and accusations, including my mother's allegedly kicking Fritzy, my grandmother's dachshund, under the dinner table, and my father turning into a goatlike man who thought of nothing but *carnal pleasure*—damning words from the mouth of Granny Fi, who came close to fainting if sex was mentioned."

Lily read in Paul's tremulous smile, as he talked about his parents and grandmother and even the irascible Fritzy, whom only Granny Fi held dear, how deep was his capacity for love. And she thought how judgmental she could be of her own parents and, at times, how unforgiving. But Paul was speaking again, and Lily savored a buttery mouthful of Chardonnay while returning her attention to his story.

He said with an amiable chortle, "My grandmother thought she could mold my mother, but Maman's . . . sexual exuberance was more than Granny Fi could handle. She waited around for me to be born, but when Maman took to nursing me at the dinner table, Granny protested by dining alone in her room. My father refused to get involved. Then Fritzy died, and that clinched it. Granny packed her bags and bought this house on the lake in Wisconsin where she'd grown up. She lived here unhappily for the next twenty-five years. Every summer when I came to visit, she refreshed my memory on why she'd left Idaho. She never spoke to my father again. They both had their backs up and, coming from the same genetic pool, neither gave an inch. One summer evening when Granny was in her eighties, a wind came up while she was paddling her canoe far from shore. She'd swum across the lake every morning when she was a girl, but when the canoe capsized she sank like a stone. On her way to the bottom, I doubt she regretted it."

"What a sad story," Lily mused as she pictured Paul's grandmother wearing Red Wing boots and wool trousers to keep the mosquitoes out and the evening chill from reaching her bones. Lily mentally dressed her in a boiled wool fedora with a jaunty feather, a plaid wool Pendleton shirt with the sleeves buttoned tight around her wrists, and an oiled-canvas hunting jacket. If she'd been wearing *that* outfit, Lily thought, no wonder she drowned.

After she went to bed that night, Lily left the door to the guest room unlocked in case Paul decided to pay her a visit. Was it the sound of the door opening that awakened her? She looked to see if Paul was standing in the doorway but spotted no one in the shadows. The moon had gone down. Feeling chilled and haunted by the image of Fiona Crisp in her woodsman's boots and layers of thick clothing plummeting downward, downward into the black water, circling like a giant ray, its wings flapping in slow motion, she pulled up a second blanket and lay in the dark room, her eyes open wide as she listened to the loons calling across the lake, their eerie wails. And she thought how Paul and his grandmother had both fled the ranch and taken refuge in this remote location. For both it was a floating world, an anodyne for grief, based on a need for escape and solitude.

For the next few hours Lily slept fitfully. She dreamed that she could hear her parents' voices raised in argument through the thin cabin walls. They had taken Leo from her and bound him with cords to the back of a loon. She tried to rouse herself enough to get out of her bed and rescue the baby, but she, too, was strapped in tightly and could only watch in horror as the loon carried her son across the rippling moonlit lake. The bird's tremulous cries sounded like the distillation of all loss and sorrow.

In the morning, sunlight once again played over the leaves of the silver birches and infused the air with an almost palpable shimmer. The lake lay placid and smoothly sheeted, like a gleaming blue reflective cover that had been pulled tightly over the water and would be rolled back later in the morning to accommodate the swimmers and water skiers, after they'd climbed out of their beds and finished their breakfasts.

Paul brought Lily a wide round mug of café au lait where she sat at the kitchen table. "This is as good as any I've ever tasted," she said after taking a noisy slurp. The foam had settled softly beneath her nose. She licked her upper lip clean and sighed. Delicious! As, too, were the slices of papaya dribbled with lime juice, and the croissants Paul had pulled warm from the oven and placed in a basket in front of her. There were homemade butter curls and raspberry jam precisely aligned on the tabletop, on a faded but neatly pressed floral cloth, the kind Lily's grandma Fern used to unfurl for Sunday dinner.

"Did you hear the loons last night?" she asked as she dabbed at the flaky remains of a croissant with moistened fingertips, which she licked with pleasure.

Paul observed her, smiling with amusement. "They sound

like wolves, don't they? Sometimes I can't sleep for the howling. They're like spirits out there, the voices of loved ones."

"Voices and spirits? Isn't that a little—outré?"

"You heard them calling last night?"

"I did," she confirmed, and felt affection for the man welling up inside her. There was something gentle in his manner, something contained and shimmering, like a drop of mercury that formed a perfect ball when trapped inside glass. If the glass broke, the mercury skittered and ran, no longer one ball but many.

"But loons aren't wolves," she said.

"They didn't sound like wolves to you?"

She shook her head no.

"Have you ever lost someone you really loved, some shadow you've wiped off the slate of memory? If you had, you'd know."

"I know," said Lily sharply, the camaraderie she'd felt moments earlier draining from her.

"You do? I wonder, then, why you can't hear the wolves."

"Does it matter?" she snapped, surprising herself and, from the look in Paul's eyes, surprising him as well. She glared into her empty coffee mug. "Don't tell me I don't know loss or pain."

"I'm sorry," he said softly. "I would never suggest that. We all know loss and pain—it's the human condition. I simply meant—"

"Fine," she interrupted him. "That's fine. We can drop the subject now."

"I simply meant . . . ," he began again and then stopped, grown flushed in the face, plainly exercised by the sullen note his houseguest had introduced into a pleasant conversation. Lily could guess what he was thinking: Why did women do this, become prickly and drag emotions into a perfectly innocuous discussion? Surely two people of different genders could chat about a loon's eerie call, howl, whether it was wolflike or not, without taking it all so personally.

"I'm sorry," she said. "You touched a raw nerve."

"Don't worry. I have them too."

"You do? You're so down-to-earth and well adjusted. Like bedrock. Like the Idaho batholith you've been telling me about."

"If I were down-to-earth and well adjusted I wouldn't be here," he said.

"Sometimes we all need a break from our lives. I took one."

"Sweden?"

She nodded. "And Italy. What about you? Have you ever been to France with your mother?"

"She didn't go back for forty years," he told her, "until after her father died. Then she said there were too many ghosts. She had an aunt who hung herself. When Maman walked up to the goat shed at La Pierre Rouge, the house where she grew up, she reported a ghost hanging from the rafters. She was convinced it was her aunt Giselle. Maman has always had a histrionic bent. Life is an explosion of emotion when you're around her." He drew in air noisily through his nostrils and then opened his mouth and exhaled in a great release of whatever it was—the need for autonomy, distance from memories—that had taken him away from the ranch and his mother and landed him here, in this temporary base camp.

Although *was* it temporary? Lily asked herself. Maybe this had become Paul's future. Maybe he would never choose to leave here. And who was she to speculate on what a person did or did not choose? What was Lily Fern doing tapping her toes in Wisconsin?

"Was your mother upset when you left the ranch?" she inquired briskly to change the subject and distance herself from the concept of temporary base camps and personal soul-searching.

Wasn't it always easier and more satisfactory to explore the life of a fellow misfit?

"As I said," Paul reiterated, "my mother does nothing without carrying on. But she wasn't the only one. When I left for Wisconsin we were both crying."

"You cried?" Lily blurted out, astonished.

"Why not? Most people cry when they're leaving someone they love. I'd lived with her all my life. I knew I'd miss her and she'd miss me. So we cried."

"I've only cried once in my life that I can remember," she admitted.

"When was that?"

"It's a long story. You don't want to hear it." She was teasing him now, echoing his earlier disclaimer when they had first met and the mention of sordid details had piqued her interest. But there was a brusqueness to her tone of voice.

Paul responded by suggesting amiably, "Would you like to walk down to the dock with our last cup of coffee?"

"No way," she said. "The mosquitoes will eat us alive. Anyway," she added, standing up and taking his hand, "I have a better idea." And leading him into his bedroom and pulling him down onto his rumpled bed, she caressed him with a lingering gentleness that said, Thank you, Paul Crisp. Thank you for never rushing me or overwhelming me with demands, never prying into my life where I would prefer that no one forced an entry. And he touched her in ways and in places that kindled desire, that somehow melted the parts of her steeled against the touch of any man who possibly loved her, somehow cleansed from her body the rigorous, chilling, self-punishing embraces of her Swedish partners.

When they lay together, slick with sweat and sated with what Lily recognized was a sexual exorcism of an ex-wife and an ex-lover, she said, her voice hoarse and depleted from the depths of their lovemaking, "Remember when we were talking about the loons at breakfast?"

His hand slipped over her breast and enclosed it, like a muff of warmth. He groaned with contentment. "Should I?" he asked.

She rolled up on an elbow and looked down into his eyes. "I was wondering, Paul, if *you* lost someone you loved so much that you wiped him, or her, off the slate of memory?"

"Yes, I did," he said. "Or I thought I did. My wife, Melinda."

"But now . . . ?"

Turning his head to gaze out the window, he addressed a sailboat below them on the lake, heeled over and skimming at breakneck speed across the water. He spoke quietly, avoiding Lily's eyes. "I don't expect an answer soon, or ever . . . ," he said, hesitating before going on, "and this has nothing to do with her, with Melinda, I promise you . . . or I think I promise you . . ."

Lily put her hand on his cheek and turned his face toward hers. She said, "Spit it out, Paul. I'm here. I'm beside you," never suspecting what was sticking in his throat.

He said, "Will you marry me?"

Nine

It was shady where Lily sat at the table on the terrace, soothed by the soft buzz of bees in the lavender and the convivial chirping of a few tiny birds. Alonso, spread-eagled beneath a mimosa, emitted a sound more vole- than catlike: a rasping peep. Beneath a pink and gray spotted nose his mouth curled up as if a dream mouse, fat and spunky, were being tossed high in the air by sharp little teeth—to the accompaniment of Mozart. The Belgians had turned up the volume on a flute sonata, not one Lily recognized. Not Paul's shaving music.

She had dreamed one night that she was digging toward China, and if she dug deep enough and long enough she would find Paul alive, wearing blue pajamas and humming Mozart in Beijing. The dream had soothed and charmed her. Is that where he had landed, the whirling cloud of dust that had been her husband, reborn as a Chinese musicologist?

She needed sunglasses to observe the sea as sunlight struck its water obliquely and sliced its surface into shimmering mirrors. Thank God for the counterpoint of the sea! Today, in her writing, she would face a rather bleak and uncomplimentary passage in her life. It would be typed onto the page with the help of her trusted friend, Madame Olivetti, to whom, since the weather had warmed, Lily had returned her cashmere shawl, for dust protection. But for now, enjoying her solitude, she lingered over breakfast and was breaking open a warm croissant when she heard the chugging of Yves's truck laboring up the hill. She felt a sting of irritation; how peaceful it had been, slipping into morning with a sleepy disregard for appointments and commitments, with only a cat for company. But when Yves appeared around a corner of the house, his cap in hand, looking, as always, well fed and affable, Lily's pique at being disturbed vanished.

"*Bonjour, Yves. Ça va?*"

"*Oui. Ça va,*" Yves said, but the smile that had lit up his face upon seeing Lily twisted into a frown. "You look . . . overtired. Exhausted."

"I don't doubt it," she admitted. "I was up most of the night writing about my husband." She patted the seat beside her. "Here. Sit down. Would you drink a cup of coffee?"

He surprised her by accepting, and, slipping onto the bench beside her, he laid his cap on the table, spinning it with his fingers while she filled a second mug from the thermos. He took a sip of coffee, pronounced it excellent, and remarked matter-of-factly, "I can see in your face that you loved him."

"Can you?" she said. There was a softness to her smile as she confessed, "Actually, I don't remember *being* in love when I married Paul, but I was tremendously fond of him."

"Maybe it was lust," Yves suggested with a self-deprecating snort of laughter. "I was married once. I saw Marie's ivory skin, just a slice of it through a break in the curtains, and I became enflamed. When she withheld the slice from me, I quickly married her."

Lily laughed. "With Paul it was friendship. I simply enjoyed being with him. He seemed so grounded by the ranch in Idaho and his upbringing. He was suffering through a few years of estrangement from his mother . . . but that didn't seem to shake the solid core of him."

Yves grinned over the rim of his coffee mug. "I am thinking that friendship builds a firmer foundation for marriage than lust." His eyes crinkled up. "But there must be . . . it has to be agreed upon . . . how does one say this? Sex must be a part of the friendship package."

"In our case, it was," Lily said, and then blushed at her own presumptuousness. "You know, Yves, I hired you to fix the problems with my roof, not the problems with my psyche."

"I have offended you, Madame?"

"Oh, please," Lily said, "don't call me Madame. My name is Lily. I may be old enough to be your mother, but surely—"

"My mother!" Yves snorted. "You are too young and beautiful to be my mother! My sister, perhaps. . . . My mother has a nose like the prow of a great ship. It can part the wind in two directions. When she talks and talks I imagine the waves breaking over her nose, endlessly. You see . . ." He pointed at his own nose, reminding Lily of Paul jutting his nose into the air, as if it were on exhibit. What was it with these Frenchmen and their noses? she wondered. But Yves went on, "I have my mother's nose, although fortunately it is the three-quarter-size model." He chuckled heartily while Lily joined in, reminded of a breakfast with Paul at the lake, after they were married, when over bowls of cereal grown soggy with milk they had jiggled with laughter, heaved with laughter. Because of what? His nose? His mother? Loons? She had no recollection.

"Thank you, Yves," she said. "Thanks for making me laugh and for listening. I guess I needed to talk. I've been living so much in my memories." She placed her hand warmly over his and for an awkward moment neither of them spoke; they seemed paralyzed, mesmerized by her small, smooth hand looking naked and vaguely erotic perched on top of his. She removed hers promptly and, to ease the transition, gestured at Alonso, who crept silently toward her. "Have you met this foolish cat?"

"Whose is he?"

"He belongs to my neighbors, the Belgians who live below me."

"I believe he is presenting you with a liver or a kidney. From a mouse, by the look of it. He must be in love."

Lily peered over the side of her chair, and, indeed, a small, fresh organ leaking purple blood had been left by the cat. *"Merci,"* she called to him as he marched away, tail erect. "He looks like a Buddha in cat's pajamas, doesn't he? Remarkable eyes. I wonder what he knows, what he sees."

Yves tipped back his head and finished off his last swallow of coffee. "He sees meat," he said, "with fur or feathers. There's no Buddha in that cat."

"You think not? He's got our number. Believe me. They all do, these animals. They've reduced life to its simplest elements. Eat. Sleep. Purr."

"But they suffer."

"Dogs—but not cats. Think of the time they spend curled up in absolute stillness."

Yves thrust back his chair. "Think of the time I spend talking to you when I should be working!" He stood up, as did Lily.

"The bed?" she said.

"The bed . . . ?" Yves hesitated while, amused, Lily read the confusion on his face. Which bed? he was probably wondering. The one with the white linen sheets and the alluring comforter? Ah . . . non! The one that had fallen apart in her daughter's bedroom.

Together they crossed the terrace, Lily leading and taking down an old iron key from a hook on the wall, and unlocking the door.

"Voilá, the bed," she announced with a flourish of her hand. "It belonged to my husband's great-aunt."

"This room . . ." Yves paused, shaking his head. "It resembles the cell of a nun."

"Yes, it does," Lily said as she looked around her at the white-washed walls, the narrow bedstead, the pair of straight-backed chairs standing stiff as sentries flanking the ancient washstand that had belonged to Giselle. While Yves crouched to examine the bedstead, Lily crossed to the window and cranked it open. She imagined the young woman staring bleakly down the long sloping vista of treetops to the sea, sobered by her visit, by her sister's husband and her sister's children.

While Yves hefted the mattress from the bed and carried it one-handed, like an overlarge dog transported by the scruff of its neck, to the far wall, Lily recounted the story of Justine Lafond, the attempted rape, and the tragic history of Giselle Godard. Yves tapped his nose, intrigued, as he listened to her tale. When she was finished he said:

"It's your classic ménage à trois, but it sounds a bit darker."

"It was," Lily admitted. "I've always wondered why Giselle stayed on with Monsieur Lafond."

He suggested mischievously, "Perhaps she slept with him after Sunday luncheon? He was a vigorous man, a stonemason, *non?*"

"But why didn't she run off with her nephew, Paul?"

"Perhaps she wasn't invited. Perhaps her love went unreturned. This frustrates you, not to know, doesn't it?"

"Not to *understand.*"

"What is there to understand? Maybe she despaired. Much as we desire it, love doesn't always show us its kindest face. Perhaps the pain was too much or . . ." He hesitated, casting his eyes toward the empty bedstead, his lips curled up in a bold grin. "Perhaps she could not endure another Sunday in bed with Monsieur Lafond."

"Perhaps she couldn't," Lily agreed.

"Was she beautiful?"

"I can't tell you, Yves. I don't think I've ever seen her picture. There are some old photograph albums in the armoire in the living room. I've been meaning to go through them, but I always put it off since the cupboard could use a good cleaning. There are boxes of cornflakes Monsieur Lafond must have put there over twenty-five years ago."

His face lit up in a knowing smile. "There, you have your answer! Giselle was fed up with making love to a man who ate cornflakes!"

"I've never thrown the cornflakes out," Lily confessed, laughing, "like they're some kind of shrine or memorial. Maybe it's time I did." Then, spotting something on the floor beside her foot, she stooped to pick it up—a leaf that must have blown into the room the previous autumn. It crumbled in her hand. She heard Yves's voice close behind her. How close . . . ? She was wearing shorts and suddenly grew conscious of the backs of her legs presented for his inspection. Well, let him discover what he would. She made no apologies.

He told her gaily as she turned to face him, "I should not mention this since you are my employer, but you have lovely legs, Madame. Lovely. They could belong to a woman half your age."

"Oh, I think not," she said. Her tone was mildly bantering. "But here is something for you to remember, Yves. I am not Madame, I am not half my age, and my name is Lily." With a quick smile, she left him to his work and stepped across the terrace, made buoyant by his compliment and the sexual badinage, lighthearted and innocent, that had passed between them.

Returned to her bedroom and her desk, Lily vowed that now she would not stop. She would continue her writing until she and Paul were married and had moved to Idaho, and Pierre was born. She would see this segment of her story through whether Alonso waylaid every bird flitting through the Belgians' orchard, whether he paraded beneath her window day and night screeching in his exultant cat's voice, "I have killed another mouse for you, my darling" (she would not halt the carnage); whether Yves announced it was time to fix *her* bed, which was not broken, and coaxed her into it—she would resist all interruptions and temptations, bolt the doors, and entrust her mental well-being to the low-slung carriage and squeaky return of Madame Olivetti.

She warned Yves at lunchtime that she would be immersed in her writing for a day or two and, hence, unavailable. She told him after he had shimmed the joints on Justine's bedstead and replaced the broken panes of glass in the upstairs bathroom, while he was packing up his tools. They stood together in the driveway, in the heat of early afternoon. She noticed a sheen of sweat on his nose and cheeks, and touched a finger to the moisture pooled in the hollow of her neck. They shook hands and wished each other a pleasant day and a delicious meal—his would be tastier, she assured him—and then, on impulse, she rose on tiptoe and kissed him on one cheek and then the other. His eyes caressed her from under his cap and the shock of black hair that tumbled across his forehead. His hands hung empty at his sides. He clenched and unclenched his fingers. She thought: He is a great deal younger than I am.

Yves opened the door to his truck, and the measured tempo of his movements as he slipped behind the wheel betrayed the pull of desire. He looked into her eyes and Lily felt a frisson of recognition pass between them. He said he would return, the day after tomorrow. He was not yet finished with his mending.

"I'll see you then, Yves."

"This is not as healthy as you think it is, Lily."

"What isn't?"

"All this writing."

She said, "I suspect it isn't."

Ten

*L*ily sat alone in a room of lengthening shadows and golden light, dust thickening the air and glimmering as the sun slanted in through the window and painted her arms in points of light—Seurat arms, she thought, and smiled at the memory. Paul was always comparing parts of the female anatomy to paintings. Esther had the hips of a Renoir. Philomena tended toward the thick, solid limbs of Gauguin's island beauties. Lily was Goya's *Maja Nude*, with a little less breast. A week after they'd first made love at the lake, Paul had remarked on Ingres's *Odalisque*. He'd said he felt fortunate to be sleeping with a woman who was not so long-waisted and cool.

Fortunate! How little Paul knew at the time, or suspected.

At the end of August, when the Cassatas' second child was safely delivered, Lily had unwrapped her nephew from his blanket, tilted him this way and that, and peeked at his bottom. "What on earth are you doing?" Philomena had inquired languidly, in a rosy daze, as she lay in her hospital bed, radiant after delivery.

Lily answered her, "It's a cute little rump. Just checking to make sure everything's in the right place." She surveyed the rest of him: spindrifts of red hair, gray-green eyes, and skin as rosy as parboiled shrimp.

Just then Antonio cracked open the door and peered around it to find Lily wrapping up his newborn son in a hospital blanket. He walked over and kissed his wife on the forehead, then gave Lily a hug. "I raced home to check on Gina," he reported. "Esther seems to be keeping her busy and fed. I told her you'd be there soon to spell her, Lily. If she wants she can swing by later with Gina. Did you notice his hair? It's red like yours, and he's got your eyes."

Lily said, "I noticed. He's wonderful."

"Did you tell Lily what we named him?" Antonio asked his wife, sliding into the chair beside her bed and reaching out with his large right hand to stroke her shoulder.

"Not yet." Philomena beamed at her husband before turning her quiet green eyes on her sister. "We've decided to call him Leo, after Leonardo da Vinci. And there's something else." She gave a little giggle. "We figure Leo's the Italian equivalent of Lily, don't ask me why."

Lily caught her breath, and then forced a wide appreciative smile to her lips. "That's a lovely name, and thoughtful of the two of you," she said as the irony of two Leos slid like a knife into her belly.

Pain struck. A small vial of pain, tightly stoppered and labeled "Cortina," had been hidden inside her until a second Leo popped into her life and uncorked it. Pain spilled into her system and trickled toward her heart. She wanted to run, to escape it. She wanted movement, change, distance from this cozy family scene. She wanted Signora Miceli's bosom. She wanted the baker's sweet kiss on her forehead. She wanted Leo, her own Leo. She wanted Paul Crisp with his solid stance, his rancher's squint, and his steady smile. She wanted to rock this small boy in her arms forever. Still cradling Leo and avoiding Antonio's eyes, she said to her sister, "I'm sure he'll be a tiger."

But she lacked the heart to add, "Like his father."

That same night she telephoned Paul. It seemed so cold in retrospect, so severely planned and formal, almost as if a third party had arranged their union. In a perverse sense a third party had, for it was a little boy named Leo who had prompted Lily to make that call.

"Are you awake?" she asked.

"Not for long," he said.

"Paul, did you mean it when you asked me to marry you?"

"Whoa there, Macduff," he replied in a voice that sounded hoarse and somewhat breathy, as if he'd been lifting weights or doing sit-ups. "What's the hurry?"

"Actually, I could use a friend."

Paul chuckled. "That doesn't require a marriage license. Most women get married because they could use a husband."

"That's what I'm saying," she insisted. "The answer is yes."

They had agreed to marry—over the telephone! *Agreed.* A word stripped of romance and the passion of commitment. And yet there had been commitment on her part, because she was a woman who did nothing lightly or by half measures. There had been passion as well, a sexual meshing that pleasured them both: there was no lack of romance in the bed department. So then, what was missing? Only this: the almost palpable shimmer of attraction, lust, complicity, recognition between two people that exploded into a light so bright it immolated such niceties as trust and loyalty, respect and friendship; immolated any communication other than the language of bodies spoken in a rising heat, in moans, whispers, and cries; immolated all but the stardust that had already fallen on Lily in a grove of flowering fruit trees, on a hot summer evening when her parents and sisters had gone to the movies. She'd become wary of shimmer and stardust and was grateful for a man who moved through life quietly, thoughtfully, somewhat formally, with only a modicum of shimmer—and yet, unaccountably, he kept her off her guard and interested. When she least expected it, with a certain je ne sais quoi that shot a veil of confusion over her perfectly ordered image of Paul, he both mystified and seduced her.

A week later they climbed the courthouse steps in Milwaukee with no family member as witness. Lily was twenty-four and looked tired, her red hair closely cropped in a Swedish style, her skin deeply tanned, for it was the end of summer. Her shoulders were bared in a sea green sheath, her legs smooth and shiny in nylon stockings. She wore spectator pumps; Paul wore cowboy boots scuffed at the heels, but the hand-tooled brown leather toes shone with polish. He was thirty-nine, stocky and vigorous, dressed in pressed khakis, a blue plaid shirt, and a knitted tie. His coarse black curls were neatly combed and tamed for the occasion.

Lily stopped suddenly, restraining him with a gentle hand on his arm. "We're early," she said. "Let's wait to go inside."

"Cold feet?" he inquired, but the teasing smile that had accompanied his question grew tight around the edges when he looked into her eyes.

Speaking quickly and without hesitation, she announced, "I have a couple of things to tell you, Paul. I should have told you sooner. I'm sorry. You're free to back out. I'll understand—no recriminations—if you change your mind."

"Only two things?" he responded calmly. His smile had unaccountably softened and widened.

"I was pregnant two and a half years ago in Italy. I lost the baby."

"I'm sorry to hear that." He waited quietly for her second disclosure.

"I'm not in love with you, Paul. Not the way a woman should be in love when she gets married. I feel tremendous affection—I love being with you, but it's not the same. You deserve better."

"Are you in love with someone else?" he asked. "With the baby's father, for instance?"

"I can't say for certain, but I hope not," she answered him.

Paul nodded, quietly digesting these startling admissions while Lily studied his right cheek, angled fractionally away from her. Then he turned to face her. He looked directly into her eyes and said quite formally, "I love you enough for both of us, Lil, but I'm not made of stone. I assume that, with time, love will become a part of the marital arrangement."

"I imagine it will," she replied, and slid her hand into his.

He bent over and kissed her on the mouth. "Shall we then, Miss Fern?" And together, with hands clasped and swinging between them, they ran up the steps so as not to be late for their marriage appointment.

Hours later, still dressed in his white socks, his khaki pants, and his blue plaid shirt (he had taken off his boots and tie), Paul lounged in the bathroom doorway observing Lily. She was standing in the shower, singing softly, washing off the grime and sweat of the long afternoon in the city, and the even longer drive home to the lake. Suddenly he stepped into the shower fully clothed, took her in his arms and, hastily unbuttoning, unzipping, shedding heavy cloth from slippery skin, drew her naked legs up and around his waist and pressed her back against the tiles. The shower had its way with them, water running into and out of and shamelessly everywhere, lubricating, heating, and rinsing away the loss of Antonio, who, after all, was nothing more than a wildly handsome, weak-willed, amoral bastard. Soaking wet and naked except for his socks, Paul made extraordinary and unforgettable love to her.

Eleven

*F*or the first few months of her marriage Lily cleaned. As single-mindedly as she had worked in the bakery in Cortina and, afterward, had packed up and moved to Sweden, she scrubbed the pine floors of their house by the lake. She swept down the log walls, vacuumed the upholstery, and washed the curtains. She aired the down comforters in the cold October sunshine and, after shaking out the summer blankets, stacked them alongside the linens in Fiona Crisp's cedar wedding chest. She oiled the antique sideboard and the chest of drawers in the corner of the dining room. She dusted the books on the library shelves. She scoured the oven and defrosted the freezer.

Late one afternoon when the telephone rang, she overheard a bemused Paul speaking to Esther. "I've never seen anything like it," he confessed. "It's actually quite frightening, all this cleaning."

Lily could hear her sister's loud voice, four hundred miles southwest in Iowa, where she was taking pictures of cornfields and writing about them for the *Milwaukee Journal*. "Is she getting any translating done?" Esther shouted. "You know, she's got a job, Paul. She needs to keep at it."

"She is. She's swamped with work. Her desk is piled with articles she's translating and a kinky book about murder in Morocco. It's not the French that's worrying me. It's her cleaning that I find alarming."

Esther's laughter filled the room. "It's Lily's awesome, untapped female anger redirected at dust and clutter. Something in her world must be out of order. This is how we Fern women

control things—by cleaning. You might find that hard to understand, Paul. When there's something out of whack you probably
watch football like other men, or waterproof your boots or—
what do I know?—call up some guy and talk about equipment.
If you're female and a Fern, you clean. So, what's out of whack
with my sister?"

"Lil says she's falling in love with me. Could that be the
problem?"

Lily ducked quickly down the hall and into an open doorway so as not to be caught eavesdropping.

Antonio was outraged, incredulous when he heard that she
was married, as if the ten nights of intimacy they had shared
three years earlier had given him the right to act like her father.
"How could you do it? You barely know the guy!" he shouted
over the telephone. "What the hell are you up to?"

"That's my business," she told him.

"What are you trying to tell me?" he cut in angrily. "Do you
love him?"

She burst out, as she had never done before. (Why now?
she'd thought afterward. Why now, when I'm married and he
should mean nothing to me, do I want to scream at the man, to
make him hurt like I once hurt?) "You're asking me about love,
Antonio? You tell *me* what it is. What does love have to do with
any of this?"

He slammed down the receiver.

She attacked the house with her feather duster. She purged
the medicine cabinet of out-of-date drugs and took all the glass-
ware and china out of the kitchen cupboards. She relined the
shelves with lavender paper and repainted their bedroom in a
quiet shade of aqua. Pleased with the outcome, she rolled a soft
butter cream onto the kitchen walls. Paul stayed out of her way,
until one cloudy weekend in early November when she announced, "There. It's done."

In celebration, they opened a bottle of champagne and sipped it, sitting close together on the couch. The well-seasoned oak and birch logs crackled and spit while heat poured into the room through vents on either side of the rock-walled chimney. They ate handfuls of olives and pecans Lily had roasted in the oven, and tossed olive pits into the flames. "Maybe olive trees will grow there someday," Paul commented.

"I doubt we'll be here to see them," she observed, amused by Paul's whimsical vision of an olive grove sprouting from the fireplace.

"What do you mean, not be here?" he asked, both sounding and looking baffled.

"I think we're leaving here, Paul. Don't you?"

"Where are we going?"

"To Idaho."

"Idaho! You think you can live with my mother?" he said, clearly trying to humor her.

Lily shot back, "Can you?" The teasing note had gone out of her voice, for she watched every evening as he poured himself a shot of Laphroaig single malt after a day of teaching and tossed it back, shaking his head and woofing and wincing with the pleasure of its peat-dark machine-oil taste. Then he would stare at the gunmetal lake, at the leafless birches and the cold gray sky, and reminisce about springtime on the ranch, the strong sweet odor of lupine on the hillsides, the aspens leafed out and fluttering in the draws, the foxes and coyotes.

Paul set down his champagne glass on the old wooden trunk in front of the couch and remarked, more serious now, "This is all rather sudden."

"We could try Idaho for a few years," Lily cajoled him gently. "Then France for a while, or Italy, or Spain. We could take your mother with us. There are cows in Spain, bulls and calves . . . Hemingway, Pamplona. It's your kind of place, Paul. You'd love it."

He studied her face intently, almost squinting with the patent need to peer more deeply into her mind. He sounded wary when he ventured, "You're joking."

"Am I? Maybe I'm just dreaming, Paul, but you've been looking out the same window at the same lake for over three years now. Your heart's not here. It's not in Wisconsin. Even I can see that. Don't you think it's time the train moved on? For both of us?"

———

For Thanksgiving they flew to Idaho as a test: Lily's first visit to the ranch, her first meeting with Paul's mother. In the bedroom where Paul had spent his childhood, they made love in the morning, slowly and soundlessly so the bedsprings wouldn't squeak and betray them. The need for stealth opened new avenues of arousal, more attention paid to the insides of ankles, knees, and thighs, leisurely, long silky touches and agonizingly slow and deliberate penetrations—while below them in the kitchen they could hear Paul's mother's husky voice and her throaty chuckle. She was saying to Blanca, who was warbling tunes of betrayal and heartache while frying the bacon, "Don't disturb the lovebirds, *los recién casados*—the newlyweds. . . ."

Afterward, Lily wrapped herself in a terry-cloth robe and curled up on the window seat, allowing her gaze to wander over the barren snow-dusted hills and up into the cobalt sky. Paul was stretched out on the bed beside her, coverless in the chill air, smug as a cat who has just digested a dimpled mouse and is contemplating another. He spoke to her in a quiet, ruminative voice. "You were right," he said. "I've missed the ranch."

She responded lazily, "I told you so. I could see it in your eyes."

"I couldn't see it in myself."

"It's easy to mistake inertia for happiness."

"When did you get so wise?"

"Not wise," she protested. "You're just an easy book to read. You're an essentially happy man, so if there's sadness lurking, all I have to do is flip back through the pages and find where you veered from the theme. It doesn't take much wisdom to track your theme. Idaho and the ranch. You were born on a horse. For me it's more complicated. I'm much more—"

"Secret?"

"I was going to say difficult."

"You don't have to stay in the pigeonhole where your parents put you, Lil."

Her chuckle was edged with irony when she replied, "I flew out long ago, Paul, in case you hadn't noticed. For me it's always been a matter of timing, fitting adventure into . . ." She hesitated, searching for words less inflammatory than "my relationships."

He suggested, "A wandering theme? A theme of wandering? I can accommodate that. We can travel together."

"Where?"

"Here, to Idaho for a start. That was your suggestion and I'm all for it."

"Growing up in Milwaukee was nothing as exotic as this ranch," she allowed. "You always put it so poetically, Paul, but finally I can see it, the long revealing twilights you were telling me about and the rocks like sunken ships. I think I could live here."

"I feel the beauty like a pain in my chest," he admitted. "I never wanted anything else. Except you. I wanted you."

"And Melinda," Lily added wickedly.

But she envied him. She could not imagine so profound an attachment to any one place, to distant cliffs peopled with pirates and treasure by a little boy who had grown into manhood witnessing, most evenings of his life, the same shattered spires and fluted prow of rock gilded by the setting sun. When Paul spoke of the land or the cows, or the sagebrush hill where his father was buried, he did so with a sense of calm that sounded as wonderfully secure to Lily as bedrock, something hard and mysterious that could not be chipped away. That first, brief visit to Idaho had affirmed for Lily how much Paul's separation from the ranch—and from his mother—had cost him.

Justine Lafond had appeared and behaved as her son had advertised: a ferociously attractive, charming, and imperious Frenchwoman. After spending time with her, Lily understood why a young wife such as Melinda, with only a year out of college under her belt and a faltering self-image, had found life at the ranch intolerable.

"My son, of course, is a most precious being," Justine informed Lily as they strolled together beyond a ranch house that resembled a log château. Smoking a cheroot, she waved its burning tip toward the lofty structure: "Chenonceau, the sixteenth-century château *en France*—you have seen it? This is *my* Chenonceau. I married an angel, my marvelous Freddy, and he built me a castle."

The extravagant structure featured glass-paned doors and high arched windows that cut slices of sunlight from the chill autumn landscape. There were porches upstairs and down with views onto and over fields, ponds, and distant hills that made you suck in the cold, clear air more deeply, as if your lungs could become drunk on the dry herbal tang of sagebrush and solitude. The house was three stories tall, a fantasia of rustic luxury, elegant in spite of its size and the massive logs that toed into each other with the delicacy of dancers. It was all so buoyantly French, with ridiculous corner turrets and niches where lovers might hide, yet built with such solid, American, masculine timbers: a foreign bride's dream of happiness surrounded by gardens that, in summer, would be overflowing with boisterously colored flowers. Lily imagined that Justine's gardens would not be tidy or clipped but, in the French manner, a profusion of blooms and vegetables overhanging and intertwining in long rows and loose spreading beds, the sweet scent of roses and lilies blowing into the kitchen on summer afternoons and mingling with the richer odors of tomatoes, spiced cherries, or gingered plums simmering on the stove.

Late that first afternoon, when Lily retired for a nap, she marveled at how Paul had turned out so well in spite of basking, since birth, in the singular beam of his mother's devotion. Was it the fresh, open landscape and the soft, nibbling nose of his favorite horse that had acted as counterweights for his taciturn father and eccentric mother? For Paul had a lightness to his nature, a sense of life's dips and quirks and its ultimate merit that saved him.

"It's not easy being the only son of the most possessive and forthright woman in the world," he quipped that night at dinner. Lily waited for the explosion, but Maman merely smiled mildly.

"Pffft! Such nonsense. You are mistaking a mother's pride. How should I feel, indifferent to my child? This little body that your father and I—"

"Enough, Mother!" Paul stomped away from the table, surprising Lily, who had never yet heard him raise his voice or speak sharply. As he exited the room, Justine Lafond laughed deep in her throat, that husky, all-knowing woman's laugh that must have reduced Melinda to a puddle at Justine's feet.

But Lily was in no way intimidated by a mother-in-law for whom perturbation and a sense of injury were two of life's most treasured diversions. She asked, "What was that all about?"

"Pffft!" said Justine. "Just ignore him."

For a while neither of them spoke. Lily simply leaned back in her chair and returned Justine's smile while Justine studied Lily. "This is fine. I do not complain," Justine said at last, laughter bubbling through her words, her eyes pinched into slits of merriment. "I approve of Paul's moving to Wisconsin to escape me. At some time in our lives we must all break free from our mothers, or there is a risk that we will become them. And he is teaching again, this is good. He is a man who delights in children. But he is all I have, you see, except for the ranch. Except for this uncivilized piece of terrain covered with these terrible bushes, not with flowers and lavender, not with the beauty that makes life so sweet to the senses, to the nostrils." And she tapped the treasured Lafond proboscis. "Do you understand what I am saying? This is preposterous, *non*? To live alone in the wilderness, *dans le pays sauvage*, with nothing but sagebrush to pull at my clothes and my fingers."

"Have you ever thought of returning to France?" Lily asked.

"Of course not, my darling," Justine replied, flailing one hand above her head and suddenly expounding on how she had raised from a sprout the fig tree beneath which she sat. "From a sprout! As I raised my son," she pointed out proudly. "With much tender feeding and singing. But he was more demanding than this graceful tree, and look at him now! He is a bull, *non*? A gentle bull, with the waistline of his grandfather, Gérard, and the beautiful bedroom eyes of his father."

Just as Lily was regrouping from this latest exposition, Justine demanded, "Do you love my son?"

"Yes, I do," said Lily, her voice holding steady.

"But not as I loved my Freddy."

"I'm a different woman, Maman."

"Are you so certain?"

"I don't smoke cheroots," Lily countered with a grin.

Justine eyed Lily knowingly, a sparkle of amusement in her eyes. "You mean you are not so flamboyant, *chérie*. But let me tell you something. If you open the vents, the steam escapes. If you keep them closed, there is always an explosion. You saw Paul last night at the dinner table? He keeps the vents closed, *non*? And you, my darling?" She posed this last question while directing a piercing gaze at Lily, as if a peepshow were on offer featuring red hair lying in frothy clumps on the floor, a fingernail scissors carving a ragged channel through a young woman's shoulder, and scarlet blood staining the white folds of a laundered comforter. Lily sighed inwardly, realizing how far she had come in two and a half years from that desperate evening when the steam had exploded and Signora Miceli had rushed into Lily's room, aghast.

Amusement shining in her own eyes this time, she said, "When I open the vents, Maman, you don't want to be there."

And Justine Lafond tossed back her head and broke into peals of rich, throaty laughter. "How I adore you," she cried. "I think we are very much alike, don't you agree? Just a little bit pushy and naughty. We will never tell Paul, but I think the poor man has married his mother!"

Returned to Wisconsin, Lily's love grew quietly. A pine needle frozen into the ice on the lake lasted until spring. A green leaf shaped like an arrow shot up through the melting snow. A minnow smaller than Lily's big toe bit her. A woodpecker tapped out love messages on a silvered snag below their bedroom window.

Twice a week Lily drove into town to the nursing home to speak French with Lucie Johnson, a Parisian by birth, who had lived in Wisconsin for sixty years. Lucie's husband was dead; she had just turned eighty-seven, and had forgotten most of her English. Each Wednesday when she saw Lily, a look of bewilderment passed across her eyes before the social graces drummed into her as a child, in Paris, filled the emptied well of her memory. She would take her visitor's hand in her own chilled, blue-veined fingers and inquire politely if Lily was her daughter. Invariably, the conversation would turn to the chair in the corner. It was her grandmother's chair, she explained, and she must take it with her, but how could she fit it into the trunk of her car when she drove back to Paris in the morning? Lily assured her that the chair could be lashed safely into the trunk, with a sheet of plastic tied over it. *"S'il pleut,"* in case it rains, she always added.

Lucie would then draw herself upright in her chair, her face softening into youthfulness as she recited her English translation lesson: *"Il pleut. Il pleut à verse. Je suis moulliée jusqu'aux os.* It is raining. It is raining cats and dogs. I am wet to the bones." She smiled eagerly, tilted forward in her chair as she awaited her teacher's approval, her scent pouring over Lily, as though a truckload of violets had overturned in the room.

Near the end of each visit, before Lily had hugged Lucie's frail shoulders and been enveloped once again in floral perfume, the old woman whispered apologetically, "Tell me, my dear . . . I must have forgotten . . . are you my son, or my daughter?"

Driving home to the lake one July afternoon, Lily's heart ached inside her breast and she blessed the good fortune of her own grandmother, that feisty, stubborn, inordinately sharp old lady who, at the age of ninety, still fell asleep each night with the *New York Times* crossword puzzle, completed in ink, tucked under the clock on her bedside table.

Grandma Fern continued to live with Lily's parents—not a household in which love flourished. Lily's father had become more demanding and self-important as he neared the threshold into his sixties, while her mother, trying to accustom herself to a chin and jowls that seemed to have lost their stuffing, had veered into bitterness. The deterioration of her parents' relationship saddened Lily because they had loved each other once; she remembered their love from those summers at the cabin. But somewhere along the way they had stopped talking and working things out, and everything that had once been a minor skirmish now escalated into a full-blown battle. It was a war of attrition, "the death of the love soldiers," as Esther termed it. "I can't save them, that's the worst part," she had confessed to Lily. "They're just as flawed as we are. I love them, but, my God, it's hell being around them."

Lily could not help but recognize the strangely weighted balance of her own burgeoning love for Paul set against the slow decay of her parents' marriage.

She asked Esther when they spoke on the phone later that evening, "Should I drive down for a visit? I'm alone in the house. Paul's mother was hiking up the hill behind the ranch house to dig out the sagebrush around Freddy's grave. She stumbled on a rock and broke her ankle, so Paul's flown out to help her. She'll recover quickly. He's the bearer of good news."

Esther yelped into the phone with unconcealed joy, "You're not pregnant, Lil!"

Amused by her sister's thunderous response, Lily repositioned the receiver well away from her ear and said, "No, I'm not. We're moving to Idaho in the fall. Paul's resigned his teaching position."

Esther's voice grew abruptly sober. "Whatever possessed you?"

"It's the beginning of our travels, Es. I'm thinking of the ranch as an exotic base camp."

"How exotic can living with a herd of cows be?"

"I'm looking forward—"

"You're crazy, Lil. Paul's tied to the earth, his *own* piece of earth. You didn't marry a traveler. It'll change you," Esther predicted. "Living out there in the desert with your mother-in-law will change you."

"Maybe," Lily allowed lightheartedly.

"So come on down," Esther urged. "I'll be in Nova Scotia

next week, if you can believe it. Some travel piece. But I'm here for the weekend. You should have been me, Lil. A camera and a notebook would have gotten you a lot farther than a couple of languages and a homestay in Italy."

A sudden uncomfortable silence dropped down between them.

"I'm sorry, Lil," Esther quickly apologized. "Losing a baby—"

"It's okay, Es. Life goes on."

"You've had a rough time of it."

"I said it's okay. We all have our difficulties. Mine were no greater—"

But Esther interrupted her with a bark that once again caused Lily to distance her ear from the telephone. "Oh, stop being such a Pollyanna, for Christ's sake, Lil," Esther growled. "Sometimes I want to take Antonio out and shoot him, but Phil's so damn happy. . . ."

"I have moved beyond all this, Es."

"I hope so, Lil. For your sake, and for Paul's. Look—drive down tomorrow," she insisted with a heartiness that Lily recognized as Esther's peculiar ability to tidily rebury unpleasantness after aggressively digging it up. "Mom and Dad would love to see you and you've always been Grandma's favorite. With you, she can get all huffy and offended about Ram Gupta and enjoy herself. You might swing by Phil's place on the way down. You know she's pregnant again?"

"No," Lily said. "I didn't."

⎯

And now the *should nevers* were upon her—the moment that Lily and Madame Olivetti, working together through the early-morning hours, had been dreading. Lily stood up from her desk and pushed back the typewriter, ran her fingers through her hair, yawned, and stretched. Then she watched through the window as a stain of rosy peach deepened in the east and flooded upward, as if the sky were blushing at all it had witnessed through the long night. A zephyr of breeze lifted the curtains and lingered, fragrant, a whiff of French violets although none were in bloom. A wave of remembrance, of youth and its miscalculations and its irresistible seductiveness swept over Lily and she wondered, Was it worth it? All these sleepless hours? All this writing about the past? This self-indulgent gnashing of teeth and bodice baring? This journalistic cleansing?

Paul should never have flown to Idaho to help out his mother. Lily should never have driven to Milwaukee without him. She should never have stopped en route to visit Philomena, who had confused the time of her arrival and taken the children to the market. She should never have lingered on the doorstep—*Run,* she'd thought. *Just turn around and run*—after Antonio answered the doorbell. Black hair. Black eyes. Lips she had longed to kiss just once, to taste . . . that jolt of desire, that irresistible chemistry. It was her fault as much as his. She should never have walked through the door he held open into her sister's house. She should never have followed him onto the porch.

"A glass of wine?" he offered.

"Why not?"

Lily took a seat on Phila's wicker couch, crossed her legs and soon realized that her right foot was nervously jiggling up and down. She stilled her foot and inhaled deeply. The jalousies were open and the smell of freshly cut lawn soothed her, as did the sight of a gray squirrel arching its tail in front of Phila's flower bed, and a pair of cardinals busily crunching up sunflower seeds at the bird feeder.

Antonio returned with an uncorked bottle of Chianti, two long-stemmed glasses, and a bowl of olives. "How have you been?" he asked. "You look beautiful. Marriage suits you."

"It does," she agreed.

"Leo and Gina miss you. They keep asking when Aunt Lily is coming to visit."

Lily nibbled the olives. She drank her wine too quickly. "It's a long drive," she said.

"Still—"

"Well, I'm here."

"I've missed you, Lily."

When he refilled her glass she didn't protest. It was almost restful: this ritualistic exchange of news, the quiet smiles, the dark wine softening the afternoon. . . .

When she reached for an olive, he caught her hand.

"Don't, Antonio." She jerked her hand away, overturning the olives, and stood up abruptly. "We can't do this. It's over."

"Is it?"

"Yes," she said, and attempting to make her exit with some measure of goodwill and dignity, she reached down and patted his shoulder, a sisterly gesture, no hard feelings, too much wine, a lapse in behavior easily adjusted. . . .

She should never have touched him—that was a mistake, because her arms went around him and his lips were instantly on hers, and there was no question of right or wrong but two bodies that had longed for each other for how many months and years? They were tearing off each other's clothes and there was no way to stop them once they lay naked, entwined on the couch, the sunlight slanting in hot and golden, the olive bowl broken, liquid puddling on the terrazzo floor. She was pressed into the cushions by the urgent weight of him. His smell, she remembered, his hot, sweet-tasting skin and his tongue, licking, traveling, whispering, "Lily Crisp . . . is that a cookie or a woman? Lily Crisp. That's a ridiculous name. A truly ridiculous name—"

And she woke up. She woke up to his whispering and saw the olives, the broken bowl, the sunlight, and before he could enter her, even reach between her legs, she shoved him off her, dislodged him with a rudeness that enraged him.

"What the hell are you doing?" he said.

"Get a life, Antonio. You're married to my sister."

He stared at her. Naked, sober, tumescent, nursing his erection, he waited for her to change her mind. But she did not.

"Do you love him?" he asked.

"Paul? My husband? Yes. As a matter of fact I do."

"I'm happy for you," he said brusquely and began to apologize for his conduct when she had gone to Italy, when he had slept with Philomena, when today, this afternoon, she had walked into his house and he had taken advantage of the wine and the heat—

But she ignored him, dressing quickly, not even bothering to comb her hair or put on her sandals, simply holding them in one hand by the straps, as if she had gone for a wade in the sea or run barefoot through the grass.

"There was never any ending, Antonio," she said quietly when she was ready to leave. "Now there is one."

Twelve

It was on one of those warm early September days when glints of sunlight freckled the lake and ran sparkling over the bark of the silver birches that Lily told Paul she was expecting a baby. He was seated in a folding canvas chair on the end of the dock, looking admiringly down at her legs. She wore shorts and was thoughtfully dabbling her toes in the water.

A powerboat towing two water skiers cut across in front of the dock, kicking up wakes that momentarily obscured her view of the island in the middle of the lake. The whine of the engine and the arching fans of spray splashing the backdrop of sun-bright water and wooded shoreline awoke her from her reverie. She lifted one foot and then the other from the rain-soft lake water and watched the sunlight that had been flirting with her toes break and skitter like a flock of miniature swallows swooping back to their nests. She was aware of Paul studying her legs, but he seemed in a contemplative humor and content to sit without speaking.

Finally, she swiveled toward him and broke the silence. "I have news," she said.

"About us?"

"I certainly hope so. We're having a baby."

A complexity of emotions she could not read played across his face, causing him to blink repeatedly and twist his rosebud of a mouth into a tighter bundle.

"A baby? At my age?"

"Forty isn't old, Paul."

"To be a father?"

"It's the best age, really. You're beyond the muddle. My life's been such a muddle."

"Life *is* a muddle," he said. "But you're clear on this"—a statement, not a question. "You're clear on us. On me and the baby."

"Of course I'm clear," she said, and then added with a laugh, "As clear as a muddled woman can be." And rising to her knees, she laid her head in his lap. He fingered her soft red hair. It had grown longer, loosening after its mannish Swedish cut, that hairdo of pain and desperation. That shout for help.

"Are you pleased?" she asked.

"More than pleased," he replied softly. "I never dreamed that life could hold such happiness." Then, in a heartier voice: "We'll have to celebrate. Can I make you a cocktail?"

"Sure, but let's bag the old-fashioneds for a change and drink something more refreshing. How about a rum and tonic?"

"With a cloud?" he inquired.

Imagining him tethering a small cloud to a highball glass and presenting it to her, she said, "I guess I married a rancher *and* a poet." Not for the first time in her marriage she found the whimsy in her husband oddly pleasing.

"A splash of dark rum on top of the Bacardi and tonic—that's called a cloud," he explained and stood up abruptly, knocking over his chair. As he set it upright, he blurted, "I've never thought of myself as a poet, but sometimes when I'm watching the loons, or listening to them, there's a sort of melodic throbbing in my head that feels like ... if it ever resolved itself into words, it might be poetry." In obvious confusion he gave a short, formal bow. "Now if you'll excuse me, I'll just run up to the house and make our drinks ... but ... do you think it's such a good idea—rum—in your condition? How about a Coke instead?"

Lily grimaced. "I'll miss the cloud."

"No cloud," he said.

She followed his retreating back with her eyes, smiling as he disappeared up the slope. This was Paul's way. He would be stepping back and processing the information, detaching from his emotions before confronting the enormity of fatherhood. She had been struck since the first time they met by the formality of his words and actions, which seemed at odds with his often outrageous unpredictability.

She waited. The boat towing the water skiers disappeared behind the island and suddenly the noise of the motor died. A breeze riffled the water. She felt the chill of autumn on her skin and she shivered with the fear that she would not be able to carry this baby, Paul's baby, to term.

A short time later he returned bearing a tray, with a Coca-Cola for her, an old-fashioned for himself, a folded shawl, and a bowl of nuts. The frosted glass he handed to her had a white paper cloud, obviously cut out of a napkin, affixed to its rim. Breaking into a smile, she blew a puff of air at the paper cloud and watched it flutter as he placed the black lacquered bowl filled with macadamia nuts on the dock beside her. "A child in utero requires fat," he pronounced, handing her the shawl and taking up his previous position beside her in the canvas-backed chair. She thanked him for bringing her shawl. He reached across and put his hand on her shoulder, and with a smile so gentle and untainted by expectations or emotions that she felt as if he were a mirror into which she looked and saw only the goodness in herself, he said, "I guess we had better discuss it."

"Discuss what?" she asked.

But he said nothing, and they sat for a while in a silence curiously unweighted by the question, still unvoiced, that hung between them. In the end, he spoke.

"You saw Antonio in July when I went to Idaho."

"Yes, I did. I told you. We discussed—" And then it struck

her and she nodded, shifting position on the dock, hugging her knees to her chest as if protecting the new life that stirred in her womb from the aura of hurt that surrounded it. Paul was asking if the baby was his, if she had slept with Antonio. "You don't mean—"

But he cut her off, the color rising to his cheeks and forehead. "I'm not a fool, Lil. I was blinded by love when I married Melinda, but I married you with my eyes wide-open. Do you think I didn't know Antonio was the father of the child you lost in Italy? Do you think I didn't worry what would happen if you ever spent time alone with the guy? I could see the bastard in your eyes before you married me. You couldn't hide it—you loved him. Okay. I could live with that. I knew there had to be some sort of withdrawal, a severance from the past. I could wait because I'd fallen in love with you, head over heels. I still am."

"Paul—" she began.

But the stillness of his manner stopped her and she reached for his hand. "I was a fool," she said. "Once upon a time I was a fool, but then I met a guy, this rancher who herded loons, and I fell in love with him. I'm having his baby."

Over Paul's shoulder Lily watched as the sun brushed its golden belly on the tops of the darkened pines and for a moment hung there as though impaled on the pointed tips. Shadows spread like an indigo glaze spilled across the surface of the lake. Then he stood up. He took her hand. He pulled her to her feet, put his arm around her, and said, "Would you mind if we called her Justine, after my mother?"

❧

Lily was over three months pregnant when they jounced down the frozen dirt road leading away from the lake, under a vault of frosted branches bowed down with snow from a freakishly early October blizzard. She had scrubbed and polished until their lakeside home was spotless, the roof was swept clean of moss, the gutters held not a single leaf, and the windows sparkled. As they turned left onto the plowed pavement, Paul remarked on how his grandmother's house had served as a welcome refuge, and Lily reminded him of their wedding night, when, lying naked on the bed, she had marveled at the number of casement windows, French doors, and airy spaces in the old and potentially gloomy structure. Paul nodded with a grin of remembrance, which Lily suspected had more do with the number of naked toes on offer than the number of windows, and he admitted that remodeling the place, doing the work himself, had been a damn sight cheaper than six months of therapy.

Before heading west they looped south and stopped in at Philomena's house. Esther was standing beside her sister in the front doorway. Paul presented them both with a set of keys to his lakeside retreat. "Now, make sure you use it," he told them while Gina, the Cassatas' daughter—turning four in April, Lily knew, for her birthday fell two months after the loss of Leo— slid her hand into her uncle's. Attached to her other hand was fourteen-month-old Leo Cassata, who, except for the rusty hair and gray-green eyes that he shared with his aunt Lily, was his father reborn: an irrepressible, irresistible charmer. Leo flopped down on the floor and crawled after Gina, who had tugged Paul away from the front door, skipping hopefully in the direction of the sunroom, where, twice in the preceding year, the two of them had sat at the table overlooking the weeping willows in the backyard, Paul entertaining her with loon stories while they shared a pitcher of lemonade or a pot of hot chocolate.

"Tell Antonio good-bye when he gets home from work," Lily said as she hugged her younger sister.

"He'll miss you," Philomena sighed. "He's devastated that you're moving away. I told him, what did he expect? With a baby on the way, your first one, after all—and you're no spring chicken. I mean twenty-six is different from twenty, right? But

I guess I know all about that! The queen of babies." She tossed her head, with its thick golden brown hair drawn casually back in a ponytail. "I hope Tonio perks up. Poor guy, he was moping around at breakfast this morning. Really down in the dumps. He said—"

Esther cut in, "These two have to get on the road, Phil." Then she pulled herself up to her full height and said loudly, with a jolly smile, "Hey, Lil, do you remember when I caught you in the pantry? You were crouching in a corner pouring thimblefuls of Dad's liquor into a jam jar. I was standing in the doorway absolutely hating you because you hadn't asked me to do it with you. I was the older sister, I wanted to be in on it, but there you were, the little redheaded brat . . . I was so hurt and angry, I snuck upstairs without telling you and knocked on Mom and Dad's door—I think they were going at it—and ratted on you."

Lily laughed. "Oh, yes, I remember."

"Where was I?" Phila asked and then, smiling broadly, she laid her head on Lily's shoulder and put her arm around her waist. "Oh, I remember now. Dad was roaring down the staircase pulling up his pajama bottoms . . . Was that the incident? You were always getting into trouble back then. What was it Grandma Fern used to call you? You little scamp?"

"Oh, hell," Esther said and started to cry, and grabbed her sisters in a bone-crushing embrace—which was how Paul found them a few minutes later. He had made the trip to the sunroom with Gina and a toddling Leo, managing, after a loon story or two, to steer the twosome back to the hallway, where the Fern sisters were carrying on as if there weren't another snowstorm predicted for that evening and Lily and Paul didn't need to get on the road soon and put some miles on the odometer before nightfall.

"Stay here. Leave tomorrow," Philomena urged. "Tonio'll be hurt if he doesn't see you. He said to tell you to wait."

"We'll call from the road," Lily said quickly, with a hollow cough, as if the air had suddenly become so dense that she could barely suck the oxygen from it. Then, hurriedly planting kisses on her sisters' cheeks and the tops of the children's heads, she took Paul's arm and walked out the door.

Thirteen

That impressive family beacon—the Lafond nose—could be traced as far back as Paul's great-grandfather, Georges Lafond. For all Lily knew, it had ennobled the faces of every Lafond who had ever walked the crystalline hills and the cork oak forests of the Côte d'Azur. She blessed the irrefutable signature of family genes, acknowledging the tawny, non-Germanic sheen of her own skin. If Grandma Fern had been beside her at that moment, Lily might have whispered in her ear, "You know damn well Ram Gupta did more than *make* your mother's bed." And the old lady might have replied, with an enigmatic smile, "Let's just say that upon occasion Mr. Gupta may have treated my mother to something more lively than sherry."

A son, not the daughter Paul had imagined in choosing his mother's name, was born six months after Lily and Paul had moved to Idaho. There wasn't a delivery room nurse who didn't remark, with a bemused grin, that little Pierre had quite a nose for a small-fry.

Upon viewing her grandson, Justine Lafond proclaimed, "Well, my darlings! There is no mistaking the father!"

Lily had clasped her newborn son to her breast and felt almost sick with the release of worry. The delivery had not been an easy one, perhaps because of the tension inside her, the almost unbearable dread about whether her baby would be ushered alive into this world, or dead. Jubilant at the birth of his son, Paul kissed Lily softly on her forehead, the tip of her nose, and her mouth while she smiled up at him, her eyelids drooping and her lips grown sleepy as words tumbled from them, making little sense. "I guess it's a boy, but let's not name him Justine, okay? My dad named me Hamlin. It's a boy's name. My daughter, Hamlin. Our son, Justine . . . I can't live with that. Can you? We'll name the next one Justine. Our daughter, Justine . . . that sounds better. And our son, Pierre. Our little big-nosed sweetheart."

Pierre was a quiet, sensitive child who trailed Blanca around the house, a knapsack on his back, bearing sketch pads, charcoal, a gaudily painted statuette of the Virgin of Guadalupe, and a telescoping feather duster. He snuck slices of Blanca's berry pies out to the barn to feed the horses, and scratched the cows between their ears while he sang to them in a voice so low one could barely hear the words of the Mexican love songs Blanca had taught him. He drew detailed pictures of birds with colored pencils, and once discovered a mountain bluebird's nest in a washbasin nailed to a cabin wall. He had run back to the campfire, where Paul was grilling the six cutthroat trout they had caught in the lake for dinner, and pulled up short in front of his mother. "There's a cabin in the trees," he'd informed her softly. "It's falling down, but there's a nest and three eggs. They're as blue as the sky. I won't touch them, but I'd like to paint them. Did you bring your paints?"

The excited look in his eyes brought a smile to Lily's face as she hurried to the tent and unearthed from beneath a pile of sweaters a battered tin box of watercolors, a metal cup for water, four or five brushes held together with a rubber band, and a small square block of watercolor paper. "You know, dinner's almost ready," she reminded him while zipping up the mosquito netting behind her and handing him his painting equipment.

"It's not dark yet," he said.

Paul remarked from the other end of the campsite, where

he was carefully flipping the fish so they wouldn't flake into the fire, "Cold trout never hurt van Gogh."

"Did van Gogh eat trout, Dad?"

"Of course he did."

"Are you sure?"

"All painters eat trout. Cold trout," Paul said. "It stimulates the imagination and keeps your paintbrush nimble. Hot trout depresses the painterly spirit."

Pierre cast a skeptical glance at his father, then looked over at Lily, who chose not to wink and tip him off. After further hesitation, obviously torn between wanting to believe his father and suspecting that trout, served hot or cold, had nothing to do with the outcome of painting a few blue eggs, Pierre said, "You're pulling my leg, Dad."

"That is an astute observation. I am," Paul confessed.

"Never believe anything your father says about fish," Lily added. "He always exaggerates."

"The light's fading, Mom."

"Go," she said.

"Great kid," Paul observed as Pierre's narrow blue-shirted back dodged between the pines.

"Great kid," Lily agreed, knowing that Pierre, with his customary diligence, would not return until he could no longer see to paint, at which point he would trudge into camp, ravenous but uncomplaining, and wolf down the cold trout and reheated Dutch oven potatoes that Paul had saved for him. He and his dad would exchange a few impromptu comments about van Gogh's eating habits, as if the painter were a close family friend. And Lily would wonder as she had so many times before how the love she bore her son could be stretched, in the event of a miracle, to include another child.

She and Paul had always hoped for a larger family, but twice after Pierre's birth Lily had suffered miscarriages, then nothing, no pregnancies, no stirrings of life. As the years passed and Pierre entered his early teens, she continued to insist brightly that *someone* had to balance the birthrate of the inner cities. Esther blamed it on margarine—a clear cause of infertility. Lily's father counseled abstinence before ovulation to build up sperm count, then deep penetration. "Up to the neck, if possible," he told Paul over the phone. "And tip her up afterward. It gives them a boost. It's easier than swimming upstream."

Each month, when the basal temperature thermometer signaled ovulation, Lily and Paul would climb into bed for a ritualistic coupling, followed by Paul's intense visualization of a tomboy daughter riding bareback across the fields while Lily tipped upside down to give the sperm a gravity head start. It took years for the monthly dashing of their hopes and that inexplicable sense of loss to shrink to a size that fit into their lives with a minimum of pain. Eventually, Lily stopped lying with her legs over her head, her toes pointed up at the ceiling, and shifted her viewpoint to a glass filled to the brim with a healthy young son, instead of half empty.

Her life had been—overfull—as she remembered it.

Those first fifteen years after Pierre was born had shaped and stamped her as a rancher's wife. Those years of planting, weeding, fertilizing, harvesting, pickling, preserving, cooking, trying to get pregnant, tiring, wilting, herding cattle, mending fences, hoping that Pierre would come out of his shell and laugh—like Blanca, his beloved Blanca, had laughed and thrown her apron over her head, and lamented, "But you are so meager, señora. You are wasting away from too few tortillas and too much housework. You have the eye bags of an old cow." *Muchas gracias*, Lily had told her. *Old cow* had done nothing to enhance her self-image, but she had assured herself that it must sound less brutal in Spanish; it must be an expression of concern used between women.

She had done it all, a rancher's wife, and did not for a moment regret it—although she wondered at times how her life had turned out so peculiar. At the start, Idaho had struck her as a place as alien and alluring and as worthy of study as a foreign country, a foreign language. "Why do you like it, the ranching life?" Esther had asked and pestered her with questions, sounding enchanted, if a little bored, by the numbing details of Lily's reply.

"The work is physical, and there's always something different. We've got three hundred cows with their complement of calves, eleven thousand acres, about fifty acres a cow, double that in a year-round operation. But we sell the calves and ship them south in the end of November, range grazing, you know?"

"No, I don't," said Esther. "Do you herd cows in French? *Dépêche-toi.* Hurry up. *Trouve ta mère, petit veau.*"

"Find your mother, little calf? Your French is abominable, Es," Lily snorted.

"I thought last time we talked you were going back to school to get your master's."

"Don't worry. I will. Right now I'm too busy."

"You're always too busy. You should be leading my life, Lil. You were the one who wanted to travel. Who ever thought you'd end up a housewife?"

Lily had grown accustomed to Esther's jibes about Lil, the adventure queen, bogged down in a sagebrush desert. She knew that Esther's prodding came more from a good heart, a true wish for her sister's happiness, than from a myopic vision of career fulfillment. Esther's own life revolved around photojournalism and the various men whose hearts she had broken or, conversely, who had broken hers.

"I'm not a housewife," Lily reminded her sister. "Running a ranch is a full-time job." Although later, she had mulled their conversation over and, yes, one might wonder how the young girl who'd streaked naked past her father and plunged, with an exultant cry of rebellion, into the water had ended up living with her mother-in-law. And one might wonder how the different daughter, who hadn't been born a boy and who slipped in her dreams (as Ram Gupta must have done) onto the steamy beaches and hammock-hung porches of a wanderer's paradise, had ended up marrying a rancher solid as a fence post. Yet *ended up* implied a shifting of course that was not only unforeseen but out of her control, as if she had been the victim of an unsolicited transformation; as if a certain critical mass of cardamom-pear chutney and bread-and-butter pickles had alchemized her. But if life was a process—and surely it was not a static arrangement—then change was the perpetually evolving fabric, not the outcome of living. Change had not *happened* to Lily; she had simply introduced new patterns and colors into the weave of her destiny.

But at a younger age she had not accepted change easily. Witness the young wife exploding at her husband: "You've changed, Paul. You won't go anywhere, not even to Boise."

"I haven't changed, Lil." His voice was as calm as ever, solicitous, his demeanor unflappable. With each breath he took, he sucked in the irreducible stillness of the land.

"I can't budge you out of Idaho. You're stuck here, just like you were stuck in Wisconsin. I thought we talked about traveling, to France or Spain with your mother. I assumed we'd go somewhere, even for a week—"

"That was your assumption, Lil. That was *you* talking."

This unlikely altercation had occurred over three pots of basil Lily had planted, handsome Italian clay pots banded with grape leaves, heavy even when empty. She had filled the bottoms with bark for drainage, poured in bagged soil, tamping it down around each tender green shoot, and then placed the pots outside. When the leaves had begun to brown and the stems to droop, she had asked Paul to move the pots to a sunnier location. He had done so, athletically, straining his back by trying to lift them, then dragging, and finally rocking them across the deck. She had winced as she listened to his cursing, before he hobbled inside and poured himself a brandy. She had followed him into the kitchen. "You don't think, Paul. You hurt your back. Why? There wasn't any need. I could have helped, you could have asked me, but your famous French pride just got in the way. You suggest I plant basil, so I plant basil, and then you hurt your back moving the pots and blame me. You blame *me*! I would like to take a trip somewhere . . . to France. To La Pierre Rouge. Is that too much to ask? You've changed, Paul. You won't go anywhere. Nothing can budge you."

I haven't changed, Lil.

She felt as if she were arguing with a person armored in butterfly wings or cottonwood fluff. His fortifications were a winsome smile and eyes that shone with a softness that could only be his love for her cushioning the rigor of his own incontestable needs—family, land, cattle, solitude, laughter. In the scope of Paul's life a few pots of wilted basil, a strained back, and a round of verbal fireworks were meaningless.

In the scope of Lily's, the first small kernel of disappointment settled inside her and began to work its mischief.

Fourteen

*L*ily had fallen asleep at her desk, her head resting on her folded arms and Madame Olivetti's bunched-up shawl. She had written through the previous day and night, and a second morning, through the birth of her son: another great hurdle in her life surmounted—but at what cost?

Her eyes ached. There was a painful lump at the top of her neck. Her shoulders were rigid from long hours of typing. Her toes had seized up and cramped. The ever-growing stack of papers had blown off her desk when a wind came up just before dawn and gusted in through the window. She had thrown up her hands in despair and wept. Even Madame Olivetti had begun to squeak; she refused to return the *c* and the *h* to a level with the other keys after Lily punched them. "*Basta.* Enough," the old typewriter seemed to groan with each halting return of the carriage. She smudged the margins and doled out thin shadows of ink. She required a new ribbon, some grease, some oil, whatever. Lily imagined her typewriter creaking peremptorily, "Ask that hunk of a warmhearted Frenchman when he comes to call. But give me my shawl first, you ridiculous woman. Go for a swim. Let me rest."

But Lily had fallen asleep instead. She was drifting in the sea, and how delicious the fantasy. The water was blood-warm, sensuous. It stroked her muscles and pulled like the strong, lotioned hands of a masseur sweeping down from her shoulders, gliding on a film of emulsion, oily, erotic, into the crooks of her elbows, massaging her forearms, her wrists, pressing into the cushioned palms of her hands and pulling at her fingers until she sighed, with an admittedly sexual urgency. The ghost of a smile played across her lips as her eyelids flickered open. She gave a little start. Yves was crouching in the doorway, a sheaf of papers in his hand.

Lily mumbled, still groggy with sleep although struggling to concentrate, to make sense of what was happening, "Is it afternoon or morning? What are you doing here? How long have you been . . . ?" Her voice trailed off.

He said, "Picking up papers? I ask you, Lily, where did all these . . . words come from? Is this any way for a healthy woman to spend her time?" He resumed his slow crawl across the floor, harvesting pages and smoothing out wrinkled corners before adding them to his pile.

"Is it you, Yves, who's been rubbing my shoulders and arms? Or did I dream it?" Lily murmured sleepily.

He heaved a sigh and said, with the mock righteousness of wounded virtue, "But of course you have dreamt it! I would never . . ."

"Here," Lily said to calm him. "Let me help you." And she dropped to her knees beside him.

"I brought lunch. I was worried," he confessed, pouring out his story while they gathered up the scattered papers. "I called out, 'Lily, are you there?' When there was no answer I ascended the staircase to your room and entered through the open door. First I saw the explosion of paper and wondered what had happened. Then I discovered you sleeping. Your face was hidden by a soft cloud of hair that seemed threaded with glitter, as if sunlight were caught somewhere within it. I couldn't help but notice. . . . Your shoulders were bare and I saw a scar, thick and ropy, as if someone had dragged a knife down your arm, or shrapnel had hit you. It is an old scar?"

"Another lifetime. Another Lily," she replied from beneath

the bed, where she had slid on her stomach, over the smooth tiles, to rescue a truant page.

Yves waited quietly until she reemerged, feetfirst. Then, caught up in the drama of his own disclosures, he said in an exaggerated whisper, "I murmured, 'Lily?' but you did not awaken. What to do? I wondered. The only honorable course of action a man might take upon finding an attractive woman asleep at her desk was retreat. Withdrawal. I must tiptoe out the door so as not to disturb you. But I rejected this option. She is exhausted, I thought, my heart clenching at the sight of your naked shoulders and their vulnerability. And I questioned as I have done since the day I first met you, since I first witnessed the fervor and dedication with which you write, with which you remember—what is troubling this woman? To my mind, you are not a person easily distressed. You are strong in your core, I can see this, a woman of experience, able to cope."

"All this?" Lily sat back on her heels and asked. "All this while I was sleeping?"

"I apologize," he said, looking chagrined, although the hint of a grin snuck through. "But I do not regret it."

"Oh, Yves," she said, with a tired but appreciative laugh. "I don't deserve you in my life at this moment."

"This is a funny thing," he said. "I was thinking the same about you."

The silence that slipped between them and hung there, building, was filled with protestations and disclaimers, although neither of them acted. Neither of them made the first move until Yves, leaping to his feet, struck his forehead with the heel of his hand and burst out, "*Mon Dieu!* The luncheon! Sustenance for a weary writer. I packed it in a hamper. It's on the seat of my truck. Two bottles of vin rosé, slices of *jambon cru*, Niçoise olives, two fresh baguettes, an entire spinach and mushroom quiche, *gateau au chocolat*—all cooking in the sun! You will eat?" he asked.

She regarded him quizzically. "Your mother? She is lunching alone today?"

"Maman and I have had a conversation. She has locked herself in her room and will not come out." He opened his arms wide and threw up his palms. "Your husband, he was in such a predicament with his own mother, is this not true? He left. I too will leave."

"When?" Lily said as her heart, surprising her, tightened in a little wrench of loss. She busied herself transferring the piles of paper from the floor to the corner of her desk and planting Madame Olivetti on top as a temporary paperweight.

Yves shrugged. "There is still work to be done here. The garden wall, replacing the trim in your daughter's room, the damp on the living room ceiling, more broken tiles. . . . This is a house in disrepair."

A *life* in disrepair, Lily thought with a sudden inward burst of laughter that chased away the melancholic ghosts that, in Yves's absence, had beset her. She suggested, "Let's lunch on the terrace. It's a beautiful day."

"Yes. On the terrace," he agreed and, with an explosive muttering under his breath, plunged headlong out of the room and down the stairs.

Lily put her hand to her breast and felt the decelerating rhythm of her own heart as she took in a calming noseful of air, then slowly released it and announced, "*J'ai faim.* I'm hungry."

Beside her on the desk, Madame Olivetti, squat-shouldered and shawl-wrapped, witnessing all and recording all, had she words to speak instead of keys to type, might have remarked on Lily's sudden and disingenuous gush of appetite.

Fifteen

*M*adame Moreau snored softly in her armchair, napping over a Dubonnet. Seeing the trembling glass in her mother's hand, Adèle Simoni rose quickly from the couch where she and Lily had been sipping their own apéritifs, and swished over in slacks of raw silk, in a pale mauve hue, to rescue the cocktail. Through the west-facing windows in the corner parlor, the late-afternoon sun beamed into the Hotel de la Plage, illuminating the old woman's face and hands and giving the impression of soft pink lights shining up through delicate parchment. Adèle absently tucked a stray wisp of her mother's silvered hair into her bun and, before turning back to Lily, stroked her mother's withered cheek, gilded and smoothed by a liberal dusting of powder and the hot splash of sunlight.

"She sleeps like an angel," Adèle whispered, although there was no need to speak softly, for her mother's hearing was failing, and often Adèle had to shout to be heard. "It grows hot here in the afternoons, but I am not allowed to pull the drapes. Maman is not like the other old people of this village, who live behind shuttered windows and seek out the darkness, as if they are testing what awaits them. Everything changes," she remarked, with a resigned sigh. "Even my mother. Now she sleeps for no reason at all, like a cat in the sun. You can see." With two gracefully extended fingers, she gestured toward her mother.

Lily regarded Madame Moreau with a long-term affection. A tiny woman, compact except for a comfortable cushion of flesh around her middle, she was soberly attired in a black dress and black fringed shawl, although she threatened someday to put on the scarlet frock that had caused her husband's cheeks to darken and his blood to rise precipitously. She was eighty-five years old; Justine Lafond's age, had she lived. Close friends since birth, they had parted long ago and seen each other but once, when Justine had returned to buy up the hillside and upgrade the plumbing. Madame Moreau described Justine's visit: "At sixty-one and a widow, she had more sex in her little finger than I had at twenty when I met my Julien."

She said of Justine's engagement to Freddy: "I was making a trip with my mother, so my friend Justine, she looked after the counter. It was here in this hotel, and it was June. There is never much business in early June. But what luck! An American, very rich, enters the hotel and asks for two rooms. Justine knows at the moment she sees him, at the moment she smells him—it's incredible, isn't it?—she will take this man from his mother and her little sausage dog. And she does!"

But now the old woman dozed, her eyelids twitching, noisy puffs of air erupting from her slackly draped mouth, and Adèle said, her smile twisted to one side by an excess of emotion, "She dreams about my father and wakes up thinking she has been romping with him, naked in the bedroom, or swimming nude in the starlight. In her dream life she is sixteen and has shed her inhibitions and her clothes. And, apparently, so has Papa." Adèle's laughter rang out high-pitched and melodic, no longer muted. Pouring more gin into a burnished metal shaker, she offered Lily another martini.

"No more," Lily insisted as she held up a hand to stop her friend in case words were not a sufficient deterrent. Lily's mouth tasted vaguely metallic and her head ached from yesterday's bacchanal with Yves.

Adèle observed her, assessing. "Yves, he is still working his magic . . . ," she queried with a mischievous lift to her eyebrows;

and then, having stretched out the pause to accommodate her meaning, ". . . repairing your rooftop?"

"The old house is sparkling." Lily's smile was broad and inscrutable.

Adèle broke out laughing. "How we misbehave! God has a busy schedule keeping track of all our transgressions."

"He has you to help Him," Lily teased her friend. "But don't add to the list what is clearly speculation"—for nothing had transpired the day before. Luncheon on the terrace had been an uproarious occasion, two bottles of wine were emptied—lingered over, that was true, yet the alcohol had entered Lily's bloodstream with alarming speed and accuracy. At one point she remembered Yves reaching for her hand. His was large and strong. He had held it in his lap with a minimum of pressure, as if it were a sacred object or a holy loaf—a fraternal caress that, nonetheless, she had found disturbing. She tried to concentrate on their conversation but all she could think about was her hand in his hand, his thigh so close it exuded heat, and her thigh, or thighs, and what was happening to her lower extremities—a melting of the legs and more, far more, for her entire body, led by the pulsating tips of her breasts, had rushed to the palm of her hand.

Yves confessed, midway through their second bottle, "I'm falling in love."

Lily had looked at him blankly, the magic dissolved in an instant. "Not with me, I hope."

"No, of course not. With Giselle Godard."

"With Giselle? But she's dead."

"This matters? One can dream, one can imagine. This is your specialty, isn't it? To imagine."

"To remember, Yves. I'm not sure it's the same thing."

"Oh, but I think it is. Who is there but Madame Olivetti—a typewriter!—to contradict you?"

"We were speaking of Giselle, not me," she reminded him vaguely, the wine effervescing in brilliantly colored motes of light that burst against the backs of her eyelids and made a shambles of her concentration.

Yves nodded. "So we were. Then tell me what she looked like, this great-aunt of your husband's."

Lily imagined Giselle plain as laundry hanging on the line, prey to the Lafonds, both father and son. Or radiant as a pale moon, their dark-eyed seductress. "I've not the slightest idea," she confessed. "Isn't that strange? Even when I heard about the ghost."

"A ghost! What ghost?"

But the sensation in Lily's legs had been overwhelming and her thoughts, wandering, dreamy. She knew where this was heading, all this wine and heat and floral-scented sunshine and this talk of Giselle and love, and she wasn't prepared to go there, not yet, not this time, not always slipping into a man's arms and finding solace there in human warmth, in the strong musky odor that was so disarmingly, irresistibly, arousingly male—Yves's big calloused competent hand enclosing her own, his black Sunday trousers coarse and pleasantly steaming against her lightly skirted thigh.

She said, moving slightly away from him and sounding surprised, as if proximity had crept up on her unawares, "Look! You've got my hand."

"But yes, you are right!" he exclaimed, and carrying it to his lips with a graceful flourish, with the utmost delicacy, he kissed it. "*Voilà!*" He let go of her hand. "This is better? A little space between us? My trousers, they have scratched you?"

"No," she said. "Yes." And then, laughing, she let out a long sigh, relieved to have hurtled over this moment, desire beating in all those tender places that a woman hides beneath her blouse and skirt but presents to the world, open and woundable, in the fragile hollow of her neck, in the sensitive skin behind her ear, inside her wrist, and where the anklebone pokes out sweetly and whispers.

Yves raised the bottle against the sun and squinted to check its level. "Almost gone," he announced. "Shall we finish the wine?"

"Absolutely," she urged him, and then: "You asked about Giselle."

"Her ghost? I did." He filled their glasses, emptying the bottle. "*Salud!* May all ghosts be as lovely and seductive as the long-dead Giselle!"

"*Salud.*"

"Yes, tell me," he said with a husky rumble in his throat, like an engine decelerating into a tight curve, noticeably repositioning his crotch and thighs on the bench, a maestro of delicate repairs and meticulous adjustments. And so she told him about Giselle's ghost, breathing deeply as she did so and enjoying the last of the wine.

"Paul's mother saw the ghost when she went to France after her father died, to inspect her inheritance. One night she was seated under the plane tree and dreaming of Freddy, when she heard a noise above her in the *bergerie*: a scuffling and a snort. *Ah, sanglier,* wild boar, she thought and walked unarmed up the steps to the goat shed. Inside, she saw the ghost of her aunt Giselle, dead for more than twenty years, dangling from a rafter. A woman of action, she bolted the door, hurried back to the house, and telephoned Paul. We had just sat down to an Idaho trout lunch when the telephone rang. I answered it. '*Mon Dieu,*' my mother-in-law cried. 'She's still there. She's still hanging in the goat shed!'

"The very next day she'd had the shed torn down."

And precisely where had this haunted goat shed stood? Yves had wanted to know, and Lily had fluttered her fingers above her head, indicating the graceful circle of fig trees that grew above the house. There. Up there in the garden. Giselle's garden . . .

"Lily? *Chérie*? A martini for your thoughts." The waggish lilt in Adèle's voice lifted Lily out of the past and landed her back in the Hotel de la Plage.

The parlor had darkened while Lily sat thinking of Yves and Giselle. A cloud like a crab's claw had pinched out the sun, and shadows tapped with chilled fingers on Madame Moreau's shoulders. The old woman woke with a start. "I think he must be an impostor," she declared, blinking steadily as she cleared the cottony residue of dreams from her head.

"Who, Mother?" Adèle called out loudly from across the room, where she was seeing Lily to the door, one arm tucked fondly around Lily's waist.

"Monsieur Dupré, of course."

All ears, Lily turned back into the room upon mention of her renter's name. She and Adèle had been discussing him earlier, marveling at how the man had maintained his anonymity over nine Septembers of renting Lily's house. Couldn't Adèle have driven up the hill on some pretext and introduced herself? Couldn't she have monitored his comings and goings? Adèle had replied with her usual good humor and equanimity, why would she have taken an interest? She was a busy woman, she had a hotel to run, and, what's more, Lily had never asked her. Madame Moreau had offered no opinion prior to her nap, but now, freshly awakened, she spoke.

"Does it matter what the man looks like? Tall or short, blond or dark-haired, clean-shaven or wearing some silly mustache, as long as he pays the rent in full and on time . . . ?"

"He speaks English," Lily reported.

"Is that relevant?" Adèle's forehead wrinkled in wonderment that Lily would say something so foolish.

"French is preferable," Madame Moreau interjected into a

conversation that was going nowhere. "French is always prefer-able. It is as I said. If he speaks English, he is an impostor. He is not a Frenchman."

"That's absurd, Mother," Adèle said.

"What did you say, dear? Speak up."

Not letting on that her mother had just bugled her question across the room and out the door, Adèle shouted, "It's what I've been saying all along, Mother. He's German."

And Lily, shaking with laughter and helpless to stop it, forgot to inquire what had been on her mind in accepting Adèle's invitation in the first place. She had been hoping to speak to Madame Moreau about Giselle Godard. She had been meaning to ask her: Why did Giselle hang herself? What did she look like?

Sixteen

The next few days drifted sluggishly by without Yves appearing on Lily's doorstep. She missed his upbeat presence around the house, his cheerful banter and his phantom orchestra, and found it difficult to concentrate, to write, concerned to the point of intellectual numbness with the comings and goings (and stayings away) of her handyman.

Had he left town without letting her know, without saying good-bye?

She looked for him when she bought groceries in the village, and even went so far as to drive past his house, a chunky stone cottage bordering the sea. Pots of carmine geraniums flashed color beneath windows like transparent eyes lidded with crisp, dark draperies. Unlike Madame Moreau, who insisted on leaving her curtains wide-open so light could wash over her and bear her away on its watery flood, Yves's mother seemed to prefer twilit interiors. Perhaps she was in the kitchen at this very moment, beating egg yolks or folding the whites into a luscious, shiny, cooling mixture of butter and chocolate. Was Yves standing beside her, cajoling her into grudging merriment while unceremoniously licking the spatula?

When Lily did not discover him at a window or on the front stoop with a watering can in hand, she drove thoughtfully back to La Pierre Rouge, vaguely disgruntled. For two days now she had been wandering in circles: pieces of paper with a word or two typed on them—or no words at all—littered her desk, Madame Olivetti had become ever more sullen and unresponsive,

and Lily, exasperated with the disintegration of her pleasant routine, felt at loose ends, transitional, caught between writing and
remembering and yearning for (why not admit it?) the touch of
a man. Since Paul's death she had felt only dullness. Nothing had
stirred within her, the flame of her sexual being, even the spark
to ignite it, notably absent, extinguished. But now a hot bead
of desire pulsed inside her chest. She longed to feel the weight
of a man between her legs and crushed against her breasts. She
longed to arch up into him and feel the thrust of his own desire
pushed deeply inside her so that only a cry and a sound more
sob than laughter could carry her with him, and hold her there,
trembling, panting, releasing.

Loneliness slammed into her rib cage. Could she crumple and
fold like the pages she had written, be lifted by the breeze and
wafted, twirling, floating across the cork oaks and the flowers?
Could she sail over the Belgians' house, flirting carelessly with
the eggplants and the peppers, and wave at Alonso, and leave
Yves behind, safely cocooned in his mother's kitchen? Could
she fly perpendicular to her life for an instant, for a minute or an
hour, and return unnoticed, soundless as a cloud borne along by
the wind, over the sun-sleepy sea, over Monsieur Léon's campground, and back into her splendid house, no harm done, no
one the worse for her little adventure? Could she fly to that
place where Paul was waiting and hold him in her arms and tell
him she loved him?

She remembered, then, with a stab of wistfulness, Paul
standing in the bathroom and shaving under his chin, his neck
stretched upward and jaw thrust forward, humming a Mozart
flute sonata. Paul pushing open the door and posing naked on
the threshold, two dabs of shaving cream spotting his chin, comfortable pods of fat resting above his hips on an otherwise muscular and well-kept body. Paul lunging across the mattress and
ripping away the quilt, an aging Lothario snorting and catching

at her ankles, tugging at the sheet. Paul chortling afterward and avowing, "I love you, Lil." Paul humming again, softly, while stepping into his shorts, the melody muffled by the sweater he had twisted around his head, his arms trussed up in its narrow body, searching for armholes; his face, flushed and affable, as it poked up through the sweater's neck, and Mozart—yes, she had recognized it then, unmistakably, Mozart's Variations on "Helas, J'ai Perdu Mon Amant"—Paul's signature tune in lively counterpoint to the lowing of the cattle and the singing of the birds.

Seventeen

*L*ily sighed and floated seaward, becalmed and expectant as the sea in its noontime torpor. The water was silken, glassy; the sun was at its zenith. Her eyes behind their lids searched endlessly for shelter from the glittering light.

But Adèle was calling. "Lily! Come back! Yoo-hoo, Lily! You must take care." The Frenchwoman hurried along the sidewalk, frantic, in a navy blue silk dress, her wide skirt billowing, feathered by the wind, her muscular calves and narrow ankles set off to perfection in high blue heels. "Lily," she trumpeted through cupped hands. "You swim out too far. Why do you do this? *Faites attention.* We are no longer young."

"What is it?" Lily shouted, kicking toward shore. Her feet touched sand at the same moment that Adèle threw up her hands in a gesture Lily recognized, one that cut through the water and into her heart: Justine Lafond's gesture, the flamboyant dismay of her mother-in-law.

How she missed Paul's mother—her power, her pluck, her determination. Not long after Pierre was born, Paul had confided in Lily that he could read his mother's death in her eyes. She had diminished in his absence, the formidable ties that bound her to her Freddy gradually sapping the life force. Sorrow lined the skin around her lips and hollowed her cheekbones, although she still held herself proudly erect, delivered pronouncements with the force of regal decrees, and sniffed mightily if Lily appeared too agreeable. At those times Justine would swipe the air as if batting the dust from a stiff carpet, bullying Lily, but with patent affection, because her daughter-in-law would not take a stand. She would state, and then underscore her point with flailing arms, "You are too good, my darling, too accommodating. Where is the edge, the sting? What is it that *you* want, Lily? Not I. Not Paul. Not Pierre, but you. You! You have become so . . . how do you say? So wish-wash. So anti-committal!"

"Humor her," Paul said. "She won't be with us long." But the four years his mother lasted were shorter than even he had predicted. Her grandson, Pierre—her *petit chou*, her little cabbage—held her as tightly to this world as any of them could. But Freddy's tug was stronger. He came to her at night and stood at the head of her bed. She made space for him on her pillow and kissed the empty air.

In the last two summers of her life, torn by longing and invaded by cancer, Justine knelt in the garden, on a folded-over towel, and wrenched out weeds while cursing the sagebrush that hedged in the lawn. *"L'herbe du diable,"* the devil's grass, she muttered under her breath as, balanced on her knees, with her back arched to stretch out the ache, she pointed a long finger in a goatskin glove at the brush-covered hills. When she finally collapsed at the end of winter, Paul and Lily rushed her to the hospital, where a surgeon opened her abdomen—too late; the cancer was everywhere. Eleven days later they drove her back to the ranch. "So I die, after all, in the devil's grass," she murmured, wrapped in blankets in the front seat of the car and coughing weakly, racked with laughter. "Because of this great loving husband, this Freddy, I die in these terrible weeds."

She lingered five months, holding on until after Pierre's fourth birthday, putting off the one event so as not to ruin the other. "I wish she'd just let go," Paul had whispered to Lily late one afternoon after he had closed his mother's door and they were standing together in the hallway.

His face looked weary and worn, and Lily had imagined

her mother-in-law replying, as if her spirit were already vapor and had passed through the woodwork, "Have zee patience, my darling. Soon I will."

And she did, on a warm, gusty night when the wind blew open the French doors in the living room and the pungent smell of wet sage swirled in and pulled Lily from the couch where she lay reading, to watch the clouds close over the moon. She locked the doors, tiptoed upstairs, and slipped into Justine's room. Paul was sitting beside his mother, holding her hand. Tears streamed down his cheeks.

"What is it?" Lily asked quietly and went to him.

Just then Justine pointed upward. "Look, I see Paul on the ceiling." She murmured the words, barely moving her lips, then gave a soft rattle, a sound Lily had never heard before and, thus, didn't recognize as that last, remarkable, barely perceptible exhalation, life's membrane parting, the long sleep beginning, the spirit escaping. Paul reached over and gently closed his mother's eyes. Justine's wrinkled face had grown smooth and white and beautiful, and her body had shrunk, deflating as if her spirit had taken up actual physical space inside her.

Neither Paul nor Lily ever knew of whom—of Paul, Justine's brother, or her son—she had been speaking.

One morning in early May, the year after Justine died, Lily was hiking up the hill to the family gravestones, gauzy ribbons of cloud strung out above her, and was reminded of her mother-in-law claiming that epiphanies—a word Justine had used often and loosely—were appropriately experienced in air, with clouds. Airplanes, to her, were winged houses of worship. Lily had never looked for the appearance of a god while airborne. Revelations as she knew them came while walking in the hills, in late spring perhaps, when the mules' ears and the lupine wove a brilliant tapestry in the awakening grasses. With the far-reaching sky overhead and the earth expanding, delivering aromas pure and sweet as a bouquet of lilies removed from the refrigerator and set in a sunny location, she felt an emptying and refilling of the spirit with a sharper, clearer liquid. Maybe the nose *was* the entry portal, as Justine Lafond had often insisted, knowledge entering the body through one's nostrils and fizzing, like a tablet of Alka-Seltzer, throughout one's system.

Pierre had plodded alongside Lily on that cool May morning, dragging his feet in the dirt and swatting at lupine. "Don't walk too fast, Mom," he'd instructed her in a loud whisper, his small hand held tightly in hers. "We don't want to wake up J.L. in heaven."

J.L.

Justine had refused to answer to *Grandmaman* or Grandma.

Slowing her pace to match that of her son, Lily had answered him, "I think she's having a good sound sleep."

"Is she snoring?"

"Like a dragon."

"Do you think she can see us and hear us?" Pierre asked, reaching back with his free hand to scratch his bottom where a twiggy branch had snagged it. He wore bright red tights. He refused to wear anything baggy. The rubbing hurt his skin, he claimed, so they dressed him in tights. He required red. This had led Paul to comment, "The kid has spirit. He'll be a wild one, *non?*"

The boy's grandmother had assessed him differently. "He suffers from a serious nature, like my father, Gérard," she had announced soon after Pierre's birth. "He will make a fine stone-mason or a plumber."

Squeezing Pierre's hand as they neared the gravestones, Lily assured him, "I'll bet J.L. is having a grand old time watching us. She's looking down that long nose of hers and thinking, 'My, but I wish I were down there with my little cabbage.'"

Suddenly, Pierre cried out, breathless with excitement, "Hey, look, Mom!" and, letting go of her hand, he sprinted forward. "There are flowers growing out of J.L.'s grave!"

The ghostly white petals of jonquils opened like rosettes of starched silk stitched together and tipped toward the sun.

"Whoa there, Macduff," Lily called after him.

Pierre turned quickly, and with a hint of exasperation that did not escape his mother (who tried not to giggle), he said, "You know, Mom, Dad's always saying that. But it's really 'Whoa there, pardner,' not, 'Whoa there, Macduff.' So what is this guy, a man or a horse?"

But Lily was no longer listening. She saw only the jonquils growing on Justine Lafond's grave. Quietly, without her knowledge, Paul must have climbed up in October or November and planted them.

—

Adèle had vanished inside the glass doors of the Hotel de la Plage and the sun had grown hotter by the time Lily toweled off, shouldered her bag, and crossed the street to collect the newspaper. Although Madame Bibot frowned at her, Lily did not take her ill temper personally. She assumed it was not because Lily was American, a woman, and younger than Madame, and it was not because she was an hour late. The poor woman scowled because her husband had made a fool of himself over some German tourist. *"Elle est énorme!"* the shop owner scoffed. "Enormous! Soft as an *édredon*, with tits like feather pillows." Lily commiserated, though not effusively, careful to disparage the charms of the German tourist without calling into question Monsieur's fidelity, comportment, or taste. What wife wouldn't scowl? Madame Bibot must be constantly on her guard, for, although she vilified her husband and expected from her listeners an outraged response, she would countenance not a word said against him. The women, according to Madame Bibot, were invariably the villains.

Lily pulled the towel closer around her own willowy figure, tucked the newspaper into her string bag, and continued down the street, stopping off at the *boulangerie* to buy a baguette before starting up the hill. Higher up, beyond a whiff of raw sewage, beyond the clatter of cups and plates being washed in open sinks in the campground and the revving of engines, she greeted the Belgian couple. She remarked on the robust growth of Jacques's pepper plants, and complimented Christine on the new pastel-striped awning that cranked out over the terrace and provided a generous rectangle of shade, which the young woman appeared to shun. Christine reclined on her side in full sun, a sumptuous goddess unfolding long, brown, oiled legs and adjusting the elastic of her bandeau top as she rose to receive her neighbor. She had been reading a paperback book while listening to Schubert—the Trout Quintet; Lily recognized the leaping theme of the fish rising.

"*C'est une abomination!*" Christine asserted and, for one moment, until Lily followed with her eyes the direction of Christine's outflung arm, she imagined the woman was inveighing against her husband's peppers. She had whipped herself into an enchanting fury. In a high, rising, tumbling voice, she railed against the Algerians on the hillside. "*Quelle horreur!* They are killing the trees!" The chain saws were buzzing, a terrible sound, the high whine of death. They were razing the oaks. They were making a golf course—*le golf!*—where nothing was flat. Just dirt and rocks and cork bark blackened by last year's fires, now piles of brush and massacred trees. "Will they put magnets on the heads of the clubs?" she demanded.

Irate and saddened by this rape of the landscape, Lily expressed her horror while Christine settled back on her chaise. Alonso, slinking up from behind a mimosa, leapt into his mistress's sun-gilded lap. "After all, *mon petit*," Christine murmured to the cat. "What more can we do? As foreigners, we are helpless to act."

Jacques ventilated noisily, as if clearing from his nostrils a cloud of insects. He addressed his peppers. "*Ah, dis donc . . . merde!* Will they glue Velcro to the balls? Will the balls stand still? *Non! Ecoute ça.* They will fly down the hill and crash through my window. My window! *Le maire!* The mayor! It is all his fault. *Fils de pute! Pardon, Madame.* I become incensed. But this is madness, *non?*"

Lily nodded her agreement and then took her leave, astonished by the sudden fervor in this quiet young man, who reminded her of Pierre, her own solemn son dressed in bright red tights. She could see him still, preparing for their first trip to France after Justine died. He had packed up his books and his paint box, rubbed the cows on their bony foreheads, and fed carrots and apples to the horses, whose lips softly nibbled at the palms of his hands, as if delivering kisses. Then he had climbed into Paul's truck and, with the face of a hero seated on hot coals, set off bravely for the Continent. Within minutes, he had been spurting sleepy air against Lily's shoulder, and smiling.

It had been Paul's idea to pay a visit to La Pierre Rouge, the familial manse that had been closed up for years, since the death of Paul's grandfather, Gérard Lafond. Lily had downplayed the enormity of this breakthrough in her husband's routine, assuming that his mother's death had jolted him out of his rut and propelled him into exploring his roots across the Atlantic. The obstinacy with which Paul had previously dug in his heels whenever travel was mentioned had always struck her as out of character in a man so agreeable.

Since July and August were busy months on the ranch, Paul had remained in France for less than a week, then flown back to Idaho. In future years this had become their routine—Paul relaxing on the beach for a few days before heading home, while Lily and Pierre stayed on. It was thus that the house and land that were Paul's on paper became Lily's through habit, through the month or more she spent there each summer. "Stay with us," she would urge him. "We could have such fun here. We could travel around and see the country." But the ranch sang to her husband in the tones of a cowgirl siren, in a language he had learned in his mother's womb and, propped upright in the saddle, between the pommel and his father's chest. Invisible reins exerted a pressure Paul was helpless to resist despite Pierre's solemnly accusing eyes and Lily's inducements. Each summer he traveled both sadly and willingly back to Idaho, a compliant hostage to his genes and his upbringing.

Hesitating partway up her climb of the gold-dust road, Lily stood with her hands on her hips. She had been making scanty headway. She had been barely moving up the hill and now had stopped altogether, so self-absorbed that she had forgotten the menace, which was not some Circe of the sagebrush calling to Paul but a team of Algerians despoiling the hillsides, the tranquility, and the view. Lily dawdled and dreamed, whereas Justine Lafond would have slapped on her hat and charged up the road, a hellfire blazing, a fury fanned into rage. She would have stopped the Algerians in their tracks. She would have torn out their hearts and the heart of the mayor. *Le maire!* Enough of this nonsense! The chain saws silenced. The cork forest rescued.

But Justine the savior, the horse trader, the queen of uproar and intrigue, was dead.

And so it was with a tremendous racket on the hillside, like a swarm of locusts scissoring off whole branches, whole trunks— the dismemberment taking place under a searing blue sky—that Lily sat at her desk an hour later. Her bare feet lay flat against the cool tiled floor, her bare thighs pressed against the satiny wood of an old walnut chair where Justine Lafond had carved her initials. Sometimes, even now, Lily imagined Paul's mother beside her, above her, within her, the scent of gardenias—Justine's perfume—on the sultry summer air, and her husky voice crooning, "I think life is a pack of cards, Lily. When you turn them over they become your history. Until then they are shadows. Shadow cards. You try to cheat them, *non*? You tuck one up your sleeve or between your bosoms, or into your sock. You shuffle the pack. But when the cards are played out . . . pffft! *C'est tout. Terminé.* You are dead. A shadow. And the cards . . . they are dealt again and again in a different order. There are just so many cards."

Eighteen

*A*lonso was up to nothing productive when Lily spotted him nosing about the edges of Monsieur Léon's domain. Fed up with wallowing in grief and longing and feeling mildly irritated with Yves, whose unexplained absence had provoked the profound and unnerving bout of lethargy with which she had been struggling, Lily had set off down the hill in the heat of the afternoon, on an unscheduled run. At the entrance to the campground she noticed Alonso sniffing out the whereabouts of Monsieur Léon's remaining pet canary. "*Va t'en.* Go away," she hissed at the cat, lunging to give him a fright and save him from himself. But Alonso turned his cool eyes upon her, bounded disdainfully between her legs, and disappeared in the bushes.

"Fine," she said. "Fine. Eat the damn bird and face the gendarmes alone. It's your life, not mine." Growling at a cat! How had she sunk so low? *Pitter-pat.* She heard him behind her, following in her footsteps. *Pitter-pat. Pitter-pat.* She stopped and spun around. He was pacing at her heels like a faithful puppy, gazing up into her face with his compassionate gold-flecked Buddha's eyes, and she melted, she melted, a cat's fickle devotion sufficient inducement to bring her finally to her senses.

That same afternoon she began again to write, punching Madame Olivetti's sturdy keys, words appearing as if by telepathic process on the sunlit pages, sentences aligning themselves with an ease that brought a satisfied grin to her face. Once again the stack of papers on the corner of her desk was growing taller, held in place now by a large smooth rock she had spotted on a walk up the hillside. She wrote about Paul, how every now and then after their first few visits to La Pierre Rouge, she would test the waters by suggesting an adventure beyond the quiet village and the seductive sea where they traveled each summer. A trip *à deux*, just the two of them, became her dream. After reading about Gertrude Bell and Freya Stark, she had a hare-brained longing to mount a camel and set off across the desert. Any desert. "We have a perfectly good desert right here," Paul pointed out when she asked if he had ever ridden a camel, ever yearned to ride a camel. "They're meaner than hell," he said. "They bite." With his habitual good cheer, he resisted Lily's suggestive barbs and gentle nudges. For her part, she refused to recognize miscommunication and emotional white lies as anything other than an inconvenience. In a marriage you picked your battles. Was riding a camel worth it?

Was Paris?

Mistakenly, she had assumed that if she presented plans for a trip, nothing startling or lengthy, say a week in Paris, Paul would snap at the chance. His response was promising, his encouraging manner and the slow, ruminative nodding that Lily would later identify as playing for time (and would never again misread as his clear intent to join her) keying into her hopes. Hours after she had given him a guidebook to Paris, he strolled out of his study ostensibly consulting a map of the Left Bank. "This sounds like a great adventure," he announced heartily. "Why not give Esther a jingle? See what she thinks. It sounds right up her alley."

Lily reached for a smile. "I had a concept of the two of us in Paris," she said, keeping her voice as upbeat as possible.

Paul responded with an equal cheerfulness, "You know, Lil, to be perfectly honest, while I'd love to be there with you, I have no desire to spend time in Paris. There's not enough—"

"Sky? Cows? What, Paul? What is so—daunting about taking a trip?"

"Next time," he promised.

So Lily and Esther, and Esther's then current lover, an invest-ment banker named Robert, traveled together to Paris. They spent a week in an old and elegant hotel, living in a suite on the fifth floor reached via a small, pink-plush elevator. There was a sitting room between the two bedrooms, a marble fireplace with fresh-cut roses on the mantel, and an antique escritoire at which Lily sat smoking Robert's Gauloises (a short-term vice) and reading Proust in French. One afternoon she set down her book and allowed her thoughts to wander.

She had been packing her suitcase before leaving for Paris, feeling frazzled and rushed. Paul had been lying on their bed, on top of the quilt, watching her with slitted eyes and a lopsided grin. "Whoa there, Macduff," he'd said. "There's no—"

"Hurry. I know." Lily had halted halfway to the closet, a black lace brassiere dangling from her fingers, and flashed him a smile. "That's what you said when I asked you to marry me."

"*Asked* me?"

"Forced you. Isn't it the same thing?" she'd teased. "And isn't it, 'Lay on, Macduff'?"

"Lay on, whoa there—Macduff killed the bastard. That's what counts."

"My, but we're being feisty this morning. Is there a reason?"

"No reason," he'd said. "I'm simply reflecting on love and death. It's the serious side of my nature."

"What serious side?"

He'd bristled in mock offense. "You do me an injustice. I'm a serious man. I listen to you and Philomena talking on the phone about the unacceptable partners Esther chooses, and it reminds me that people crystallize their love on the most un-likely objects."

"I think you're confusing Phila with Proust."

"I am? Wasn't it Phila—? Or was it Lily Crisp who said that

a woman might see a Botticelli youth, an Adonis, in a vulgar gigolo and fall in love with him? A degraded piece of fluff, but to her he's an innocent. Noble. Sublime."

"That's Proust. And you've got the genders mixed up. It's a Botticelli maiden. . . ."

"Then feel honored."

"I—"

He had held up his hand. "No, this is serious, Lil. . . ." But the shadow of a smile had flickered across his lips as he'd leaned closer and whispered, "Can't we be serious?"

"I *am* being serious."

"About what, your sister's erratic love life? What exactly is her problem?"

Grinning, Lily had cocked her hand and shot him with her finger. "She's attracted to men who travel. She didn't marry a rancher."

From Paris, Lily wrote Paul a letter:

The weather here is balmy, sometimes hot, with a cleansing downpour each morning to wash the streets clean. The rain comes out of nowhere in a great whoosh and then melts into another sunny day without you. Meals are leisurely—the ceremony of eating lunch or dinner in Paris takes on the pace and sensuality of a slow and tantalizing afternoon of lovemaking. Can you tell I miss you? Sex is everywhere, in the food and the wine, in the pain au chocolat, in Esther's eyes and Robert's chinos, in the chauffeur's wink, but not in my bed with its upholstered headboard and linen sheets. Next time, Paul Crisp, you're coming with me.

Two years later, tagging along on one of Esther's more exotic assignments, rafting a wilderness river in Honduras, she wrote to Pierre:

Aunt Es and I just returned from the jungle after three wonderful nights under a canopy of huge leaves and, here and there, a twinkling star. Each night, for about half an hour, the lightning bugs glitter. They have neon green eyes that never go out, although at times they coalesce into one larger yellow light. They land on your hair and shoulders, bright spots of magical chartreuse light. Liam, an Irish archaeologist who's a friend of Aunt Es, saw a six-foot vine snake, grass green and slender. He pointed it out. It looked exactly like the stem of a plant wound around a branch, its head swaying up and down and around, and its tongue flickering. You would have loved it. But I'm not sure this is your and Dad's kind of place. Too many trees and too much moisture. Not enough sky for you Idaho boys.

There never *was* enough sky for Paul and Pierre, except in Idaho. And so the Fern Sisters' Trips became firmly entrenched in the rhythm of ranch life, in the annual scheduling. "Esther always packs a lover," Paul joked. "Lily packs her guidebooks and airmail stationery." It was a marital accommodation that appeared to work.

Once—only once—did she drive off in Paul's truck and not return for hours. Paul was frantic, livid, his legendary composure shattered, Pierre later reported to Lily. It was gusting high winds and hammering rain when she reappeared. She, too, was angry, but had carved out the space she needed, driving the back roads, slouched behind the wheel, singing a line or two with Patsy Cline or Willie Nelson—what did it matter? It had been a somber afternoon and raining steadily, the lava fields drinking deeply of the icy downpour, but the light had been blinding, unbearably so, as if a snowy ledge or hillside, or a maddeningly cloudless sky, had amplified the brilliance so that she was forced to shield her eyes . . . from what? Simply from her own imagination scrabbling for truth, for its own ledge to cling to.

Could a good man be so selfish?

The simple facts: Rome in November, Lily's thirty-ninth birthday. She had made the arrangements and Paul had agreed to go with her. It was her birthday trip, ten days door to door. They could relax together, laugh and make love, drink Chianti in the moonlight; be young again, childless, cowless, together—this one time, alone together. No Esther, no Esther's lover, no Blanca, no Pierre, no horses gone lame or pipes breaking, no beavers damming the ponds and ditches, no parents phoning, no mother's fey laughter gone shrill, no father's grumbling or disapproval. Just Paul, her sweetheart . . . talking to Paul, giving him again her heart, her thoughts, her dreams—stacking in each other's arms that great bundle of their memories.

But in October, something came up and Paul canceled. That *something* was never clearly understood by Lily, who slipped out of the kitchen, where Paul was making tea for the two of them, pre-warming the pot while awkwardly working at a frog in his throat that took an inordinate amount of clearing, coughing. . . .

A sick cow, a sick ranch hand—who gave a good goddamn who or what was sick?

Wordlessly, Lily slipped out of the kitchen, almost running into Pierre, who ducked out of her way.

He said, "Where are you off to?"

"Somewhere."

She could hear him asking Paul, "Hey, Dad, what's wrong with Mom?"

The last word she heard was Paul's reply, "Nothing," as she slammed the front door and drove off in the truck, roaring out the driveway, her hair flying out the window.

Could a good man be so selfish? Was it even worth asking? Was she so faultless, such a gift to the male gender? Did she think Paul never questioned why he'd married *her*? Welcome to the Club of Disappointment, she thought, and then count your blessings! It's the human condition.

In the rain-drunk lava, in that shining wasteland, Lily healed herself. She felt the full force of her love for Paul and understood that she would never understand it, but somehow it meant more to her than a trip to Paris or camels in the desert. Or Rome on her birthday.

When she returned to the house her anger had passed, and she said, "This one mattered to me, Paul." She never raised her voice. And she watched as his anger, which she knew was simply fear for her safety, fear that he would lose her, drained from him.

He said, "Next time, Lil. I give you my word."

Nineteen

On the ninth of their annual trips to France, Pierre, who had just turned fourteen, kept his nose in a book and pretended not to know his parents in the airport. Confronted by her glowering son, Lily thought back wistfully to the previous May, when, returning to the ranch from a short jaunt to Sicily, she had seen Pierre not as a child any longer but as a pleasant young man teetering on the brink of puberty. Catching sight of his mother, he'd unbent his long, thin body from the fence post he'd been straightening and given her a quick salute. He'd looked so handsome in his faded jeans and old striped shirt, a sweat-grimed Stetson cocked back on his head, dark curls clipped short across his forehead. His legs were slender and slightly bowed as he rocked back on the worn heels of Paul's old boots. His feet were already the same size as his father's.

Pierre had spoken on that sunny afternoon in a high-pitched Western drawl that sounded to Lily, a Wisconsin girl, like a two-bit cowboy in a third-rate movie. "The elk came down last winter and tore up the fence, Mom. Dad's worried about the grass, they could've wiped out the regrowth." Slowly pulling off his gloves and tossing them onto the grass, he had ambled over, her thirteen-year-old son grown so adult, so tall, so confident. For an instant he had been a little boy again, pressed against her, holding her as tightly as she held him—but only for an instant. Quickly he had drawn back with an embarrassed smile. "Blanca made tamales for dinner, two kinds, *carnitas* and chicken. Your favorites." Almost as an afterthought he'd added, "How was Italy?"

Before she could reply, Pierre had returned to his work on
the fence post, and Lily, strolling toward the house, had seen the
front door opening, Blanca standing in the sunlight, waiting to
embrace her. And she'd heard Paul's truck pulling up behind
her, rolling to a stop, his voice calling out—"*Scusi*, signora. Your
baggage, I have it with me in the truck."

Even Pierre had looked up, shading his eyes with his hand
and smiling as Lily's laughter rang out with the clear joy of a
woman who has come home to her family.

But one year in a boy's life can encompass changes that occur
so rapidly, Lily almost wondered if a particularly unfavorable
alignment of the planets could account for the concussive blow
of Pierre's metamorphosis. Within a year he had grown another
four inches, his child's voice had broken and plummeted, and
he'd decided that parents were better disowned in public. At La
Pierre Rouge he sulked in his room and read books about cattle
ranching in Australia and Argentina. When he emerged at mealtimes he spoke in monosyllables, and, on his way to and from
the table, spent an inordinate amount of time in front of the
mirror. His skin had entered an unfortunate state of hormonal
transition, as had his voice and his sex, which, if the rhythmic
jiggling of his headboard against the wall was any indication, was
taking a beating.

"Where's Pierre?" Lily asked Paul at breakfast.

Paul tilted his nose toward their son's locked door and replied, "Busy."

"Do boys that age think about anything besides sex?"

"No."

"When does it change?"

"Never."

For the first time in all their summer visits Lily was relieved
when, after a week, Paul left for the States—this time with
Pierre in tow. In their absence, the silence that washed over her

felt like a warm sea offering endless directions in which to wander. She had returned to her work of translating manuscripts when Pierre had entered the third grade, and the give-and-take of stretching her mind with French translations and stretching herself physically with chores on the ranch had achieved a balance that, at the age of forty, furnished satisfaction but little time for regeneration and solitude.

Unfortunately for Lily, the delicious sensation of quietly drifting at La Pierre Rouge lasted less than twenty-four hours. At ten o'clock the next morning, as per arrangement, Philomena emerged from a peach-colored van, shapely legs first, then the soft, gorgeous, milk-white bulk of her. She called out a greeting. "Hello there, Sis! Here we are, the troops have arrived, a bit battered by your minefield. What a road! If I'd known, I would have rented a tank. Tonio's riding his motorcycle down from Normandy. He'll be here in a couple of days."

At a momentary loss for what to do—six children from the ages of two to eighteen spilled from the vehicle in a tangle of sun-browned legs and baseball hats—Lily had the unworthy thought, as the young Cassatas streamed onto the terrace, that she could lodge them in the armoire with Monsieur Lafond's cornflakes. But then she caught sight of Gina, Phila's firstborn, towering over her siblings on long, heronlike stalks of legs, and Lily laughed with pleasure.

Among her nephews and nieces Lily had favorites, although she knew she shouldn't. Gina was one of them, a soon-to-be college sophomore who saw the world in polarities of red and white. She never noticed the many delicate shades of pink—the salmons, the apricots, and the roses. Yet even at her most serious, at her most obsessed and harshly judgmental, she would break into giggles so infectious and thrilling that no one, least of all Lily, could resist her. "Do you know what it's like to go on a family picnic?" she complained to her aunt. "The number of Pampers, tissues, paper plates and napkins, foam cups, plastic forks and spoons, aluminum cans, hot dog bun wrappers, candy wrappers . . ." As the tales of unrecycled waste mounted up, Gina began to chuckle, her laughter deepened, swelled, and caught in her throat, bubbling up into her eyes, which dribbled sad, frustrated tears of amusement. "What's wrong with my parents? Three children, even four, would have been plenty."

Lily told her, "I doubt it. But every one of you is wanted and loved. That's nothing to sniff at."

"No," said Gina, torn as usual.

"We each have a gift," Lily explained to her niece, wanting to lift this overly responsible young woman to the tops of the waves where the view would be less red, lighter. "Your mother was born with a gift for bearing children. It's her passion, just like yours is saving the environment and mine is languages. Your mother is a natural. She's doing just what she wants to do."

Gina sighed. "I know. That's the problem."

"Think of it this way, honey. You have to think of your mother as a celebration. She's a marvel, really. A force of nature can't be stopped, and your mother is one."

"Then what's my dad?"

Lily paused for a moment to consider her answer, to give Antonio his just due. "Your father is a good and loving man. He works hard making sausages and you are all very lucky."

Gina said, "He thinks you're a pistol, Aunt Lily."

Angel was the other of Lily's favorites, the daughter most like Philomena: a cream-fed Wisconsin girl with clear green eyes and thick sunny hair. Uncomplicated and even-tempered, Angel romped about the house and yard, bounded into the school bus and out of it again at day's end as if life were a benign, bouncy river down which she was riding on a blow-up dolphin. She ate ice cream by the quart from the carton, with a spoon. Lily called her "my little mango," soft on the outside and hard in the center, but large as the girl grew, she never fell off her inflatable dolphin. Such steady good cheer would help to keep her mother and siblings afloat when, two months after their wonderfully successful trip to France, the chaos of unthinkable loss engulfed them.

Three days after Philomena's dramatic entrance in the peach-colored van, Antonio arrived at La Pierre Rouge, pulling up to the house in a thunderous spray of gravel, on a rented Ducati. Smiling widely he dismounted, stripped off his leather jacket, his sunglasses, and the red bandanna he had tied around his forehead, and clumped in heavy boots down the steps to the terrace, where he lifted his wife in his arms and swung her around. Then he turned to embrace Lily, kissed her lightly on the cheek, and, with her body held tightly against him, waltzed her across the flagstones, laughing as they spun and lunged and lost their balance. Lily disentangled herself quickly, laughing.

"Hey, kids. Guess who's here," Philomena shouted to the children racing around the house and toward their father in a crescendo of happy voices and shrieks of greeting. Even more handsome at forty-four than when he had cruised past the Fern bungalow in his black leather jacket nineteen years earlier, Antonio Cassata wrapped up his entire family in a giant, pulsating, irrepressible bear hug. Love spilled from the man, his salt-and-pepper hair and finely chiseled features lending him the distinguished, rugged, outdoorsy air of the paterfamilias.

As the years had passed and Lily and Antonio had spent time together on numerous family occasions, she had wondered why she had so desperately longed to keep him in her life. Once the attraction was gone—and it had died instantaneously during their protracted tussle on Philomena's couch—she questioned what had made him so irresistible. He was amusing, generous, ambitious, and cocksure of himself—a roué with a benevolent joker's heart. Had that been her recipe for disaster? She could find no acceptable reason for her previous attachment, which had lasted even after he had mated with and married her sister. But what she had felt for Antonio had nothing to do with rational explanations or essential levelheadedness. She knew from experience that desire was a trickster. It billed itself as a purveyor of fantasy, and while you were caught up in the most intimate of acts, incapable of reason, it swept aside your dreams. Paul, not Antonio, had been her dream.

Two months after that rambunctious twirl across the terrace, with Philomena and the children applauding and hugging their father, when Antonio lay dead on a dirt road in Georgia, his Harley Electra Glide overturned beside him, Lily remembered the electric presence of the man. Philomena had gathered her children around her and, taking charge with an unshakable strength previously camouflaged by her soft exterior, she'd reassembled the pieces of their shattered lives. Esther may have unwittingly spoken Antonio's epitaph many months later, after the shock had begun to dissipate and their grief to settle: "He was a charismatic Italian who rode motorcycles, made babies, and made sausage, in that order." But he had meant much more than that to Lily. Once, she had been pregnant with his son. And once, she had loved him.

Losing Antonio had shaken Lily to the core. First there had been Leo, born without breath and a heartbeat. Then the little boy's father. Paul, too, was keenly affected by news of the tragedy. Morbidly silent, he walked up the hill to his parents' graves and stood there for hours in the warm September sunshine. A few wispy clouds trailed overhead, "like the spirits of loved ones scouting for reentry into a life they weren't prepared to abandon," he told Lily afterward. It surprised her, this talk of spirits and souls, until she remembered the loons on the lake and Paul's words: *They sound like wolves, don't they? Like spirits out there, the voices of loved ones.* A few months earlier in France, during the

Cassatas' visit, Lily had wished that she could shave a corner off Antonio's sense of adventure and graft it onto Paul's steadfast nature. But the sobering finality of death tempered her wish, and the status quo had a soothing, salutary feel to it.

And then again he came, that gray old man in his flapping sheet, on his pale horse with its skeletal shanks. Again he visited families already reeling from the loss of a man who had been husband, father, brother-in-law, son-in-law, and uncle. Two months after Antonio's death, Grandma Fern climbed into bed one night and never woke up. A month after her funeral, Oscar Fern fell ill and was taken to the hospital.

Esther assured Lily over the telephone, "There's no danger. The poor guy's just corked up tight. His bladder's not functioning. The doctor says it's temporary, and it had better be. Dad'll never put up with bladder bags and catheters."

Lily's mother reported, "He's recovering nicely and feisty as a hungry bear."

But with a growing sense of malaise, Lily flew east to Milwaukee and the hospital.

When her father awoke from a post-dinner nap, Lily was seated beside him, uncomfortably upright in the armchair Esther had insisted she sit in. Lily was holding his hand, stroking it, mesmerized by the dark spots that showed up like ink stains against the pallor of his skin, the dead-feeling flesh, the raised network of veins that looked so fragile that she feared if she rubbed a fingernail across them life would seep out in a cold blue trickle, not the hot red blood of his courting days.

"So, young man," she said with a forced breeziness. "How are you feeling?"

"Ancient," he muttered. "Esther told you?"

"She did."

"It's a damn water spout, nothing more."

"Give it time."

"The old whizzer still had a shot or two in it, but now . . ."

She patted his hand. "Don't be silly. It'll be up and running soon."

"At my age? You know how old I am, Lily? Seventy-five. Let me tell you, it's a blow having a hose stuck up my privates."

"A tube, Dad. It's not a hose."

"Don't quibble. Have you been to the cottage?"

"Not lately," she replied. Not in twenty-five years. Not since she was a child.

Her father observed in a sleepy voice, "Well, it's time you went then, you and Phila. Has she married that good-looking Italian yet?"

Lily did not tell him that Antonio was dead and that Phila, soon to turn forty and the mother of six children, was coping admirably. She tried to keep her face a blank, but too much had happened in the past few months and her mouth began to tremble. "Oh, Dad . . . ," she said softly. He reached up to run a cool finger along her cheek, and she ached for this suddenly old, forgetful man whose hand dropped onto the covers, who was instantly asleep and peacefully snoring while a stream of yellow liquid ran from his body through a plastic tube into a bag at Lily's feet.

A short time later he awoke, even more confused, talking about snakes on the walls and a devil squatting behind the arm-chair. "A devil, Dad?" Lily said gently. "That's not a devil, that's a bear, a stuffed bear from one of Phila's kids. Should I move it?"

"Don't," he said. "It'll bite you."

"It won't bite me," she promised as she crossed the room and reached behind the armchair. Her father mumbled something she could not hear. "What, Dad? What did you say?" She turned with the bear in her arms. "You see? It's only a bear."

He continued to mumble, watching her closely, his eyes somewhat teary. Then he motioned her toward him. "Come here, Hamlin Lillian," he said with a hint of the old bravado in his voice, the rakish smile that had once charmed the ladies into his arms bringing a high flush to his cheekbones. Lily walked to the bed, the bear grasped around its middle, a muffler to her pain. She was bending down, searching for her father's hand beneath the covers, when his fingers closed over hers and he whispered, "Have I told you, pumpkin, how much I love you?"

When her father died in his sleep on Christmas morning, Lily did not cut off her hair or jam a fingernail scissors into her arm, or cry. Except for that one swift, violent, tearful explosion of grief in Cortina when she had lost Leo, she always mourned soundlessly. Inwardly.

Twenty

A light rain had fallen during the night, settling the dust, quenching the thirst of flowers and foliage crisped by the sun, and freshening the heat-blanched underbelly of the sky. The Mediterranean lay flat and somnolent in air sluggishly weighted with moisture, unstirred by the slightest breeze. A gecko zipped across Lily's shoes as she loped up the road past the Belgians' house. It scuttled up a nearby wall into a cloud of bougainvillea, emerged higher up from beneath a boa of colorful blossoms, then froze, its tail curved gracefully and head cocked in readiness for action, as if it were tracking Lily's footsteps.

She smiled and jogged on.

A short time later, sweating profusely from a final sprint up the hill, she crunched across the gravel driveway and caught sight of Yves seated at the table on the terrace, looking plump-cheeked and durable. His eyes went soft when he saw her and his lips bowed upward, lifting his cheekbones in a genial expression that advertised goodness—a pure clean goodness (she would later reflect) that could stop technology in its tracks and heal the confusion of the modern world.

She waved. "Yves!"

"Lily!" He leapt to his feet and came toward her.

"*Bonjour*, Yves," she said warmly. "Have you been out of town?"

"Across the border. To visit my mother."

"Your mother? I thought you lived with your mother."

"I do. But she went to Ventimiglia to visit her sister."

"I would have thought—"

"I would have stayed at home? Certainly this was a possibility but I determined—we—you—needed—"

"This embarrasses you? Tell me. I am waiting. I have heard it all at one time or another."

"I tell you this," he blurted out thickly. "I wasn't coming back."

"After you weren't going in the first place?" she teased him softly and slipped past him, unlocking the door and leaving it open behind her. Once inside the kitchen she poured herself a tall glass of water and drank it down. Then she poured another, wiped the sweat from her forehead, and, leaning back against the counter, turned to watch as he strolled across the living room. In the doorway he stopped.

"Come on in," she said. "Sit down."

Smiling uncertainly, he covered the kitchen in two long strides, pulled out a chair from the table beneath the window, and sat. He said, his face stiff with emotion, throwing his hands wide apart, "Look at me. Look at me! What you see here is a man whose mother feeds him too much, who loves him too much, and who swears that she cannot live without him. I went home the night of our memorable luncheon—you remember?—on the terrace, and my cheeks were on fire and there was wine in my veins and you, Lily, were in my thoughts. Maman had prepared no dinner, no dessert. She sat in the darkened room sobbing. I threw open the curtains that she always keeps drawn as if we live in a tomb, and I said, 'For God's sake, Mother, why are you sobbing?' No grown son can stand this, his mother damp and sagging like an old shopping bag someone has dropped in a puddle and stamped on. And then I see her, Maman, in the light from the window, and the longing in her expression, her fragility, her age—when has my mother, so busy with her cakes and custards and pastries, grown this old and vulnerable? It is a hammer blow to my chest! I am reeling! Maman, I cry, what has happened? And she says that she knows I am planning to leave her, to go to my uncle's farm in the Perigord, where the women are plump and willing, and if I leave—please, will I take her with me? What can I respond? This is unreasonable, I tell her. She is being perverse. How can you leave someone and at the same time take her with you? But she is sobbing. She is my mother. So when she boards the train to Ventimiglia in the morning, I follow in my truck. These two good women, my mother and my aunt, feed me squid and risotto and veal so tender that I think, What's the hurry? Maybe next time I will leave her. Next time I will drive to my uncle's. *Next* time— But I bore you, Lily."

She shook her head and laughed. "On the contrary, you are so much like Paul, I find you infinitely amusing."

"Amusing?" His eyes narrowed, doubtless at the perceived slight to his masculinity, but, regardless, he looked relieved and smiled and wiped his forehead with the palm of his hand and said abruptly, more cheerful now, "I have the wall to repair, that won't take long. Your daughter's room, the baseboard—two hours. I can wrap this all up in a day or two at most if this would please you."

"Of course it would please me, but . . . look, Yves," she said, then pressed her lips together and glanced up at the ceiling, where a spider was busily spinning its web. A fly blundered into it—and somehow the sight of this intimate world proceeding without her, the routine of killing mutely enacted above her head, made her choices clearer. She was fifty-two years old, no innocent, no youngster, and she had missed him.

As if reading her thoughts he said, with a husky catch in his voice, "You know what I—"

But she broke in gently—"You know what *I* think, Yves?" And she reached over and touched his cheek so tenderly, and

said with such quiet goodwill that she cinched the outcome
without even asking, "I'm sick to death of thinking."

The next instant he was on his feet and pressed against her;
his hands were upon her. A spaghetti strap plunged, and with
it Lily's T-shirt, caught for a moment on her breasts. But Yves
released it, pushed it down to her waist and later discarded it,
or pulled it over her head—she couldn't remember when, afterward, it lay like a collapsed bundle, like a bruised rose, on the
floor beneath the table. The heat of his body finished it for Lily:
her grappling with clarity and composure. She reached for his
belt buckle and unzipped his fly. She ran her hand inside his
trousers, and, without a word, he picked her up and carried her
through the living room and up the stairs to her bed. He tossed
off the quilt with a sweep of his hand and laid her down on the
white linen sheet that had been flapping through Lily's mind for
the past ten days.

Was it only ten days?

He ran his lips along the length of her body, arched and open
to him, pausing for a leisurely nibble on her breasts. She cried
out softly and spun into a blinding white oven of light. Yves har-
nessed the burden of his pent-up desire and applied it slowly.

Lily, pressed beneath him, felt washed in forgetfulness.

Twenty-one

This is what happened. She still jogged down the hill before breakfast, and she swam in the sea. She still wrote in the mornings and the afternoons, but in the evenings, after work, Yves came to her, and they made love, and then they talked; in French if it concerned the present. If it concerned the past, Lily spoke to him in English. She told him her story, and because she was lying naked beside him with her head on his shoulder or sitting propped up against a pillow, the obsessive nature of her ramblings was blunted. Everything—not only the inward eye that scrutinized her history but her skin, her hair, her lips, her breasts, even the soles of her feet grew soft with Yves's loving. He said to her, "Just talk to me, tell me whatever is on your mind and maybe this will make the process easier"—whatever the process was. He didn't ask.

He said, "Speak to me in English. I prefer it. I can watch your lips and kiss them if I wish, and I can read what you are saying in your eyes." When he strode into her room and found her still at her typewriter, he swept the shawl off the chair where she had tossed it, and he draped it over Madame Olivetti so she could not see them exposed in their intimacy. He serviced her as well, the typewriter—soon her type heads were clean, her keys shot up and down with the lubricity of youth, and each time Lily reached the end of a line, before she shoved the carriage back, the refurbished Madame no longer grumbled in her old metallic bones but sounded a lively chime, in the encouraging fashion of those new electric models.

Lily said, "So you've overhauled us both, the two old ladies."

And Yves replied, caressing her, "The compensation is generous."

For fourteen evenings he drove up the road in his Deux Chevaux truck while below him, in the village, in his neat stone house overlooking the sea, his mother's smile grew more bitter and her desserts more darkly voluptuous. For fourteen evenings Lily aroused him with her feast of whispered memories and words she knew he did not understand—Chiapas, San Cristóbal de las Casas, *posh, chechem, la selva*—and the two syllables he would come to recognize and repeat to Lily, spoken over and over with an enchanting sexual quaver, or a firmness of tone that Yves admittedly found inflammatory, taunting—Victor; a name; a man's name; Victor.

Then he would push her legs apart and take her with such energetic joy that, when they had finished, they would lie on their backs panting and laughing. Laughing! It would break Lily's heart, for laughter with its capacious joy was a frosting she and Paul had always spread on their lovemaking.

Each evening, before Yves departed, Lily would pull her lover back onto the bed as he was buckling his belt, and she would say to him, in French, "Tell me, Yves, slowly, while I am putting on my clothes, what your mother is preparing for dinner."

Twenty-two

*V*ictor: She had met him in Mexico, while visiting Esther.

At the last minute Paul had not come with her, and they had argued—or she had argued—lashing out in the first violent and damaging exchange of words in almost eighteen years of marriage (exploding over three pots of basil or roaring off in Paul's truck seemed like love taps in comparison). She had been sitting across from Paul—each detail of that breakfast tableau remained with her still: the waxed pine table, the bentwood chairs with their floral pillows, the blue and white polka-dot cereal bowls that Justine Lafond had treasured, the dark red café-au-lait mugs rimmed with foamed milk from what had been, until Paul quietly delivered his news, a most pleasant breakfast. The sun had just lifted over the graveyard hill.

"I'm disappointed," Lily said carefully. "This isn't the first time, Paul. This is the third time, the fifth time—I can't even remember how many times you've backed out on a trip we've planned together."

He nodded and stood up and began to clear the table. When he had stacked the dishes on the counter and, having turned on the faucet, stood waiting for the water to grow hot, he took a sudden interest in the frost patterns on the kitchen window.

Lily spoke to his back. "Hello, Paul. Are you listening?" Her voice remained steady, but her eyes, if he had bothered to look, were lightless. "Do you understand that this trip means everything to me? My grandmother is dead. My father is dead. Antonio is dead. I'm forty-two. You're fifty-six. . . . Who knows how long it'll be until we're both dead? I'm a fortunate woman. I lead a blessed life, but I'm human, Paul. I still have dreams."

He shut off the water and turned to face her. She could see by the slight puckering around his lips and the furrow between his brows how much this disagreement was costing him. "I'm not looking to block your dreams, Lil. You can travel with Esther—"

"I can what?" The explosion rocked them both. "You are a thoughtless stick-in-the-mud and damned selfish! Don't you ever intend to leave this goddamn piece of godforsaken, fucking sagebrush?"

Fucking. That was a first. Until now she had lived so affably inside her marriage, accepting happiness, enshrining happiness, loath to cause ripples. She had no practiced vocabulary for voicing needs and frustrations, or addressing difficulties.

"You don't mean that, Lil," he replied calmly. "We go to France every summer. I can't go to Mexico now. It's the timing."

"Timing! You were all set to go yesterday," she retorted, angrily slanting her eyes not at him but up at the cookbook shelf, where a miniature clay man riding the back of a ceramic toucan stared her down. He seemed to know everything; small cracks fissured his forehead, connecting eyebrows that arched in unremitting amazement, acceptance, and the will to endure.

(Later, in Mexico, Lily would regret not having walked over to Paul and touched his cheek, brought up short by the keen-eyed little man on the bookshelf. What would it have cost her, a simple gesture that might so easily have reshaped their lives? But the moment hung between them, clamoring for revelations, shouting for some sort of acceptable closure.)

Paul said, "You'll have a great time with Esther. You always do."

"Pierre is at school," she countered. "He's a boarder, for God's sake, he can get along without us for a few weeks. He'd love it.

You might find this hard to believe, but there are telephones in Mexico so we can call our son. We can call Blanca"—her voice was rising—"we can even call the damn cows and find out if they're pregnant."

"We'll talk about it when you come home, Lil. I can't deal with it now," he said softly, enraging her further.

"I would like to deal with it now, Paul."

But he turned his back—he turned his back—and walked away.

They slept in separate rooms that night. Lily, alone in their bed, lay stony-eyed and helpless to act, paralyzed by the enormity of their argument. She wondered how other couples survived such damage—there was no other word for it. Damage. She felt that if she touched her breast, over her heart, the skin would burst into flames. The pain scorched her, it stunned her, and she imagined Melinda, Paul's first wife—trapped, marginalized, and isolated by a landscape of glorious hills and a herd of cows that wasn't even there in the winter, that went south to California.

So Lily, too, went south, to Chiapas, where Esther was on assignment, writing a piece on the town of San Cristóbal de las Casas. Esther had rented a house for two months. Conveniently, it had a tiny upper story with an extra bath and bedroom.

"You look like hell," Esther announced when she picked Lily up at the airport in Tuxtla Gutiérrez. "Where's Paul?"

"Something unexpected came up. He changed his plans."

When Lily did not elaborate, Esther said with an aggrieved smile, "The first thing you'll do when we get to the house is call him."

The road to San Cristóbal de las Casas had no guardrails. It climbed in switchbacks up a steep escarpment that rose abruptly, as if a giant piston had violently punched up layers of rock from the valley below. Crosses with fresh flowers laid beneath them and small painted shrines fashioned from cement marked the *curvas peligrosas* where the cars of loved ones had missed the corner and arced in flames over groves of oaks, or flipped and rolled. Lily did not look down. She dared not look down at the wide plain stretching empty and bright as if morning light had burst from the dammed-up blue of sky. Light flooded the flat lands, rose like smoke from the gorges.

As if summoned, a bus that had been hugging their bumper swung out to pass with an S curve approaching. The wall of silver metal hurtled alongside them, forcing Esther's Volkswagen Bug to the lip of the precipice, where branches scraped at yellow paint already crisscrossed by scratches. Lily peered over the cliff's edge, a glimpse that jolted her back in her seat, hands braced against the dash. Then the bus shot around them.

Wrenching the wheel to the right, Esther steered the car off the pavement onto a wide crescent of dirt, where she cut the engine. Silence floated down upon them like a gentle cloud. They sat for a moment, savoring the quiet and the lull in the traffic. Then Esther pushed open her door and stepped outside and Lily did the same, picking her way through a pile of garbage: wadded plastic bags, beer cans, soiled diapers, sheets of cardboard, shredded paper, used toilet paper, feces—human feces.

"Welcome to Mexico." Esther grinned as the two of them unzipped their shorts, pulled down their panties and, squatting behind the car, closed their eyes and held their breath.

Lily commented wryly, "Mom would have stayed in the car with a full bladder and counseled her daughters to do the same."

"And Phil would have obeyed her," Esther said, and they both broke out laughing as, in unison, they pulled up their shorts and perversely scuffed the soles of their sandals in the dirt to clean them.

Then they drove on slowly through boulder-strewn hills

barren of trees, the slopes nearly vertical, the soil dry and lifeless. Dead cornstalks poked up between the rocks. These were
the *milpas* of the Maya, the family cornfields hacked out of hillsides only desperate farmers without better land, or better pros-
pects, would think to clear and cultivate. Ahead, a massive white
church overshadowed clusters of brown-walled huts, tiny black
doorways, and specks of red and pink—Mayan women drifting
toward the smooth white walls and great black doors where the
Catholic saints, white-faced and rosy-cheeked, awaited them.

San Cristóbal, when it appeared around a tight bend in the
road, hid its rush of colors and sounds beneath the distant mono-
chrome of urban sprawl. Lily rolled down the window. The air
felt chilly. She smelled wood smoke and dung. A firecracker exploded like a gunshot nearby. The harsh blare of a brass horn, or
a burro's cry, set off the jubilant peal of church bells, which died
suddenly. Esther looked at her watch.

"Is it noon already?" Lily asked.

"It's twelve thirteen."

"It makes no sense, church bells ringing at twelve thirteen."

"We're in Mexico, Lil. Time is no longer a precise commodity."

"Such perspicacity in a sister—it scares me," Lily said.

Later that afternoon Lily telephoned Paul. She informed him
somewhat formally that she had arrived safely, the house Esther
had rented was beautiful, pink stucco, surrounded by jacarandas
and Montezuma pines and a brick wall breached by a blue-
green door the color of the sea in baking sunlight. They had to
jiggle the pillows to keep moths from laying their eggs on the
covers. There were dog prints in the floor tiles, tortilla-sized spi-
ders in the bathtub, and mice who grew fat on rice and frijoles
in the pantry.

Paul said, "I love you, Lil. Please forgive me."

And her heart lurched and dropped into a velvety pit of regret. She wanted to reach out and hug him and say the words she

somehow found impossible to utter over the telephone: At some point love isn't enough, Paul. I need to know you're listening.

She said instead, "I wish you were here."

He told her he couldn't talk now, and although he was thousands of miles away, Lily felt him close down. After they had hung up, she gazed thoughtfully at the telephone for a while before walking into the kitchen, where Esther was preparing dinner. "He says he can't talk now," Lily reported.

Esther replied, "Godammit it, Lil. Pull yourself together. It's rough for all of us. It's been a rough year. At least you've got a husband." And that was a hit only a sister could deliver, smack on target, dragging Philomena and her six fatherless children into the picture. Lily felt diminished, as if overnight she had turned into a whiner. But what did Esther know about long-term commitments and husbands, with her gunshot approach to lovers who never lasted longer than a year, and in the end were deemed too young or too old, too forbearing or too self-absorbed, too emotionally uptight or too sexually kinky. Lily catalogued her ammunition, but she was wise enough not to load it, or fire it, at her sister.

That first night in San Cristóbal Lily lay awake for hours, oblivious to the wrenching squeal of tires on pavement, the blast of horns and the screech of brakes, the popping of firecrackers and the sobbing cadence of *ranchero* music that filled the night with its weighty lament of faithful wives chained to their pedestals, missing out on the fun while the *chicas* rutted with the faithless husbands. Her mind churning, Lily thought about Paul turning his back on her and walking away. Was it his age? she wondered. Was folding unapologetically inward something that happened to men in their fifties? The fifteen years between them had never mattered when they were younger, but now the two of them talked about nothing more intimate or important to their marital well-being than the weather, cattle, wildflowers,

Pierre, and what books they were reading. She accused Paul of turning into a curmudgeon for whom mending fences or moving water was a preferred mode of escape from any meaningful discussion. Somewhere, somehow, they had lost touch—or was it she, a sphinx when it came to examining relationships, who had lost touch? And wasn't it always easier to spot the shortcomings in one's partner than to turn the glass of introspection on oneself?

For whatever reason, a wrinkle had formed in their marriage, a slight malaise, little bouts on both their parts of unspecific melancholia: all par for the course in any long-term relationship, any fool could have told them that. But unlike Paul, Lily had grown skittish in the years leading up to her father's death, for she had witnessed the unraveling of her parents' union, ultimately held together by little more than a shared history and inertia. Her mother had turned into a sniper. Her father had girded himself with unbreachable armor, proof against the bullets that were his wife's words, his wife's despair.

A tiny crack in their marriage, Paul and Lily's, and yet . . . Was it any wonder that Victor slipped through it?

Twenty-three

He appeared at the blue door in the garden wall, a tall man whom Lily took to be German. (Esther would later explain, joking: "You can see it if you bite him. It's pure German blood coursing through his American veins." And Lily would not ask the obvious question because even then, a few hours after she had met him, she didn't want to know the answer to when and where her sister had bit him.)

When she heard the garden bell tinkling, she ran up the steps two at a time to unlatch the door, expecting a Mayan selling kindling or a ladino with a story about a stolen watch in Comitán and could she lend him twenty thousand pesos, but she did not expect the man whom she saw: lean and well muscled, his runner's legs projecting from wrinkled khaki shorts, a faded blue tank top baring wide shoulders, a well-worn knapsack in the dust at his feet, which were dust-covered as well in leather sandals. His pale blond hair, cut short—spiky—resembled a hedgehog's bristles. He peered down at her from the alleyway, from the step above the stone landing where she stood, and his bright blue eyes, translucent as water underlain by pure white sand, held hers for an instant before he said, "Lily? You're Esther's sister. I'm Victor Piontek. Is Esther home?"

"She's not, but you're Dr. Wrinkles. I know," she said and laughed, and opened the door wider. Esther had told her about Victor, an orthopedic surgeon—knees or hips, Esther couldn't remember which, but she called him Dr. Wrinkles because he didn't own an iron. He was always heading off somewhere, to the jungle or the beach, with a kayak and his knapsack, an attractive woman in tow. He was in Chiapas for a month, training doctors in the local hospital and doing grassroots medicine in the villages.

Victor lounged in the doorway, staring at Lily. He didn't look as if he'd be leaving any time soon, nor did he ask when Esther was returning. He appeared somewhat stunned, or bemused, so Lily finally asked, "Do you want to come in?"

"Sure," he said and stooped so as not to hit his head, waiting while she closed the door, then following her down the stairs and into the house, where she sat on the bench in front of the fireplace and gestured for him to take the only comfortable chair in the *sala*. He leaned back and stretched his long legs in front of him.

Lily smiled and cleared her throat. Then she said, "I can't stay long. I have an appointment at ten."

It was nine o'clock in the morning. Sun streamed into the living room through a bank of open windows. On the lawn sloping down from the patio, Faustino, the gardener, flitted carelessly, birdlike in his bones, from one garden perch to another, whistling all the while. He ripped up weeds with fierce little hisses, and overwatered the flowers. "That's too much water. *Bastante.* Enough," Esther would explain to him every Thursday when he came to work, miming with drooped hands and a convulsed mouth the flower heads gasping for air and expiring. Faustino would laugh and whistle and continue to water.

But this particular Thursday, catching sight of the señora's sister entertaining a male visitor, he turned off the hose and drifted uphill toward the patio, climbing the steps and picking up the broom Esther had left propped beside the back door and beginning to sweep, every now and then directing a sharp look in through the nearest window.

"Would you like something to drink?" Lily asked Victor.

"A beer?"

As if she could think of nothing more refreshing than a beer after breakfast, she said, "Sounds good," and walked to the pantry, bare feet slapping against the clay tiles, took two Negra Modelos out of the refrigerator, pried off the tops, and handed him a bottle. "Would you like a glass?"

He took a long drink of beer and wiped his mouth with the back of his hand. "No," he said.

Struck by the hollow note in his voice, as if something essential, some spark that ignited emotion or feeling, had blown out, she responded, "Is anything wrong?"

"Not really," he said. "My mom died a month ago. I'm sorry if I've been staring, but she had red hair like yours, and hazel eyes, and quite honestly I find it unnerving to be talking to a woman who looks just like my mother did thirty years ago."

"It can't be easy," Lily said, sitting down on the bench and confessing that she had lost her father a year ago December and, cantankerous as the old guy had been, she missed him. Victor nodded and smiled but said nothing, and for a while they sipped their beers in a silence that lay pleasant and unrushed between them. Then Victor spoke about his mother, and Lily, surprising herself, told him how her father had assumed she would be born a boy, so he'd chosen the name Hamlin. Oscar and Hamlin had been slated to play catch together in the backyard, to go to baseball games where they'd root for the Braves, to take fishing trips to Canada (no women invited), and to sprawl on the couch with their feet up, drinking beer and whooping loudly, pounding on the armrests when the Packers made a touchdown. "But Dad had me, a girl. Hamlin Lillian," Lily noted, ending her discourse with a shrug. And once again Victor was speaking, inquiring, murmuring responses to her replies and posing more questions while Lily observed him.

There was a certain northern drama to his looks: his piercing blue eyes deeply set under sturdy bones that projected like eaves, his thick blond eyebrows angling up and away from the bridge of his nose, giving his long, narrow face a look of studied intensity—until he smiled. Then the mischievous bow of his full upper lip and the gap between his front teeth instantly disarmed her.

"So you read a lot," he said at her mention of Proust's *Swan's Way*. "You don't look like a woman who buries herself in literature. You look . . ."

"How do I look?"

He replied, after a moment's consideration, "I'd have to say . . . the wife of a painter, sort of a summertime breeziness, white sheets hanging on the line and flowers in the garden, armloads of hollyhocks and lilies—but then there would be lilies, wouldn't there, since your name is Lily? Lillian. I like that, it's a little old-fashioned."

"You have quite an imagination, Dr. Wrinkles."

He chuckled and ran a hand down the front of his tank top to smooth it. "I have no imagination really. But you must."

"I must?" She looked at him curiously. "Are you always so opinionated about what you don't know?"

"You interest me," he said.

She laughed at his bluntness. "Why do I find that so alarming?"

"You mean unsuitable? Because you're married?"

She replied graciously, an expeditious hint of retreat in her voice, "Married or not, I'm still a woman, and the fact that you find me interesting is a compliment."

With another of his beguiling smiles, he acknowledged the distance she had so adroitly and discreetly slipped between them. Then once again, as if scripted, they fell silent. Lily studied Faustino, who stood motionless as a garden statue, a stone elf grasping a watering can that spilled endless moisture on a pot of geraniums. Meanwhile, Victor gazed across the room at a trio of wooden *santos* lined up on the mantelpiece. They were sturdy figures, the paint peeling from their chins and foreheads, flakes of carmine bright as bits of shell clinging to their cheeks. They looked staunch in their mission, braced for eternity. With a smiling salute, he eased himself upright, then glanced down at Lily, who had stretched out her legs, her toes pointed upward; she leaned back on her hands. He teased her gently, "You can't stay long, remember?"

"I said that wrong. *You* can't stay long."

"That would make Faustino happy."

"He's protecting my honor," she told him, and then went on to describe how Faustino had arrived at the back door one morning while Esther was still in bed. A loud knock had brought her up quickly, and when she'd opened the door, this tiny man with a scrubbed face and a fringe of black hair under a cowboy hat had been standing below the kitchen window, whistling. He introduced himself as Faustino, who worked in the garden every Thursday. Only on Thursdays, he explained, because on other days he worked in other gardens. Then he listed the names of the señors and señoras, all *estranjeros*, foreigners, for whom he planted and watered and weeded. Esther told him, as politely as she could in her limited Spanish, that he seemed very nice and honest, and hardworking she was certain, but she didn't need a gardener. He replied, with a wide smile, "Yes, you do, señora." When she offered him a cup of coffee he knew she was hooked. And she was.

Victor laughed and said, "He's a good man, Faustino." And, as if by prearrangement, the gardener gave a tip of his hat and, replacing the watering can beside the broom, glided down the steps and across the lawn to the bed of roses where the hose lay curled. Whistling again, he bent to turn on the flow of water and douse the roots of flowers screaming for air.

"I guess we've passed muster," Lily said, and then, noticing Victor's empty beer bottle, she asked, "Are you thirsty? There's more beer." She stood up and started for the kitchen, but he stopped her.

"No, I'd better be going." He stretched his tanned arms with their thatch of pale hair above his head, fingers locked. Then he groaned—and Lily felt the release of air from his lungs as a fevered blend of gases, longing, and raw masculine heat. He set his empty bottle on the counter.

She said, "Esther will be sorry she missed you."

"When did you say she'd be back?"

"I didn't." She grinned.

He laughed softly. "I know."

They walked together out of the house, through the garden, and up the steps to the blue door, where she opened the latch and stood aside. Instead of ducking through the doorway, he turned toward her. She stepped back.

"Any messages for Esther?" she said as Victor held out his hand to say good-bye. She took it.

"None." He smiled, still holding her hand.

She looked at him, searching his eyes for answers, but all she could see was a handsome man wearing wrinkled pants and a wrinkled shirt.

He let go of her hand.

Lily slid the lock closed behind him and took a deep breath. Her heart was beating so fast, one would have thought she'd been running.

Twenty-four

The taquería had been Esther's idea. "The guy's alone in town. Dinner at the fat man's will do him good."

During the two days since Victor's visit, Lily had accomplished little: refreshing her Spanish, punching pillows to discourage moths, saving from Esther (who had threatened to kill it) the spider in the bathtub, and setting out poison for the pantry mice. She cleaned doodlebugs out of the intake filter to the washing machine, boiled water for twenty minutes because Esther refused to drink the purified water in jugs she claimed were filled from the local tap, and then waited on the sidewalk for forty-five minutes to toss out the garbage. The truck never came, but while she waited she thought about Victor.

There had been a frisson, a sexual shiver—although she wondered if the shiver came from anything more than the juxtaposition of a grown man and a grown woman in an empty house.

After returning the bags of garbage to the kitchen, she strolled toward the *zócalo* in search of Victor, to invite him to dinner. All gringos eventually ended up in the plaza. As she turned the corner onto Comitán, the colors began: the pink and green houses, the turquoise and yellow houses, the red and ochre houses. Chamulan men wearing fluffy white tunics and brown leather belts walked in single file along narrow sidewalks. Their women followed, barefoot, dressed in black woolen skirts and embroidered blue blouses, folded blue shawls draped over their heads. On the street corners tortilla women, seated on their stools, rose like hummocks from the crowd. Burros trotted past them, loaded with kindling. Tourists with their pale legs exposed and scissoring briskly stopped to buy mangos skewered on sticks and cut into petals. Mestizo girls, their buttocks encased in tight orange skirts and breasts surging over stalwart brassieres, strutted in pairs. They wore high black heels.

After crossing Insurgentes and reconnoitering the plaza, Lily chose a bench under a plane tree across from the cathedral, checked her watch, and sat down to wait. A determined group of Chamulan women hurried over. They flanked her on three sides, engulfing her in multicolored belts, bracelets, shawls, striped hot pads, and tiny dolls pinched out of clay, and cried, *"Compra-a-a-lo, compra-a-a-lo."* Buy this, buy this.

At twelve fifteen a tour bus pulled up beside the plane tree. To Lily's relief, the women surged toward it. Afterward, to pass the time, she bought Chiclets chewing gum from a boy who reminded her of Pierre as a child, paid the boy's brother three thousand pesos to shine her sandals, and fed white bread to the pigeons. At one, when Victor ambled past in his wrinkled pants and wrinkled shirt, she stretched her legs and queried, "Would you care for a Chiclets? Or better yet, a beer?"

He responded amicably, "It's a little late. I start drinking at ten."

They shook hands as if this meeting in the plaza were a daily occurrence. Then Victor took a seat beside her and they basked in the sun, like two cats on a park bench, watching the *gringitas* in their Guatemalan shorts, with their milk-white legs. They talked for an hour.

"May I ask you a question that may be indiscreet?" Victor said as he stood up to leave.

"Sure."

"Who shined your sandals?"

Lily's eyes crinkled. "Who greased them, you mean?"

He saluted and sauntered toward the kiosk in the center of

the square while she called after him, "We have an iron. You're welcome to use it." Without breaking stride he waved. Lily, avoiding a pod of young Chamulans floating in her direction, ducked under the plane tree, angled at a jog across Guadalupe, and, before the light changed, turned up Utrilla.

The round-faced brothers from Mérida, walking south, spotted her on the corner of Adelina Flores. Hammocks woven in warm ocean colors draped over their muscular shoulders and beefy forearms. As she had every day for the past week, she smiled broadly and told the men she had already bought a hammock. She'd bought two, in fact, and they'd fallen apart. As always the brothers spilled their wares onto the sidewalk, uncoiling, in waves of pastel, hammocks much larger and finer than the ones she had bought. *"Matrimoniales . . . más anchas, más grandes."* They smiled in unison, their teeth flashing white against dark golden skin and thick black mustaches. Lily laughed and thought how Paul would enjoy the daily ritual: the shoe-shine boys, the Chiclets boys, the Chamulan women, the hammock sellers who never let on that they'd seen her before. Or perhaps all gringos did look alike.

"No, gracias," she said cheerfully while stepping over hammocks and feet and proceeding down Utrilla toward the market. She stopped by Esther's favorite bakery, then crossed over to Comitán, walked east toward the hill, up the dirt road, and into the alleyway, where she paused outside the blue door, pulling from her pocket a balled-up tissue and blowing her nose.

It was then that the wasp stung her.

Later, when Lily tried to isolate the moment when her feelings for Victor had shifted, she settled on that morning when, walking back from the plaza, she blew her nose, a wasp was in the Kleenex, and it stung her. She cried out, cursed, and kicked the blue door that guarded their house, then flattened the wasp with a vengeance that scared her. She knew she was going to pieces in some way, and if she had any sense at all she would run inside and pack her suitcase and telephone Paul and kiss Esther good-bye and catch the next bus to the airport. She knew that for some peculiar reason she was falling in love with Victor, and it was not a healthy reason: Victor as catharsis. Victor as bludgeon. Victor as an implement potentially as damaging as a nail scissors.

Pressing a finger to her mouth to lessen the sting, she unlocked the door and hurried down the steps into the garden, where Esther was pulling shirts and underwear out of the laundry basket and pinning them up on the clothesline. "What ate this?" Lily scowled as she inspected the sleeve of her favorite yellow shirt. "Did you beat it on the rocks?"

Esther straightened up, squinting at Lily and stretching her back, her hands on her hips. "Are we having dinner with Victor?"

"Indeed we are. At the taquería."

"You might want to sit with your lip to the wall."

Lily punched her on the shoulder and mouthed an obscenity. "I blew my nose and a wasp was in the Kleenex. It stung me."

"I thought Victor might have bitten you," Esther said, and broke into sudden laughter as she held up Lily's shirt, two fingers poked through the holes in the sleeve. "The washing machine eats shirts. You saw?"

Lily smiled thickly through her swollen lip. "No kidding."

———

Victor was already seated when they arrived at the restaurant. Recently shaved, his skin held a smooth, ruddy, tropical glow. He wore pressed gray pants and a pressed cotton shirt in a shade of aqua that matched his eyes. Not by chance, Lily thought, walking through the doorway. Not by chance that aqua shirt.

The taquería's walls were painted a bright pumpkin yellow. It was the flamboyance of the color, Esther explained to Lily, that had first attracted her. The restaurant occupied a single large echoing room with a warehouse-sized opening in the front wall. On Sunday and Monday nights, when a metal curtain was cranked down over the doorway, it looked like every other building on the unlit street: shuttered, locked, with a slim, tantalizing line of light visible beneath the metal curtain. The floor was cement. Here and there Formica-topped tables and vinyl-covered chairs had been placed in no apparent order. A few of the seats had been mended with tape. Lightbulbs screwed into sockets in the ceiling doubled the firepower of the pumpkin walls.

A brightly lit food cart topped with a ruffled canopy and draped with plastic flowers was parked inside the vast doorway. It was here that the fat man greeted his customers. To the left of the cart a slender youth with a sketchy black mustache and dreamy brown eyes slouched at the grill. A chalkboard menu leaned against the counter. "Tacos," it read: "*Al pastor*, beef, cow's udder, pig's head, tripe." A *telenovela* played to the empty tables—and to Victor. This was the kind of eatery where one took a few steps inside, heard the television turned up full volume, saw that there were no candles or shadows, and headed for the door—where the fat man waited. One patronized the taquería for its tacos and its owner and, if one favored pumpkin, for its walls.

El gordo was a man of girth. He wore tight pants, pointed black shoes, and a white nylon short-sleeved shirt with the four top buttons undone. Catching a glimpse of his satiny brown chest with its single curl of black hair and dangling golden crucifix, Lily had little wish to see more. The man's stomach appeared to buoy him up, as if attached to or harboring a fishing float. He walked on tiptoe, bobbing between the tables, the television set, and the back of the restaurant, where he leapt up a low step into the room where the beer was kept chilling.

When Victor spotted the Fern sisters, he rose to his feet with a grin and pulled out two chairs. Esther kissed him on both cheeks. Lily shook his hand firmly. She wore jeans, sandals, and a muted green sweater that, not by chance, matched the color of *her* eyes.

"You found an iron," she remarked.

He answered with a faintly ironic smile, "I found my land-lady."

Esther nudged him with her elbow. "Whatever happened to male empowerment?"

"I think that *was* an act of empowerment."

"For whom? Your landlady?" Lily asked, their conversation cut short by the fat man, who arrived carrying iced Coronas in eighteen-inch glasses with bulbous bases, narrow bodies, and flared rims. The glasses came from Vera Cruz, he told them.

Esther inquired, "Is the cow's udder fresh?"

"I am so sorry," *el gordo* replied. "Today the udder is old and tough. It must be tender and soft, and then ... but not today, señora. Today it is tough."

"And the pig's head?"

"Riquísimo!" He turned his eyes to the ceiling and kissed his fingertips.

"When I was a kid," Victor continued in Spanish so as to include the fat man, "I went down to the kitchen for a snack one day and there, on the counter, was the head of a pig. I asked my mother, 'What's that pig's head doing here?' and she said, 'Oh, it's just here for a visit, *liebchen*.' She gave me a cookie and told me to run back upstairs, so I snuck down later to visit the pig. In its place was a stack of freshly made sausage."

"So?" Esther demanded expectantly.

Lily said, "I don't find theorizing about pig parts all that interesting."

She ordered four pork-and-pineapple tacos. Victor ordered

five. Esther glanced up at *el gordo*. "I'll have two tripe and two pig's head, *por favor*."

Victor turned to Lily. "What happened to your lip?" he asked quietly, brushing her elbow with his.

"A wasp," she murmured.

He placed his finger, gently, against her mouth. It happened quickly, this pressure, this unexpected touch.

When Esther looked over, they were drinking their beers.

The tacos arrived, transported by their host, who slid the plates onto the table with a grandiose flourish. Lily bit into a tortilla, small and tender, with diced pork wrapped inside. She chewed slowly, savoring the rich, fatty meat in its spicy sauce, then ran her tongue over her teeth, licked a dab of salsa off her lower lip, and took a second bite—into the cold, sweet surprise of a slivered pineapple. She glanced over at Victor. His eyes held hers, a connection that offered exquisite promise, the sensation of pain coalescing with pleasure as the hot sauce burned and her lips caught fire.

Beneath the table, Lily's legs turned to liquid.

Twenty-five

O ne could argue, Lily supposed, that in a country where sex heaved at the walls and made the *mole* chile sauce dark and voluptuous, she had merely succumbed to her environment. But that would make her a victim, and it was *she* who fell in love, if not irretrievably with Victor, then with Mexico, with Chiapas, with pig's-head tacos on Wednesdays, fresh snapper on Thursdays, hot tamales on Saturdays. With black beans, tortillas, and beer for breakfast. With the hammock sellers, the shoe-shine boys, and the Chiclets boys who dogged her footsteps. With the Chamulan women selling hot pads in the plaza. With the muscular dogs lunging and barking on the rooftops, and the hole-in-the-wall shops selling iced Coca-Colas, *pan Bimbo,* and jalapeño chips.

Almost overnight, and with Esther's unwitting collusion, Victor became a fixture in their lives: the two sisters and Dr. Wrinkles grown virtually inseparable. Early each morning, before Esther headed off with her camera and notepad and Victor walked to the hospital, the three of them would study the calendar, then pencil in future drinks, meals, and excursions *à trois.* Over coffee after lunch, they would work crossword puzzles together and read the newspaper, lamenting that they couldn't buy the *International Herald Tribune* in Chiapas. They'd talk about hiking in Idaho and hunting in Montana and dream about mountains, deserts, the sea, always the sea, in Mexico, Honduras, France . . . and this, in due course, led to Lily's bringing up La Pierre Rouge. "The Red Stone—that's a strange name for a house," Victor said, and so she told him about Georges Lafond's young Italian bride and the story of the red stone set off-center in the wall because no marriage was perfect. Victor said he'd never forget that story, it confirmed what he'd always thought about marriage: If it wasn't perfect, he wanted nothing to do with it.

Often, before dinner, they would rock in hammocks in Esther's garden, with books on their stomachs and eyelids fluttering, languid, dazed, doing nothing constructive—*a volar palomas*, letting the doves fly—as if the heat were too much. Three hammocks, three books, three pairs of glazed eyes, and three ice-cold bottles of Negra Modelo on the grass. After eating, they would dress in heavy sweaters and, tucked under a blanket they had bought in the market, sit lined up on a bench on the terrace, Lily in the middle, or sometimes Esther. Or sometimes Victor. Arms linked beneath the blanket, they would tilt back their heads and gaze at the stars.

On other evenings they would lounge on deck chairs, squeezed in between columns and foliage in Victor's courtyard. He lived in a small apartment off Dr. Navarro, behind high yellow walls, a dilapidated turquoise door, and peeling turquoise shutters. In his long-neglected garden where bougainvillea ran riot over crumbling pillars, geraniums sprouted between the paving tiles, and tough-skinned succulents took hungry bites out of the bricks, they drank freely of wine and margaritas. *"No más."* No more, Lily would say to Victor, smiling up at him with Esther between them, Esther blurred between them. Lily would have talked with Paul earlier in the evening; they would have chatted happily, their argument swept under the carpet as the sensory overload of Lily's holiday existence filled her with tales of adventure. She was bursting with stories—Paul could no doubt hear the excitement in her voice, which spilled over with affection as well. Love was stacked in generous layers and Paul, at a distance, was included in the exotic overlay.

On a cloudless afternoon partway through Lily's visit, Esther and Victor drove off in Esther's rental car and returned in a chartreuse Volkswagen bus. Bounding up the steps into the kitchen, Esther announced, "We're going to the rain forest, Lil," and she danced her sister, swooping and spinning around the kitchen table. Victor looked on, smiling halfheartedly. When Lily inadvertently brushed against him, twirling weightless in Esther's arms, he gave a small salute, as if to say, I'll see you tomorrow, and walked out the door.

Lily threw up her hands. "What now? What have I done?"

Esther said, "The poor guy's got it bad. You better watch it, little sister."

The three of them bantered like schoolchildren playing hooky as they drove out of town the following morning, the van rocking as Esther took the corners a little too quickly. She slowed for two bicyclists pedaling alongside the traffic. A flatbed truck with slatted sides pulled out in front of them and rumbled down the Real de Guadalupe, workers standing in the back, wedged in vertically like sticks of kindling in a high wooden box. The men swayed, only their heads visible, and the tops of their shoulders, which jiggled in unison. Farther along, as the road wound upward through scarves of vapor, Lily caught glimpses of black-boled trees and whitewashed houses; imagined entire villages dissolved in a soup of thickly swirling mist. She squinted out the window at pine trees, eroded earth, and barren cornfields that quickly gave way to lush vegetation and bright orange flowers that burst from the foliage like showers of sparks. The sky bleached white in the sun's glare.

Esther braked for *topes* if she saw them in time, speed bumps in the road that the chartreuse bus could barely negotiate in low gear, at the lowest of speeds, without overstraining springs that had lost their resilience. Once the pavement ended, ruts in the track kicked the van into fits of almost uncontrollable juddering.

The road had become more pothole than dirt by the time Victor took over at the wheel, steering a snake's path into the rain forest. He swerved to avoid the deepest holes, jamming on the brake as trucks hurtled past them, veering into the mat of underbrush that rose up beside them in a living, trembling, vegetal wall. They picnicked in the dust, backs wedged into the bushes, eating cheese and tortillas, slices of tomato, avocado, papaya, and melon that Lily and Esther had pulled from a basket and presented on a striped cloth. Dust billowed up and settled over their feet, their legs, their shoulders, their arms. They inhaled dust, chewed dust. Victor gave Lily's knee an avuncular pat. "Exquisite," he said. "An exquisite luncheon. *Déjeuner sur l'herbe*, without the nude and without the grass."

As they were packing up what was left of their meal—a few slices of cheese, half a soggy papaya—a truck swayed toward them, barreling past and engulfing them in a beige spray, soft as talc. They were beige as the trees, as the lunch basket, when they climbed back into the bus and set off southward on their snake's trail through the potholes.

Eventually, Victor turned down a grassy track barely wide enough for the bus to wiggle its way through the foliage. In an hour the sun would set. Lily asked if he knew where he was going.

"I spent a week here once," he reminded her. Husbands had brought their wives to the clinic that he'd set up in the meeting hall. When he'd asked the women what was wrong, where it hurt, their husbands had answered for them. Nothing intimate. Nothing about vaginas, bleeding, or menstrual cramps. Nothing about growing sickly and thin after the second or third—or fourth—baby. Their stomachs ached. They were constantly tired. They wanted pills, as many and as colorful as possible. How could any man speak openly to a doctor about his wife's sexual parts when the entire village was hanging over the sides of the meeting hall, kibitzing, squint-eyed with curiosity?

At last they came upon a clearing in the trees, and a hut thatched with thorn-palm fronds and palmetto. It had wide silvered planks for walls, with built-in ventilation where the planks did not meet. Two small girls wearing red print dresses flashed like tropical birds as they turned, aflutter, their skirts flared out, and fled into the forest. A barefoot woman leaning in a doorway waved laconically at the chartreuse van, with its gringo faces carried past in windows, like displays on a TV screen. Victor swung the bus left across a grassy common neatly sheared, as though readied for a game of croquet. The trees grew taller here, thicker, like sheeted emeralds. The trunk of a giant ceiba shot skyward, naked as a peeled radish, its branches extended like exultant arms.

"Hah," Victor said, delighted. "Hah."

Lily asked, "Is that some foreign language?"

"Hah," he said again, in his element now, she could see that; in his element in the rain forest, where no one cared if his sandals and feet were dusty or his shirt was wrinkled.

"Hah!" said Esther.

Lily observed that she was driving into the jungle in a chartreuse bus with two imbeciles.

Victor said, "I am charmed by your sister, *amiga*, do you mind?"

And Esther clapped him on the back. "Dr. Wrinkles, I assure you, I could not be more delighted."

Mateo, Victor's friend, was waiting, alerted. He sat in a state of magnificent calm on a backless mahogany bench, his arms folded across his chest, his knees spread wide, his white cotton shift stretched tightly across them. He was a full-figured man, thickset about the middle but solidly so, with high-muscled calves and arms; he wore plastic sandals. Victor honked twice before calling out the window in Spanish, "My friend! How good to see you."

"It is the doctor?" Mateo broke into a wide and welcoming smile, his mouth like a chalice with square golden inlays. Without shifting position, he waited, magisterial, the imperturbable lord of his clearing. The arrival of three gringos in a chartreuse bus was evidently a minor ripple, an inconsequential speck of turbidity in the long-breaking wave of his evening.

Within an hour they had set up their tents and strung their hammocks between the columns of the open-air shed where they would cook and eat their meals, and while away the afternoon hours of soul-drenching heat and insects and torpor. But now it was dark; night had fallen without so much as a tender warning. At a stately pace, Mateo wandered between their tents, fingered the nylon, inspected their white-gas stove, counted and opened the coolers and, by candlelight, surveyed their contents. His curiosity decidedly whetted, he took a seat on a round of wood and, pointing at Lily and Esther, asked how much Victor had paid for them. How many years of laboring for their father?

"Nothing. No labor," Victor reported. "They came free."

Mateo scowled, and there were chuckles all around before he demanded, "Free? Is there something wrong with them?" Along with his visitors, Mateo laughed uproariously. He clearly enjoyed the doctor and the two sisters, the cooler of beer, and the congenial bantering. He was probably thinking, Is there nothing one cannot ask a gringo? Have they no sense of honor or outrage?

"Tomorrow," he announced, "I will tire you out. I will lead you through the forest at my hunter's pace, to the *cascada*."

⸺

The two little girls in red dresses were Mateo's daughters. Giggling, they gamboled about the dawn-lit compound, pulling the dogs by their tails and kicking them with their bare toes. They piled palm fronds and flowers, and finally their own thin bodies on top of them. Fascinated by Lily's pearl earrings, they drew close while she drank her coffee, then fled in shivers of laughter when she asked them, "Where is your mother? What are your names?" They chirped, making little clicking sounds in the backs of their throats, like small birds in a tizzy of fear and excitement, before scurrying around the side of the hut and peeking out at Lily with shy brown eyes. If she made a move in their direction, they pirouetted toward the arroyo where the water coursed out of the jungle, rollicked, and fell into a pool cold and deep as a stone cistern.

The girls seemed drawn to Victor. They crept toward him, behind his back, their slender brown hands cupping mirrors of water that fractured into droplets of wild delight when they splashed his neck and T-shirt. They had aimed for his head. He smiled his pleasure, although he dared not turn around lest he scare them. He jiggled instead, and flapped his arms, like a heron's wings. Lily mused to Esther that he reminded her of Paul; fooling around with the kids, it was something Paul would do. He still dreamed of a daughter, the small weight of a wondrous female sleeping softly in his cradled arms.

Esther said, "You can't help but love the guy."

"Who? Victor?" Lily asked.

"No. Paul, you idiot." Esther's eyes were laughing, but there was something perplexed and sad behind them. "He's a peach. He's a peach of a guy. You should think about that, Lil."

"I do. I do," said Lily.

Half an hour later they set off—Mateo in the lead, carrying a machete and a bag filled with oranges, then his two little daughters, the three dogs, Victor, Lily, and Esther—across Mateo's father's corn patch. After skirting the backs of two huts, they plunged into a wall of shrubbery that opened into a latticed wonderland: leaves the size of dragons' ears; lianas draped over tree limbs shot with beams of milky light; cedars and *chiclezapotes*, whose bark had been slashed and bled for gum. Mateo led at a healthy clip, testing their stamina. Sure-footed in plastic sandals, he skimmed over narrow logs bridging creeks and shallow rivers, and waited patiently on the far sides, with a smile both indulgent and disdainful of these lesser beings. Often he would stop to explain the marvels and the perils of the forest: wild cane that the villagers cut for the shafts of arrows, a tree that held liquid one could drink in a pinch, leaves to salve snakebite and vines one could weave into baskets, the thorn palm, whose spines would prickle and fester in the palm of a hand. And *chechem*, the weeping tree, whose sap would blister your skin, make it swell up and burn. Dabbed in your eyes, *chechem* would blind you. "If you wander off the path in search of the tiger," Mateo cautioned, "do not grab hold of the weeping tree or use its leaves to clean your bottom. Please follow me now. You are safe. I am always guarding." And he sprinted ahead of them up the trail.

At the ruins of a temple in the forest, his colt-legged daughters rolled down the hill over the fern-cushioned stones that had crumbled long ago from the walls of their ancestors. They landed, squealing, on the ferret-eyed dogs at Mateo's feet. He pushed them away, these capricious females. They scrambled up, arms waving, clambering into the tumbledown shrine, over the limestone blocks that the roots of an enormous tree had torn loose and shattered. Mateo, at his ease, reclining in a sideways posture, made inquiries of Victor, who sat cross-legged between Esther and Lily.

"Why do you never kiss these women in my presence? I have met other gringos, much younger, whose bodies pushed and rubbed. Busy hands," Mateo said with a chuckle. "Extremely busy hands. They were immodest in front of me." He slapped Victor's knee. "Is it middle age that accounts for your different behavior with these women?"

"No," Victor answered him. "It is not middle age but a matter of courtesy. As I've already explained, these women are not my wives, but even if they were, I haven't seen you, Mateo, caressing *your* wife in public."

"How could you? She remains in the house," Mateo pointed out. "You have not seen her because she is occupied with the baby and the cooking. Tall people white as bones walk into her dreams and upset her nerves. But this thing about middle age . . ." He forged on with his agenda. "My wife no longer cares for my kisses. She claims that the stubble that grows on my cheeks rasps her skin, and the odor that comes from my mouth is like the stench of a rotting *paca*."

Victor diagnosed him. "It has nothing to do with middle age, *amigo*. You need a shave and you have bad breath. They're both curable."

The hunter's teeth flashed golden as he jumped to his feet and, slinging his bag over his shoulder, grunted at the girls and the dogs, shooing them with his hands until they spun and ran back down the trail. "Go! Go!" he cried. Then he turned and said to Victor, "Good. You will cure me."

The forest swallowed him up, a patch of white cloth growing fainter as they hurried after him.

At the waterfall, Mateo cut open oranges with his machete and passed them around. He ate four at a crack, shoving them between his lips. Then he climbed up over the terraced falls, sloshing through green, earth-smelling water, and slipped in behind a thundering liquid curtain. One muscular brown arm winked out and beckoned them in. As they picked their way up and over the ragged ledges, water ran rain-soft over their ankles and feet; moss sponged their toes. The heat was building, blanketed under the forest canopy, drifting in layers, the sun beating paths through the interlaced branches, light dissolving, billowing into heat, shade, heat, and then water, sheets of water so cool it raised goose bumps on Lily's forearms and thighs. She felt pale, ghost-thin, evaporative, beside Mateo's brown, hard, stout body.

He said, pushing through the falls, "I go now to search for the tiger."

"What's this thing about tigers?" she asked.

"The call of nature," Victor explained. "A euphemism."

"*El tigre* calls me as well," Esther conceded, and she left them drenched and chilling—chilled by the black cliff at their backs that streamed with river and moss and leaves, sucked the heat from their flesh while the water thundered overhead, drummed down on their feet and bathed their bodies in a stone-cold spray. Lily shivered, her T-shirt wet against her nipples. Victor stepped sideways and reached his arm around her, pulled her against him, his hand grasping her shoulder, the flesh of her arm, her elbow. They were joined, chastely bundled from rib to waist to hip; no sound but the tumult of the water that cloaked them. Victor turned his head, bent down, and she raised her lips and gave them, cold and wet with the fern-scented water, to him. For a moment, or moments, they streamed through a black sky, cool rain pelting their faces and a warm wind strumming at their knees and flanks, unconcerned, disembodied, although pinpoints of heat burned like splashes of sap from *chechem*, the weeping tree, that would blind them if they touched it.

When the kiss ended they stood as before, unspeaking. Lily still shivered. Victor's arm encircled her shoulders like a shawl, to warm her—which is how Mateo found them. Dipping his head through the watery veil, he broke into a smile of collusion. Victor squeezed Lily's shoulder, thrust his body through the falls, and was quickly gone.

"Come," Mateo said, a delighted party to their secret, offering her his hand. "The sister is waiting."

Twenty-six

A raucous screaming woke her, intermittent hoots and wails from the forest, the squeaking of a hinge, shrill and metallic—*crrrk, crrrk*. An ani squealed, and squealed again. Lily heard the reply, a deep chuffing call; then the raucous chattering of old biddies disparaging the young, who did nothing but open their beaks and screech for food, food, exhausting their parents. The forest sounded stacked high with birds in their leafy tenements.

Lily knew relief, for already the cooling had begun, a complicit withdrawal into a zone of comfort where she and Victor were lighthearted friends, nothing more, no damage done—a tender lip that a wasp had stung, the touch of his finger upon her mouth, his arm wrapped around her, his hip against hers, his lips surely touching her, softly touching her—she would forget all this, tip this one great soup of sensation, this soup of sensation that was Victor and Mexico, into the river that poured from the jungle over travertine ledges, pale limestone shining up through clear sheets of liquid, bright and dazzling. It had dazzled her. It had dazzled her, all of it.

She gave herself over to the surrounding clamor, to the rattles, screeches, and growls that had built to a crescendo. In his tent Victor slept, or lay awake, five yards from her. She had tilted up her face to meet his kiss. Why? What had drawn her to him? No matter. No matter now that she had tipped out the soup, the delicious, sumptuous, sensory rush of it masked in the hidden roar of water, diving and tumbling. She forgot it all: her body's pleasure, her mind's uninhibited response, attachment without strings or process. For the wild sweet clamorous hours of a single morning, she forgot.

Mateo was seated on the bench in front of his hut, a baby in his lap, when Lily emerged on her knees from the tent she shared with Esther. She stood up and walked over to him, sat down and placed her finger in the tiny brown fist that closed around it, warm and weightless as a petite-sized eiderdown pillow. The three of them rested for a moment in companionable silence as the mist smoked in the matted grasses, curled and vanished. Birds piped and chirped and went about their business of gossip and preening and feeding. Lily asked after a while, "Can I visit your wife, Mateo?"

"I think not," he replied, with a slight sideways cast of his eyes. "She has fear at this time, from the birth of the baby. Her nerves. . . . The doctor will see her."

The baby's grip loosened, and his heart-achingly small hand released Lily's finger as quickly and softly as the stir of air from a hummingbird's wings. Mateo grunted, smiled, and, raising his son to his chest, embraced him and rocked him in his thick-muscled arms. Lily watched as Esther unzipped the tent fly, swiveled through the low opening, and stood up with a jerked, stiff motion, hands braced on her buttocks. She stretched and yawned with a great trailing sigh of enjoyment, then tilted back her head to drink in the fragrance of the morning. Turning, she caught sight of Mateo, the sleeping child, and Lily beaming like the Madonna—the bench empty beside her. Shouts came from the direction of the arroyo, where Victor was bathing.

Mateo replied, some time after Lily had asked about his wife: "I am called Mateo, but this is not my name. I search for a second wife because this one shrieks in the night and lives in nightmares. We have a son and two daughters but my wife will not kiss me. The evangelicals give me a Spanish name, then preach that one wife is sufficient. But I have forty years, I am still strong. I have vigor. My wife has a sister, as you have a sister. She will come here to live, and then I will have two wives."

Lily said, "There must be a reason why your wife lives in nightmares, Mateo. You think her sister will cure it?"

"She will cure me." His laugh was airy and unrepentant as a child's.

Long afterward, Lily was haunted by the woman whom she never met, whom she imagined drifting listless in the murk of the plank house, lit in strips where sunlight filtered through and sectioned her body as it swung in her hammock, one leg trailing on the floor, murmuring to her baby who sucked at tired breasts. Victor had given her bottles and bottles of vitamin pills rich in iron, he had told Lily. The woman had allowed him to touch her wrist and neck and to listen to her heart and lungs through the thin fabric of her red dress; red like her daughters' dresses. The little girls had crouched in the dirt at their mother's feet, watching the doctor's hands and face with hushed and tremulous eyes. Throughout the examination Mateo had squatted in a corner of the hut, testing the blade of the razor and popping one by one from their wrappers the breath mints that Victor had given him.

That same afternoon they left Mateo, his lovely shy-eyed daughters, and his cringing dogs. He warned them that the sides of their van would grow hot as a *comal*. They would fry inside it, like tortillas. He announced this with enormous relish and a hearty laugh that revealed four golden teeth gleaming like satellite suns in his mint-scented mouth. He slapped Victor on both shoulders, embraced him vigorously, stepped back and looked him up and down, and then, in one forceful stride, pressed him again to his sturdy chest. *"Amigo mio . . . el doctor. Qué te vayas bien."* May you go well, my friend the doctor. He shook Lily's hand and then Esther's. Lily called *adios* to the little girls, who, giggling, wiggled their fingers in timid waves and bolted. The dogs followed. Mateo shouted them back; with sour eyes they slunk to their master's side. Then he turned and strode into the forest.

Struck by the abruptness of his departure, the surreal setting, the heat—the sweltering, suffocating, unbearably wet heat—Lily climbed into the back of the bus, sat down, and closed her eyes. Esther followed her in while Victor extended a parting wave to his nimble admirers, who darted from tree to tree, wispy and gleeful as scarlet fairies. He fired up the bus, which coughed and sputtered in heartfelt disapproval of this sudden call to action. Haltingly, it performed its functions while Lily fell asleep and dreamed of blackened tortillas and pinch-nosed dogs wearing limp red dresses, of Mateo pulling tail feathers from a stack of parrots' carcasses, of a woman shaping clay into tortilla-flat figures that had cone-shaped breasts and forest seeds for nipples. The woman was transparent, gel-like; Lily could track the blood pumping under her skin, bright red liquid patterned with flowers, like little girls' dresses, purple where it flushed through a garden of veins, and black and weeping where it entered her heart and fell in steady drops onto Lily's hand. Something somber and menacing slid under her fingernails and shot like hot ash up her arm. She cried out, and awoke.

"What's up back there?" Victor said, cocking his head to one side as he spoke. His eyes remained fastened to the road, to the potholes.

"Something bit me."

Esther said, "It wasn't me."

"Spit on it," said Victor. And once again they chewed dust, sighed dust; spit dust. They reacquainted themselves with the powder-thin texture of beige: beige skin, beige eyelids, beige saliva; beige stripes buckling over Esther's nose; beige tips to the spikes of Victor's hair. Beige armpits. Halfway through the journey the sisters exchanged places. Soon Esther fell asleep on the backseat while Lily, in the front of the van beside Victor, called out the location of potholes as if she were guiding a raft through a particularly nasty stretch of white water. Two bad ones at three o'clock—monster at five—*bache* that'll eat us alive at eleven. When Victor reached over and stroked her leg, she warned, "Hand on my knee at two o'clock. Watch out there, *amigo*."

Twenty-seven

*H*e was waiting on the corner of Guadalupe and Utrilla, a spectral figure—pale hair, dark arms and legs and knapsack at his feet, the rest of him obscured by fog. A rush of cold air entered the van as he climbed in beside Esther, shut the door, and turned his head to greet Lily. "I could sit in the back," he offered.

"In my lap?"

Victor grimaced theatrically and returned his gaze to the windshield. "The fog's a bitch," he remarked to Esther, and, indeed, as they drove out of town, the hills looked as if they had been sunk up to their necks in a steam bath.

They were going for a hike in the cloud forest. A few days earlier Lily had telephoned Paul. She had told him about their trip to the *selva*, Mateo and his dogs, and the two little girls, and had sounded so wistful that he'd asked, "Is there something wrong? Is there anything I can do?"

Lily had replied, only half in jest, "I think you'd better pull yourself together, Paul Crisp, and get down here."

But he did not come down, and Esther, whose good humor was fraying, threatened a trip to Guatemala. "I've got a friend there. He wants to do a story," she announced cryptically. Yet when Victor suggested a hike in the cloud forest, she said yes. Yes. The bromeliads would be flowering, they must go, it would be lovely, pushing forward Victor's plan as if she were fate's accomplice; a handmaiden of disaster.

And it *was* lovely, as that quiet moment of not yet knowing, not yet taking the step that for better or worse will change your life, is so often dewy and sun-shot in remembrance. By ten o'clock the mist had burned away and shafts of sunlight struck down through the branches. The tall oaks rustled as if the touch of warmth had caused their leaves to shiver, while beneath the trees—not the young ones that shivered but the giants on the hillside that lived in the clouds—the shadows fled. The earth was wet, slippery. No rain had fallen but the fog had been thick; it had fallen like rain.

Esther led the way up the steep, slick trail into the cloud forest, through the smell of damp earth and sodden leaves and the eerie intertwining of branches and sounds. The woodland was hushed but not silent; their footsteps thudded softly on the pathway and their breathing grew labored. Lily tipped her head up: The oaks on the hillside had tremendous height, tremendous girth, their trunks and branches tufted with moss and brome-liads flashing purple and red. Brilliant yellow flowers winked amidst the ferns. Esther vanished above them. Victor coughed, a dull, woofing sound muffled by moisture. He spoke easily to Lily, for he could not see her eyes.

"I'm falling in love with you," he said. "Romantically in love. If I were my patient I'd call it acute transitional lust."

"And if I were your patient?"

"I'd advise you to avoid me. I *advise* you to avoid me." And he came up behind her, slid his arm around her waist, and pulled her against him, parting the hair at the nape of her neck and putting his mouth to the dampness of skin that was heated from the climb, tangy with salt. She did not resist the luxuriant swivel of breasts and hips as gradually, gently, he turned her. "We can't," she murmured, and he whispered that he knew, he understood, they would certainly, absolutely, not ever . . . even as his repro-bate's hands slipped beneath her shirt and caressed her.

"Don't. Not with Esther—"

"So near? I know"—and he kissed her a deep, unequivocal, leisurely kiss. Her arms went around him, a fierce little rush of desire sloping down from the base of her spine through her buttocks to her legs.

"Is that a yes?" he asked.

"Is it?"

"That's *my* question."

But seventeen years of marriage weren't as easily shed as the shirt Victor reached for and began to unbutton. His hands, trapped by Lily's, pressed into the softness of her breasts. Tenderly, she raised those captive hands to her lips, released them, and watched him in silence as he watched her.

Then, one by one, she did up her buttons.

——

Esther was doling out peanuts to two squat men in *huaraches* when Lily and Victor reached the top of the ridge. Upon seeing their faces, she handed them each a small bag of M&Ms. "*Amigos mios.* You look in need of sustenance," she said.

The two Maya, sharp-featured men wearing dark pants, pink serapes, and flat-brimmed straw hats, were jabbering in harsh clicking sounds with an old woman, smaller even than her companions but straight-backed. She had the face of a shriveled chestnut, wore a dark brown wool poncho, and pink plastic slippers.

"*Á dónde vas?*" Where are you going? the older of the two men asked. A smile lit up his burnished face, creasing fleshy cheeks and curving open beneath a long nose, exposing two silver-capped front teeth. Colorful ribbons dangled from his hat.

"We are taking a hike in the forest," Esther answered in Spanish.

"It is prettier higher up," the old woman urged, her black eyes snapping.

"We are going to the crosses. *Sigue*, follow," Silver Teeth instructed as he and his companions set off up the hill at a rapid pace. The three friends fell in behind them, never once breaking stride up the nearly vertical trail, slipping on leaves and in the mud, warding off snapping branches; Victor plucking a sprig of salvia and playfully poking it into Lily's hair; Esther muttering, "I can hardly bear not to take a picture," as the two men appeared above them, swatches of bright pink and scarlet—the woman a smudge of deepest brown against the many shades of green.

In a small clearing on the mountain's summit, three wooden crosses rose from an altar built of stone and cement. The younger man, carrying bundles of freshly cut pine boughs and red carnations, untied his load and set to work decorating the crosses, which were tall as the old woman, painted turquoise, and carved at their tips. Meanwhile, Silver Teeth ignited stacks of shaved wood in a pair of clay braziers, then placed the vessels beneath the crosses. Thick, aromatic smoke twined up through the pine boughs and the flowers.

The old woman knelt before the crosses and began to chant. Silver Teeth joined her in a doleful, dark, vibrating song that carried in its darkness the tremendously moving depths of belief. The younger man filled a shot glass with *posh*, a locally distilled rum, and offered it first to the chanters. Silver Teeth poured his measure into a wineskin; the old woman drank sparingly. Next, the glass was proffered to Victor and then Esther, who tossed off their rations. Finally, when it came Lily's turn, she grimaced, closed her eyes, and downed the spirits in a single gulp.

Her mouth flew open, she gasped, her eyes filled with tears, and her throat exploded in a river of flames that roared down her esophagus and into her stomach. Victor shook with silent laughter. Esther slapped her on the back while Lily blew gusts of hot air from her open mouth. Silver Teeth, unperturbed, shuffled to the far side of the crosses and pulled a dead chicken out of a leather bag. The bird—pink, limp, and plucked—was deposited on the altar alongside a twelve-ounce bottle of Coca-Cola. The younger man polished the bottle with a long red scarf before carrying the braziers around the altar and fanning the incense to produce more smoke. Then the chanting resumed.

The combustive mixture of *posh* and ardor rushed to Lily's head. Sensation overwhelmed her: the chanting like hollow bones being blown in the wind, the breeze caressing her bare arms and legs, the yellow light splashing the turquoise crosses, the bristles of Victor's hair shining like fluorescent filaments, and Esther's tan shorts dissolving into leaves. The smoke curled upward while the old woman sang, rich in her visions, an unwavering note. Silver Teeth popped the cap off the Coca-Cola and drank it down, all twelve ounces. He did not share. Lily laughed, and the laughter hurt. To burn for one instant as the *posh* had burned, to not say no . . . Belief can do that. Incense and flowers. The vulnerable body of a defeathered chicken. The presence of gods. Wind, smoke, and a Mexican sun. A hummingbird whirring, an old woman chanting, chanting, her voice a drum: in the clearing by the crosses, in the clearing on the mountain. . . .

A gift had been presented.

And Lily, recognizing herself in the offering, in the plucked chicken, said yes.

Twenty-eight

"What about Paul?" Esther had become her brother-in-law's advocate.

What about Paul?

"Go to Guatemala," Lily told her. "Don't change your plans."

"I damn well will if I please. This is my house. Victor is my friend. Paul is your husband."

What about Paul?

Lily had no answer, and when Esther left for Guatemala, Lily examined the course she had chosen and made a second choice: not to examine it.

Nor did Victor ask when he came to fetch her—"What about Paul?"—which might have brought her to her senses, hearing her husband's name on her soon-to-be lover's tongue.

And so she went with him, and they drove seven sweltering impatient hours to the beach, not a glamorous beach but the closest beach, and they waded into water so shallow and tepid that Lily asked, "Can there be cholera in seawater?" There were no other gringos in sight. The solid brown bodies of Mexican women rose from the shallows like glossy, well-fed goddesses. They splashed their stomachs, their breasts, and their flanks as they chattered and laughed, while on shore their men swaggered, not wanting to exert themselves, to swim or jog or lie like women gossiping in the foam. They barked at their wives, short manly outbursts meant to impress, and sucked in their bellies and laughed *¡Ayyyy hombre! ¡Con las manos en la masa!* laughs. But Lily was lost, gone—what did she care?

"It's hot," she whispered.

"We can take a room," he said.

—

She lay beside him with her hand on his skin. A slim, sultry breeze blew the curtains inward, and they breathed in the salty, fish-sharp smell of the Pacific, and the smell of lovers in a sweltering room where the air is rich and redolent of pleasure and the sheets, scrubbed to a transparent thinness, dried stiff in the sun, are soaked with sweat. She lay with her hand on his skin, on the hot, tensed flesh of his thigh, which slowly gave way to the pressure of fingers kneading, circling, and stroking as they moved without haste or immediate purpose. "Is this north or east?" she asked. "Am I heading north or east?"

"Does it matter?" he said.

Her eyelids fluttered and closed. It was Victor who spoke. "You're a woman made for love. Do you know this, Lily? Can you see your own beauty?" He turned and lightly touched her breast. "Can you see this?" he asked, and more softly, "This . . . you have so much beauty. I can't take it in."

"Try," she said. And through the open window, borne on that same slender, luxurious breeze, she heard the clinking of silverware at restaurant tables, loud voices, laughter, and marimba music. She smelled salt and fish. Then *comida* ended and the sun was lowering, forcing its heat across shimmering, blue, blinding water to the whitewashed walls where brightness struck, rebounded, and fell to the streets below. Heat and sunlight poured into the room with its wood-frame bed, its painted table and straight-backed chairs, its carafe of boiled water, two glasses on a metal tray, and *jarra* filled with bougainvillea. Victor pulled her over him. She knelt, her body so warm and open to his touch that she plunged without warning into the black space behind her eyes, and she lost not only the blue-walled room and the clamor of cutlery, voices, and music, but herself as well. There was only the man beneath her, inside her, who said, "Lily, yes, Lily, Lily," as if her name were a stream of light, or an idiot's rhyme. Or a prayer.

She studied the room as dusk filled it. The walls were painted cerulean blue, although stark white plaster gleamed through the pigment, luminescent, wavering, like water charged with ghostly light. In a touch of whimsy, clouds had been brushed across the ceiling—they were rimmed with silver—and in one corner, above a yellow paneled door, a bird or angel, or a winged voyeur, gazed down on the bed. The furniture was squared off, roughly built: the table a ripe tomato red, the chairs cobalt with yellow edging, the bedstead persimmon, the tiles of the floor a pink-toned sienna. The room held everything, even gaps for silence. Lily spoke and regretted it. Victor pushed back her hair and, like a feather touching down on the skin behind her ear, brushed her with his lips. "Here, Lily. There's here, and here. Does there need to be more?"

Evening cooled the room, and the heat, which had been suffocating, rose to the ceiling, where it hovered, unable to escape. And the wind, growing stronger and sweeter with the night, washed the sun from the air; and darkness drifted down, and floated up, and met where they lay in a single embrace, all details merged: lips and toes, eyelids and noses—only long mounded shapes and their languorous rhythms in the dusk remained. And the curtains streamed inward. And the flowers on the table curled up for the night.

In the morning Victor said, "I'll order breakfast," and told the waiter in the *palapa* restaurant beneath their window: "Fried eggs, tortillas, beans, *queso*, salsa, and two Negra Modelos, very cold, and coffee, *por favor.*"

"I shouldn't," she said.

"Does that imply guilt?"

She answered him dreamily, "I suppose it does."

"Then you should eat this breakfast. You'll see."

"I'm ravenous. I'll be drunk on the beer."

"We're going nowhere."

"That's fortunate. My body feels boneless."

"That's precisely why you need this breakfast. Haven't you ever lived for a day or a week without doing anything required, just made love and ate and slept, and made love again? Haven't you ever done that?"

"For days?"

"For a week?"

"Yes. Have you?" she said.

———

After breakfast they swam, wading into the ocean until the shelf of sand tilted and broke. The sun burned higher, grew hotter, and with hands that rolled like oil across her skin, he peeled off her suit. Their toes touched sand. "Do you know," he said, "in your sleep, you speak French?"

"French? Did you understand?"

"No."

"But you speak French."

"Yes."

"And Spanish. And what else? You're an educated man— with these hands . . ."

"Does it matter?"

"Yes. It shouldn't, but it does."

"It shouldn't. Did you enjoy your breakfast?"

"Immensely," she said. "Victor, what do you do? Just float in the water and make love to women?"

"That sounds like a reasonable occupation."

"It's not."

"Would you like something better?"

"More believable."

"A construction worker. How's that? With these hands."

She kissed each finger on its salty tip. "Have I told you," she said, "this story about Paul's mother? She was standing in the water once, just like this, and Freddy ... he was young then, not even thirty. His mother was watching, she was holding her dachshund and spying on her son. He was fondling Justine. They were under the water. . . . I used to dream about that scene. I had this image—it was so clear—of Mrs. Crisp standing on the balcony in a flouncy robe. She was ill and overwrought, and holding that terrible little dog, while Freddy broke all the bonds in one provocative act. He dove down to look for his glasses and found Justine—her body, her breasts, whatever it was he found—and with his mother watching. . . . It's fantastic! He dove down for more."

"Time's circular. Did you know that?"

"Why? Because you've been here before? You've made love in that room? Please, spare me the details."

"No," he said. "Because we've been here before."

She regarded him strangely. "What are you talking about?"

"In your dream, you just said—"

"But that was Justine, my mother-in-law. It was only a dream."

Victor touched her cheek. He drifted against her and asked, only half teasing, "And this is real?"

They stayed in the room for three days while below them the waiters set and cleared tables, whistled and laughed, and cursed over broken glasses or silverware dropped on the polished floor. The diners toasted, calling out compliments, insults, and greetings. Maids tittered in the hallway, blushing when the lovers emerged, soft-eyed in the morning, and drifted out to swim, like angels on clouds. All played a part—the muted giggles, the raucous laughter, and the reek of fish no more foreign than the ardent perfume of the lovers' tongues and hands, Lily's legs, her breasts, his lips. They drank beer and ate fried eggs for breakfast. They splashed into the ocean. They took long walks on the beach, their fingers brushing, and made love through the wild, slow, sating afternoons that became a drug. In the heat that became an addiction.

He asked no questions and she made no promises. They spoke of dinner, if the wine was drinkable, which sunset they preferred, and was the lobster fresh. Only once, when they were driving back through San Cristóbal, was their future mentioned, and this by an uncle of Mateo's, a graceful figure whom Victor spotted moving smoothly, unsmiling, as if threading a jungle path through the crowded street. Victor pulled into the curb and called out a greeting. Tall and thin-boned in a bleached white tunic, with skin the color of light-roasted coffee and toes like the horned roots of trees, the man leaned in through the window and inquired bluntly, "Is this your woman? Will you be taking her home with you?"

Lily wondered, was their lovemaking so obvious? Could he smell it on their skin or see it in their eyes? How did he know?

The man addressed Victor, "Do you say to all the señoras, I love you?" And while Lily was digesting the import of "all the señoras" and Victor was searching for a politic answer, the man rapped his knuckles against Victor's forearm and winked (or a speck of dust lodged in his eye and he blinked to remove it) and walked away. Victor put his hand on Lily's knee. Neither of them spoke as he steered the car away from the curb and drove up Francisco Madero, turned left on Vicente Guerrero, and crossed to Comitán, where he floored the accelerator, roared up the hill, and screeched to a stop.

He took her face in his hands. "There are no other women. There's only you, Lily. Do you hear me? We have three days left."

"We agreed that we wouldn't . . ."

"And we won't," he said as his arms slipped around her, the taste and scent of heat and sun and sand on his skin, in his hair.

"Don't do this to me, Victor."

"Be patient," he said. "I'm in denial, that's all. It will pass."

"You're certain?" She kissed him fiercely and said, "Come back in an hour. I'll be waiting." Then she opened the door to the car and walked down the alleyway, her feet barely touching the ground, and, turning to wave, put the key in the lock. But the blue door was already open. Faustino? Was it Thursday? Or had Esther returned from Guatemala? She glanced down the street. Victor was gone. She ran down the stairs and noticed the kitchen door ajar and the windows pushed back on their hinges. There was a bowl of fruit and a book on the table. She stopped to listen: water was running, and through the sound of the water—Mozart.

She sank onto the window seat. Soon with an almost audible rush the sun would set and blackness would fall to refresh the night, but it would not be cool, only cooling. Only less hot. Pain slammed into her chest. She breathed in quickly, impounding the tears that threatened to spill from her eyes, to flood the garden and run down the grassy slopes, overflow the lawn and lap at the flowers tucked into their beds. *Mozart!*

Her vision cleared. Why? Why now? She bit back an impulse to scream.

Then she stood up and walked to the bathroom, where she opened the door. Paul saluted from the shower, his member at attention. "I came down as you requested, Lil. Or should I say, up," he said, gesturing downward and smiling broadly.

"When did you get here?"

"A few days ago. I rented a car. Where have you been?"

"Esther called you?"

He nodded. "From Guatemala. She didn't say—" His face

collapsed, as did the manifest joy of his seeing her. He turned off the shower and stood naked, red, young looking, flushed in the face and earnest—like Pierre. Their son. Unbearably earnest. "I love you, Lil," he told her quietly. "I have never loved you as much as I love you right now."

She leaned heavily against the doorjamb, unable to speak.

His voice was low and tender. "You've been gone since before you left Idaho, Lil. Since before your dad died. I'm sorry."

Her throat choked up with a sudden fullness as she turned and walked out of the bathroom and into the bedroom, where she sat down on the bed. She stared sightlessly at the crimson and yellow walls. There was blankness inside her; all lights had been extinguished. Paul appeared in the doorway, a towel wrapped around his waist.

"Lil?" he said tentatively.

"It's all right, Paul."

"Can I get you something?"

She smiled up at him briefly. "Get me something?"

"To drink?"

"No, thanks."

"Are you sure?"

"I'm not thirsty. Thanks. I have a headache. That's all."

He moved toward her. "Shall I rub it?"

"My headache?" she asked with a little laugh.

"Lil . . ."

"I'll lie down now, for a few minutes."

"Can't I help?"

"No, really. I'm just tired. I'll just sleep a bit."

Then quietly, so as not to disturb her, he opened his suitcase and took out a shirt and a pair of clean shorts, the blue ones, she supposed. They were his favorites. She listened to his movements, the sounds of ordinary life, her husband choosing clothes and getting dressed. There was no need to open her eyes to be certain of the shirt he selected, to recognize his bare-foot stance—his left hip thrust out and left arm crooked at the elbow—nor to watch while concern darkened his features and drew down his eyebrows, making them blacker, denser. Routine closed over her. Paul shut the suitcase and, breathing softly, tip-toed across the rough tiled floor to the bed. He bent down . . . as Victor had done. She felt his heartbeat. She felt the heat of his body falling gently on her skin. Then brushing his lips against her forehead, he whispered, "I have missed you so much."

She did not move. His hand closed over the quilt, gripping her toes, which he wiggled back and forth in a gesture so un-studied, so intimate, that she almost sat up and took his hand and told him everything. Had he stayed, she would have. Instead she fought the numbness, the urge to curl up inside the black-ness that engulfed her. The fetal position, alluring though it was, would in no way foster clear thinking. Nor would closed eyes. She opened them. The sun had gone down. A cooling breeze riffled the bedroom curtains. Soon the bell would tinkle, and on the other side of the blue door Victor would be waiting, the hint of a smile tugging at his lips. He would have showered and changed his clothes, the salt smell of his skin replaced by the fresh scent of soap, his pale hair standing on end, clipped severely like a boxwood hedge. Softer than she had ever imagined. . . .

When the doorbell rang she threw off the quilt, pulled on jeans and a sweater, raked her fingers through her hair, and rushed into the living room.

"I'll get it," Paul called back as he hurried out the door.

"No, Paul. I'll go."

But he didn't hear her, or chose not to hear her, so she took a seat beside the fireplace and waited, sitting very still and listen-ing to her husband and her lover conversing pleasantly as they walked together down the pathway. They were laughing. Paul was telling a joke. She heard Victor's low chuckle and her heart began to pound. Yet, when they strolled into the light out of the darkness beyond the doorway, she said with surprising calm, "Hello, Victor."

"Lily," he said lightly. "Paul and I have met."

"I can see that. A beer?" she offered.

"No." Victor shook his head. "I can't stay long. I'm leaving in the morning."

"That's a shame," said Paul

"You're leaving?" Lily asked him.

Victor confided quietly, "Some problems in Seattle, at the hospital. I've let things go too long."

"Why?"

"Why?" He hesitated as if her question was an odd one, and it was.

Paul said, "Did I miss something here?"

But Victor had dropped into the chair across from Lily and was answering her question. "There just hasn't been time."

He settled down comfortably, crossing his legs and leaning toward her as if *now* they were going to converse. Now they were going to discuss their predicament. But of course they couldn't. He slouched in his chair, visibly relaxing so that she quipped, "So you're staying?"

"No, I'm going," he said abruptly, and pushed himself to his feet.

She took a deep breath. "It's too bad this came up."

"What came up?" Paul asked.

"A summons from the hospital. A man has to work," Victor said as he shook Paul's hand. "It's been great to meet you."

"Likewise."

"How long are you staying?"

"A couple of days. Lil and I'll fly back together."

"I'll see you out," Lily said to Victor, who had already turned and was heading out the door. She followed him up the garden stairway past poppies mottled in washes of purple. Victor walked a few paces in front of her, cleared his throat once, and coughed—she waited for the words that somehow would erase the pain and make the future bearable. But they reached the door in silence, and he pulled it open. He held out his hand. "Good-bye, Lily. Say good-bye to Esther."

They stared at each other dumbly.

"You understand," she began. "I can't . . ."

"Be patient. I'm in denial, that's all."

She took his hand. "It will pass."

"Will it?"

He kissed her lightly on the cheek, then turned and walked down the alleyway toward his car. It's over, she thought. It can get no worse.

Blessedly, the future is all delusion. Only the past is known, and even then we tamper, we distort. But that moment she saw clearly: the heart's great pulse of desire, undiluted. Nothing more. So she watched him leave, and when he had left, she closed and latched the blue door behind her.

Twenty-nine

*A*fter Victor's departure Lily and Paul dined quietly, a stiffness between them, their words chosen warily. Tortillas were offered and accepted—a metaphor eliciting hidden sighs. But most of the food they had laid on the table remained untouched, their appetites diminished, aluminum foil crimped over earthenware dishes tucked into the refrigerator. They went to bed peaceably, with no recriminations. Paul pressed his lips to her forehead and rolled away, a gesture more of weariness than of resignation. They said nothing, but watched as the glowing hands of the clock marked off a long and sleepless night. Lily wondered if the house on Dr. Navarro was already empty, the turquoise doors bolted and chained, the bougainvillea spreading like a purple fog across shuttered windows, the feral vines climbing the wall to lasso the hapless drunk or the late-night passerby. She tried to imagine silence in the garden where the voices of desire had clamored in the foliage and seduction had trilled and sighed as if penned behind glass. The hours stacked up. The quiet grew weighty in which they lay, unspeaking, and memories sparked between the darkened walls, beneath the black-eyed windows, with the isolating beat of Mexico beyond.

And the healing began.

At dawn, they made love to the raucous chattering of a flock of parakeets that had landed in the chayote tree outside their window. Afterward, when the telephone rang, Lily motioned for Paul to answer it, wandered into the bathroom, and turned on the shower. She stepped over the high, wide ledge into the tub and crouched under the nozzle that jutted from the wall at shoulder level. There was no curtain to keep water from ricocheting off her body onto the tile floor, or to obstruct her view of a sun that blazed in through the windows, struck fire to the orange walls, and lent a shimmering nastiness to the painted scales of a wooden snake that lay coiled on the counter. Hot water sprayed her back as she closed her eyes and slipped into conversation with an imaginary Paul, to whom she confessed her affair with Victor, realizing, too late, that confessions of this sort were unnecessary acts. There was no need to paint a picture of what a man most desired not to see.

"Dreaming?" he asked her.

"Paul?" Her eyelids flew open. He was leaning against the sink, his eyebrows pulled into a worried V. His face looked haggard from a night without sleep.

"That was Esther calling from Guatemala."

Lily turned off the shower. "Is she on her way back here?" she asked as Paul handed her a towel.

"Not for a week. She didn't tell me what she's doing there."

"She's lost her bearings again," Lily said, with a faint attempt at humor. "Some guy she met in Copán is setting her back on course." Paul forced a chuckle while she climbed out of the tub, the towel wrapped around her, and stood dripping onto the floor, a puddle of water forming at her feet. She stared bleakly down at it, struggling to read in the random pattern of moisture Paul's future and her own. Then she pulled the remaining towel from the rack and, with an almost ritual slowness, bent down and blotted up the pool of water, scrubbing and scrubbing until the tiles were dry and gleaming, and Paul finally stopped her with a hand placed gently on her shoulder, his voice so quiet that she strained to hear him.

"Whoa there, Macduff. We haven't lost our bearings, if that's what you're thinking."

She replied, looking up at him with eyes mirror-bright as the tiles, "Haven't we?"

———

She recalled little about the weeks that followed: flying back to the ranch; flurries of activity; snippets of conversation; images of an Idaho landscape; cleaning, cleaning, always cleaning, as if an undusted surface or a clouded window would cleave her marriage and grant Victor entry. She cleaned and cleaned until nothing was left but chattering silverware, chattering voices, the tang of salt on his eyelids, in his hair, which lasted on her tongue. Sound and taste lingered—the sight of him went first as she forgot the shape of his chin and the tilt of his eyes, how they narrowed into slivers like slices of sky, or slices of glacier where the ice is bluest. She lectured herself: At some point, Lily, one's inner anguish is no longer admirable. Or bearable. But her truant mind strayed to naked limbs in a tumble of sheets; streaming white curtains worn thin, transparent, through drubbings on the rocks; a *palapa* restaurant beneath an open window; golden-skinned men with shiny well-fed bellies and women whose bosoms heaved and swelled with each forkful of rice, *pollo*, pineapple so sweet the juice beaded in the heat, on each perfect slice.

And all the while she tore into the closets, she weeded out the medicine cabinets, she dusted off the books and then the bookshelves, she scrubbed the refrigerator and reorganized the kitchen drawers. She bound her head in a scarf and tackled the attic with a broom. She knocked down cobwebs; she mined the floor with mousetraps. She watched out the window as patches of green on the hillsides grew larger by the minute, as though the rain were viridescent. And she forgot, she forgot, because forgetting was an act of will she had determined to master as the spring days moved toward a darkness that came later each evening. Often she would lie awake for hours, studying Paul's face as he snored softly beside her. She would match her breathing to his, her body cupped toward him, echoing the inward curve of stomach and thighs like the duplicate halves of a shell; and she would ask herself how you could feel such love for a man and yet sleep with someone who meant nothing to you. How you could put this face, this hair, this nose, this mouth, so known, so dear—all *this*—in jeopardy.

Then one day Paul asked her, "Don't you think you're over-doing it just a bit, this frenzy of cleaning?" and his words pushed her, like a gentle hand nudging her around a corner she had sought to avoid. She sat down heavily at the kitchen table. She stared out the window, all urgency vanished, dust, water spots, what did they matter? What had they ever mattered? Outside, Paul and a small troop of ranch hands and neighbors rode in circles, flapped their hats against their thighs and called out to the milling, bawling cattle. They herded them up the road and away from the house, into the pasture that lay plush as a tufted green salad of parsley and clover and edible blossoms. Such a life! To wander knee-deep in flowers, to bellow one's longing! She took a deep breath and blew it out, as though a strong wind had scoured her insides. All clean now, all gone. All gone . . . and her cleaning wound down.

In the mornings she slept. After ripping out weeds, she re-warded herself with half-hour naps. She washed the downstairs windows, but abandoned her program for scrubbing the walls and the floors in the basement. She left the vacuuming for an-other morning, another week, and fell asleep reading on the couch. She helped repair fences; the fields rippled and tilted. She told Paul she felt carsick. "On a horse?" he asked.

Then one morning, with the sky still black as a drowning pool, Lily awoke with a headache that lanced down the back of her neck and connected in pulsing waves of pain with her eyes. She stumbled out of bed and paced the floor. Paul went for an ice pack and paced the floor with her. "There's something familiar about all this," he observed. "Do we have an announcement?"

She said, "What's the smile all about?"

"About you, the weather . . ."

"Did it freeze last night?"

"Sure did."

She sighed, burrowing back beneath the covers and exhaling puffs of warm air like a draft-horse blowing after a long pull. "Did the peonies freeze?"

"I've seen them happier. I've seen you happier."

"I'm fine," she assured him.

But when she heard his boots clump down the wooden staircase, and, a short while later, his old Dodge truck snort into life, she threw off the quilt, slipped out of bed, and looked in the mirror at her startled eyes. Then she picked up the phone and called the doctor.

———

Dr. Arden was a squat, pinch-faced, compassionate man who had fitted Lily's first diaphragm, delivered her son, fielded the long, grief-driven arcs of anguish fueled by her miscarriages, and rooted for her fertility when she and Paul had given up hope. He entered his office, almost at a trot, Lily's chart tucked under one arm, his smile slicing open his bunched-up features. "The best of news, my dear," he exclaimed. "You're pregnant."

Lily said nothing at first, although the look on her face caused him to stop, mid-stride, on the way to his desk and hasten toward her. He took her hand, limp as a hank of dough. He massaged life into it and peered into her eyes, which she curtained from him because Victor was mirrored on each convex surface, Victor slouched in the deep well of each pupil. The doctor's own eyes were puppy-dog brown and soft. To him, Lily's pregnancy was an unexpected toot of life at an age when some women were knitting grandchild-sized cardigans.

She said quietly, "This is a surprise, Dr. Arden."

He gave her hand a squeeze, released it, and walked around his desk, taking brisk little steps and nodding his head from side to side, damping down his smile to match the restraint of his words. "It's an adjustment, of course."

Afterward, she managed to drive without incident from his office to the market, where, in a languorous haze, she explored a mound of underripe fruit and came up with two radiant, rose-washed mangos. These she placed in her cart, solicitous, as if they were bruisable infants. Someone called to her. Without turning, she waved. Her shopping list was gone; it lay curled atop the Braeburn apples. In the act of retrieving it she lifted an apple, unyielding as marble, and, lost in wonderment, picked up a second and a third, balancing them in her left hand while trying to recall what it was she had forgotten. . . . She reached for her list and an apple tumbled, it fell to the floor, but instead of bending down to pick it up, she nudged it with the toe of her shoe and sent it rolling across the aisle. Then she began to drop plump-bodied apples, one after another, into a brown paper bag. *Plunk, plunk*—like ones heavily beating heart. *Plunk, plunk*. What had they done, Victor and Lily? Paul and Lily? Whose child did she carry?

She thought back to San Cristóbal then, birds hooting and shrilling, keening their waking calls as the darkness melted into a drenching mist, the cries secret and wild, the heat coming up. And Paul descending on her body, the quilt tossed over him like a sapphire cape, the sheets swept aside; her sleep-soft skin exposed. And Paul reawakening in her the warmth of familiar love, yet not so familiar, for they had lost each other and were timid at first, then hurried as each slippery thrust became a recommitment, a new and desperate connection.

Exhausted in her arms, he had said, "Now if that doesn't create life by the sheer friction of it, nothing will."

Perhaps it had. Perhaps she could learn to believe that it had, for she needed to desperately.

In late December, during a cold snap so severe that the pipes froze in the log chateâu and the timbers of the great house groaned as if the souls of living trees had been trapped inside, Justine Fleur Crisp arrived in this world loudly objecting to the slap on her bottom and the loss of the liquid warmth of her mother's womb. She had bright blue eyes and a fuzz of blond hair, the sight of which settled like a stone in Lily's stomach. But Paul was thunderstruck by his daughter's beauty. His eyes shone and his smile was seraphic as he held her tenderly in his arms.

When Pierre viewed his tiny red-faced sister he asked, "Are there blue eyes somewhere in our lineage, Mother, or did you sleep with the milkman?"

To which Paul replied staunchly, untruthfully, and joyfully, "She resembles the Fern side of the family."

Thirty

"*Y*ou are feeling sad this evening?" Yves asked, in a post-coital show of solidarity that never failed to charm Lily.

"Bittersweet," she allowed. "Like your mother's pots de crèmes. What was it you told me your mother said? 'I weep bitter tears into the custard and it turns sweet, for I have so many memories.' "

"My mother overdramatizes her status as a widow, which you do not."

She drew a finger along his well-padded breastbone and touched him lightly, as if planting a blessing over his heart, above and below his navel, and on the tip of the rising center of his being.

Rising?

"So soon?" she asked.

"*Oui*," he admitted gruffly, and with a great roar of happiness, pulled her on top of him and lifted her hips to accommodate the motion he required. The provocative easing of her body up and down settled him snugly into his warm berth inside her.

Afterward, he said, "I have read that Mexico is a land of grit under the fingernails and steaming passion."

"Where do you read this stuff, Yves? It's sexual pabulum—or do you make it up? You remind me of Paul. Every once in a while he used to say something that was at the same time ridiculous and beautiful. It stunned me."

"It stunned you? I am amazed at how attached you were to your husband. I am filled with admiration."

She said, softly chuckling, "I suspect you wouldn't be if you understood English."

"*Alors* . . . this Victor—" He broke off and stared at her, pointed his nose at her as if that magnificent organ, attuned to sex, had sniffed out the danger.

"You disapprove, Yves? A Frenchman in a country where marriages have revolving doors?"

"You compare chocolate to oranges—" And he cuffed the mattress with his fist, but gently, as if testing the firmness of a woman's buttock. "I have read that in America all doors and marriages are locked up tight for the evening."

She acknowledged, "I'm afraid mine wasn't."

"There is no need to act quite so chagrined," he said, sounding quietly amused. "I am not your husband."

Thirty-one

What else was there to tell? Did the sea have an answer, or the softly folded sky? The plane tree's sunny leaves? Alonso, lazing on his back with his paws in the air in the shade of a mimosa? Whether Justine was of angel or devil born—or of Victor Piontek—Paul loved her madly. What else was there to tell? That ten years can pass as swiftly as a single hour spent on a terrace in the south of France, in a lounge chair, watching the ice melt slowly in a glass of lemonade.

Lily had purchased an awning, striped green and white, such as Christine unwound in the heat of the day. Yves had installed it. It cranked out over the doors to the terrace. Bougainvillea wafted across the sloping canvas like a fuchsia-colored cloud, while beyond the shifting square of shade that the fabric cast, two stone steps led up to her daughter's bedroom.

In summers past, to enliven the atmosphere, Lily had set vases of gaudy hot-weather flowers about the room. A painting, not a good one, adorned the east wall: a family dined *en plein air*, a house that resembled La Pierre Rouge stood on a hill behind the diners, while the muscular trunks of cork oaks protruded from the tops of the children's heads. The colors were brilliant, the work had that to recommend it. When on a hot August day Lily had discovered the painting in a closet where she'd thought only linens were stored, Justine had set up an uncharacteristic wail of desire, of possession—a child previously contented with stones and feathers. She'd implored, "*Maman . . . il est très joli, tu ne trouves pas?* It's so pretty, don't you think? Can I have it?"

When Justine spoke French, Lily thought she must be some-one else's daughter, that a fairy child had been placed in her arms at the moment of its birth. There was something so unattached and light about her. Yet, if her eyes weren't so blue and her hair so bright, if the bridge of her nose weren't so high and its lines so straight and sharp—indisputably German—Lily would say she resembled Paul's mother. Paul claimed she did, a sanguine assessment. "See that sly hooded glance? That trembling upturn of the mouth?" he was quick to point out. And Lily would smile, even laugh, and nod with a complaisance she did not feel, and wish that she could believe him.

From an early age Justine was given to dramatic flourishes and exotic costumes, pirouettes around the kitchen table or the living room chairs. When she was five she announced that she was moving to France because the bread tasted better and no one seemed to mind if there were crumbs all over the tables and carpets. When she was six she donned a black cape and, with a turned-down mouth and driblets of tears, mourned for the dead birds her father and brother brought home in the fall, especially the small ones, the doves and the quail. The hunters must pro-vide them with a proper burial. So Lily wrote a mawkish poem, Paul read it with appropriate grimness, and Blanca prayed while Pierre covered the shoe box in which the feathered bodies lay with clods of dirt. Then, while his sister slept, he exhumed the corpses, cleaned them, skinned them, breasted them out, and tucked them, sealed in plastic, into the freezer.

The next September, when Justine asked her father to take her hunting, he replied in surprise, "I thought we were into funerals."

She made a wry face. "That was last year, Daddy. I was a lot younger."

"So you were," he agreed. "By a long shot. Here, you can help me. You can sweep up the feathers."

Giggling, she chased the feathers around the floor with a broom and a dustpan, then streaked into the kitchen and returned with a finger dipped in honey. "Here, Daddy. Bend down," she commanded, and he did, smiling benignly as she painted a honey stripe down the bridge of his nose. She pressed feathers along it. "We'll have to roast you, too, feathers and all," she proclaimed as she trailed him to the outdoor grill, where she climbed up on a stool and, with the kitchen tongs, turned over the legs and thighs, and slathered the breasts with marinade.

"Whoa there, sweetheart. Go light on the sauce." Paul covered her small hands with his, and together they applied the marinade in stripes and swirls and dots; he dabbed it on her cheeks. Bundled in a wool jacket, Lily poked her head out the door and laughed to see her daughter's cheeks daubed with marinade, her husband's nose frilled with feathers. Paul beckoned her over with the basting brush, Justine's hand accompanying. "Come here, Lil. Let's put those hips of yours on the barbecue. They'd taste great with a little chipotle butter."

"Honestly, Paul . . . ," Lily said.

"Honestly, Daddy . . . ," Justine echoed, and he lifted her from the stool and sashayed her around the terrace. "Come on, Mom," Justine shouted, and Lily joined them, put her hands on Paul's shoulders while Justine placed her feet on the tops of his boots. They whirled, the three of them, through the peony bed and onto the lawn while the birds on the grill sizzled and charred. Faster they spun, Justine screeching with the rapture of a child danced round and round by her parents, who were holding her, holding each other, and laughing so hard she thought they must be crying, so she cried, too. Why not? Why not? Even when Pierre rushed out and opened the grill and tossed the birds from the grate, fully incinerated; even when he shook his head (though he was smiling, smiling, her wonderful brother), they continued to stumble and giggle and shout.

Those were happy years, the best of years ... strange! For Lily was always fearful. She had so much to defend: her daughter, her son—not least of all Paul. What if Victor should arrive at the ranch, unannounced, and ring the doorbell? She conjured scenarios. He would surprise her in the garden with Justine, his spitting image, digging in the dirt beside her. Or he would drive up to the house, knock on the door, and Justine would open it. In the preferred version, Victor would recognize in the lovely blond child who stood before him his own Germanic features, turn quickly (eyes brimming with tears), walk to his car and drive away—and stay away. In an alternate version, which made Lily's blood run cold, he would pick Justine up and amble into the hallway, calling Lily's name, but she would not be at home and Paul, rushing downstairs to see who was there, would discover his daughter in the arms of Victor, who would look not vaguely but exactly like her.

At times Lily's fears grew unmanageable. Then, determined to locate and neutralize Victor, she would telephone Esther and they would discuss the situation and search for solutions. Victor had vanished without a trace, Esther reported, but he would write. Oh, he would write. She was worried about the guy, you could bet your boots she was. You could see it in men's eyes when they couldn't cope, they couldn't even keep their hair combed properly or match up a pair of socks. They were that far gone—bruised, she called it. They looked bruised, purple around the gills. That's how Victor had looked after Lily left and Esther returned from Guatemala. He'd been hunkered down on a chair in his garden, on Dr. Navarro, with a half-empty bottle of Scotch on the armrest. He was moody and pale. She preferred a man with a bit of heft so a sneeze wouldn't blow him over. Victor was thin. You could see the ache in a thin man's chest; there was nothing to blot the tears. She had seen it in Victor. She could see it in Lily.

"In me?" Lily demanded, surprised, and Esther caught her breath, as if stifling a thought, a question. No need to voice it. After all, they had already talked it over. They were family, women.

What about Justine's hair, Justine's eyes?

What about them, Es?

Paul knows the truth?

His mother thought truth was dangerous in a marriage. He still plays by her rules.

And you, Lil?

Leo Cassata has red hair and green eyes. Are you telling me Antonio wasn't his father?

Touché, little sis.

Lily had taken comfort in those long, convoluted, affectionate chats with her sister.

Thirty-two

*F*or as long as Lily had been coming to La Pierre Rouge, a small painting of the Madonna had hung over the stove, beneath the pots and pans, to bless the cooking. It did not seem likely that Gérard Lafond had placed it there. Nor his wife, who had worshipped at the altar of brassières and corsets and run off with the man who sold them. Nor his son, Paul, whose ideal woman was not a virgin. Lily liked to think that Giselle Godard had brought the picture with her from St. Tropez when she'd arrived, summoned by Monsieur Lafond, to inject some level of refinement and female rectitude into the lives of her in-laws.

The kitchen Madonna slipped from its nail as Lily's hip slammed into the stove on her way out of the kitchen and into the living room to answer the telephone. She had just broken off from her writing and was assembling lunch. *"Merde!"* she snapped. She had valued the picture as a homely blessing, imbued it with healing and protective powers: now the glass had shattered and the Madonna's plump, compassionate face was torn.

"Mother? Are you there?"

"Pierre!" Lily exclaimed, relieved to hear her son's voice. "The kitchen Madonna fell off the wall."

"Into something you were cooking?" he asked with his customary gravitas.

"Onto the burner," Lily told him. "The glass broke. She's ripped. I guess duct tape will repair the rip."

Silence from a son who could sit a horse without speaking, without moving, watching cattle or clouds for hours on end.

She said to tease him, "Giselle's ghost seems to be keeping her head down nicely."

He rose to the bait—this man who had once worn red tights! "Are you all right, Mother? Are you sure it's . . . salubrious being there alone in that house?"

What could she do but laugh as she thought, Who's the parent here? What have I produced? But instead she said, with immeasurable affection, "Oh, Pierre. You're such a worrier. My life here's more than salubrious, dear. It's exalted."

Then he shocked her by asking, "Are you alone?"

And she dithered as if he had surprised her naked in Yves's arms. "Of course I'm alone. How's your sister?"

Another silence, tinged in this instance with awkwardness. Why? Lily wondered.

"Justine has a lot of energy, Mother." Just that—the reply of a young man more emotionally equipped to deal with the needs of cows and calves than the requirements of a bright, articulate, wily and enchanting, insubordinate sister. Pierre wrapped up his end of the conversation, grumbling about "those damn women." He was surprised they hadn't painted the cows pink and tied bows on their tails.

"What women?"

Pierre paused briefly before replying, "Justine and Aunt Es and—Sara. She's a girl I've been seeing."

"For a while now?" Lily asked, assuming an airy indifference. "Yes."

"I haven't been gone long."

"No, you haven't."

"A little over a month."

Pierre conceded with what sounded to his mother's amazement like a giggle, "A month is long enough." Then the timbre of his voice changed—had she imagined the giggle?—as he reported on the cows and the weather and, just as quickly, hung up.

Ah, Lily thought. A woman. Sex. Love. The "why" of it.

Standing thoughtfully in the doorway, massaging her bruised hip and putting the torn Madonna, the half-beaten eggs, and the vegetables chopped and waiting to be tipped into a frying pan out of her mind, she hummed quietly to herself with a growing satisfaction, for things were calming now; this river of pain and grief that had been churning within her was calming. Humming quietly, she stepped down onto the terrace and stooped to retrieve the mail she had tossed onto the foot of the lounge chair hours earlier. A pale blue envelope postmarked Alicante caught her eye. She picked it up, ran a fingertip under the flap, opened the letter, and read it.

Every July when Monsieur Dupré wrote to confirm his September stay, he enclosed a check for the month's rent and asked, "Shouldn't I pay more?" Then he took matters into his own hands. "It makes three years now (or five or seven) that you do not raise the rent. This is not good business, Madame. For this reason I have added five percent." His envelopes, with their enclosed payments, were always postmarked Paris, where Monsieur Dupré made his home. Lily imagined that he lived in a small, immaculate, exceedingly well-ordered apartment. Just as her friend Adèle, whose adherence to routine—which included a lover, though not always the same lover—gave Lily a sense of stability, Monsieur Dupré gave her a sense of comfort. He was punctual, predictable, and kind. Until now, he had never left Paris in mid-July.

He wrote that he was on holiday in Spain, in Alicante, citing his four-day stay as an "apéritif, a nip of Spanish sherry to whet my appetite for the banquet in September, the sojourn in your marvelous house." He composed his letters in flowery French prose, as if writing in a more formal century. His elegant script had an artistic flair, with curlicues and flourishes where Lily would have expected a banker's cramped style and meticulous hand.

The previous winter Pierre had suggested it was time to re-
tire Monsieur Dupré. He explained that he would enjoy spending a few weeks in France in September, and urged his mother,
"Give him fair notice. He has more than a year to make other
plans." Then he added in his somber-toned voice, "I can get
away then," as if confirming that September would be a suitable
month for the removal of a kidney or the gassing of his favorite
dog. But Lily had stood firm: As long as Monsieur Dupré requested it, September would be his. She had been surprised to
discover the odd allegiance she felt toward her renter, as if he
were an old friend, although she knew him solely through the
letters he wrote, the wine he drank, and the books he left her.

It had been her idea to rent out the house. "An empty house
is an easy target," she'd explained to Paul. "We only use it for a
month each summer. There have been some robberies."

"It's been mostly empty for twenty years," he protested.

"The world's changed in twenty years. As have we."

"We have?"

But with Paul's grudging approval, Lily pushed her scheme
forward, and had no sooner placed an advertisement in the *International Herald Tribune* than the inquiries poured in. From the
stacks of applicants she chose three renters: a sedate-sounding
English couple for June, an American family for August, and
a Parisian banker for September. The banker wrote: "The rent
seems eminently fair—in fact, too fair. I believe, Madame, you
have not realistically totaled your expenses."

The English couple brought with them a needle-toothed
puppy that chewed the red couch to tatters. The Americans left
saucepans on the burners and the bathtub running so that hot
soapy water cascaded through the living room ceiling, ruined
the plaster, and stained the Persian carpets. The banker won their
hearts by stacking six bottles of Chateau Lynch Bages in the *cave*,
and by leaving, wrapped in gold foil on a corner of the long

wooden table, a collector's edition of *Madame Bovary*. Paul was charmed by the man, who reminded him of a cozy old aunt tippling claret in the afternoons and spouting poetry. He and Lily agreed they would keep him, and they had—although something disturbed her. Was it his unexpected jaunt to Spain? The shaken routine? The long-kept secret of his fluent English? Or was she remembering the black silk panties under the red couch and in the lavender, and the perfume in the sheets—unmistakably dark, full-bodied, and voluptuous?

His letter was polite, delightful, and, as always, brief. He would arrive on the first of September, at ten o'clock in the morning, and trusted that the road would be negotiable, the potholes filled, and all the pointy rocks removed so that he would not, as he had done once before, puncture the oil pan on his Peugeot. He was pleased that she had labored through *The Yellow and the Green*, as Justine so charmingly called it. "But, my dear Madame," he concluded, "your daughter has hinted that you might delay your departure so we can finally meet and shake each other's hand. Is this possible?"

Folding up the two sheets of onionskin paper that were so hard to read, Lily pushed herself up from her lounge chair and strolled barefoot into the sunlight, where she caught a dazzling glimpse of a sailboat, like a child's toy skimming the wildly blue sea. She sighed—how could she not?—and then padded up the stairs to Giselle's garden. It lay above the house where the goat shed had once stood, an intimate, sheltered space floored with slabs of gray-green slate and bordered by fig trees. Justine Lafond had once told Lily that her aunt Giselle had had two lasting passions: her nephew, Paul, and ripe figs. Upon dismantling the shed, Justine Lafond had ordered the site paved over and fruit trees planted. "Surround them with love, hold down the dust, and hope for the best," she had said of ghosts. To Lily's knowledge, Giselle, capped by slate, content with the figs, had never returned. At least, Lily had neither heard nor seen her. What she sensed, instead, was the infinite peace that death had conferred on her broken heart.

Wheeling an old garden chaise of sun-bleached wood and creaking joints into the shade and sitting down on it, Lily faced the sea, her legs swung up and crossed at the ankles, her arms lifted, cradling the back of her head against a chintz-covered pillow. The fabric, faded to a blur of pastels, exuded an odor of hot dust and sunshine. With the soporific smell in her nostrils, she closed her eyes, Monsieur Dupré's letter resting lightly in her hand. Perhaps it was the pale blue sheets of folded paper (when her eyelids fluttered and for an instant she glimpsed them) that brought to mind the letter she had received from Victor, his sole communiqué since they had parted in Chiapas eight years earlier. It had arrived the week Paul died.

She had gone into town and Paul had collected the mail, as was his custom. Returning home, she had noticed an envelope, pale blue and somewhat battered, one corner torn off it, on the blotter in the middle of her desk. She had bent to check the postmark—Denia. In Italy? In Spain? Now who would be writing?—the questions barely formed in her mind when she noted the sender: V. Piontek. She slit the envelope open and extracted a single sheet of water-stained airmail stationery. The paper was wrinkled. Dr. Wrinkles.

She read the letter calmly, as if scanning an X-ray.

Dear Lily,

I'm living in Spain, in a small coastal town named Denia. I work in a clinic. It's a simple life and it suits me. The mothers here are trying to marry me off to their daughters. The girls are lovely, but when I look at the size of the older women who come into the clinic, I can only think that their daughters have

inherited these same time-triggered genes. As soon as one of them
marries me and produces a baby . . . Anyway, that's not for me.
I still worship at the altar of La Pierre Rouge. Since marriage
isn't perfect, I don't want it.

   I hope you and Paul are doing well. I haven't seen or
talked to Esther.

Qué te vayas bien. *Go well.*
Victor

She had reread the letter—twice she'd reread its meager
contents—and a conversation they'd once had, meager as his
letter, a forgotten fragment of the time they had spent together
in that little beach hotel, played itself out, images forming in the
ice-clear November air, sounds that were the barest whisper of
a breeze rattling the aspens.

She'd slipped quietly out of bed while Victor lay sleeping,
taken a shower to rinse off the sweat from their lovemaking, and
was pulling on her panties when he'd awakened with a grin of
consummate pleasure softening the chiseled lines of his face, his
eyes an aqueous, pulsing blue, as if the sea beyond the windows
had leaked into them. He'd spoken lazily to Lily.

"Love reminds me of a stolen season, a time you shouldn't
have taken in the first place, but it was so damn sweet you
couldn't help yourself. You couldn't resist it."

"That's a cynical approach to a noble emotion," she'd told
him. "Seasons always come to an end."

"Love doesn't?"

"You see, Victor"—she'd regarded him candidly as she tugged
her T-shirt over her breasts—"that's the difference between us."

In the remaining days before Paul died, before he loaded the
dogs into the back of his pickup and drove off with Pierre, coffee steaming in his mug, into a steady fall of dark rain, and, hours

later, tucked the limp warm birds into the cooler and headed for home, agreeing with Pierre on how they would shower and shave and enjoy that dense chocolate layer cake Lily always baked, even on her own birthday—and the next instant a heart attack killed him—he never mentioned Victor's letter. Nor did Lily. Instead, she tucked it into a drawer of her desk, under a stack of paid bills, and it lay there forgotten.

Eighteen months after Paul died, when Lily was cleaning out her desk, she came across the letter. Calmly, she tore it in half and then into pieces and held the bits of paper in the open palms of her hands as if they were blood that had stained her.

How much had Paul known?

That she had slept with Victor?

That Justine was Victor's daughter?

The questions caught in her throat as she felt her heartbeat skid to a stop. Barely aware of what she was doing, she ripped out the drawer where Victor's letter had lain and hurled it across the room. It tore a chunk out of the wall and shattered, and she kicked it. She kicked it! As if the drawer lying in splinters on the cozy threadbare carpet was somehow responsible for the pain that shredded her heart, that clawed at her insides; pain that had a voice and shrieked and was terrifying in that empty house. Empty, because her children had ridden out across the fields toward the hills to watch the sunset, to drift in silence on the silent hooves of horses. She had tried to cry, to wash the grief from her, but no tears came, only dry heaves and that terrible shrieking that was not, after all, the house.

Lily had pulled herself together before Pierre and Justine returned from their ride. She had tidied the room and her hair and splashed cold water on her face and then walked with a marvelous false gaiety down the stairs and into the kitchen, where she poured herself an overlarge glass of red wine. Then she sat down on the couch in the sunroom to wait. As that first revivifying gulp of Merlot spread warmth through her system, she felt the shaking inside her subside. Only then did she stop to question if the havoc she'd just wreaked on a drawer, a wall, and a sheet of airmail stationery was any more sane or therapeutic a model for dealing with loss than plunging a fingernail scissors into her shoulder, or sleeping with Victor.

The following morning she booked a flight to France for the end of June. She telephoned Esther in Milwaukee and spoke some nonsense about human loss and a wall and a drawer that needed repairing. She dusted off the Olivetti portable she had bought in Cortina when she was pregnant with Leo and writing letters to Esther, gabbling on about the sizes and shapes of all the breads and pastries she sold in the bakery while never once mentioning the size and shape of her own stomach. Then she drank a cup of tea at the kitchen table and thought about Paul, remembering the first summer of their marriage, when she'd told him she was falling in love with him, and he'd said, "That's a damn good thing because I'm hooked on you, Lil. I'm a goner."

Back inside the house, seated cross-legged on the red couch, Lily peered down at the atlas and located Denia on the map of Spain. It lay partway down the coast, on a point of land that jutted into the sea south of Valencia. She tapped her finger on the spot, imagining Victor, feeling the fishing boats beneath her flesh, smelling the squid and cuttlefish tossed into a frying pan and served crisp with a glass of white wine, hearing the German and English spoken in bars—the endless southerly migration.

She ran her fingertip down the coastline, along the scenic road, not the freeway, and arrived at Alicante, a sizeable city eighty kilometers south of Denia. Coincidence? Could this be coincidence? The postmark, Alicante, on Monsieur Dupré's most recent letter. His phone call to Idaho. The panties left under the couch and in the lavender, the perfume in the sheets. And suddenly after all these Septembers—when Paul was dead—Monsieur Dupré wanted to meet her.

Her mind reeled as she remembered Adèle standing on the hotel terrace. *Ah, the renter,* she said. *I believe he is German.*

Lily felt violated, as if someone had been peeking through the window at night when her light was on and it was black outside. He was invisible; she could not see him. He had been opening her closets and sleeping in her bed, picking up silver frames and gazing at pictures of Justine as a baby in Paul's arms, as a toddler with chubby thighs and white-blond curls, as a hard-boiled seven-year-old with her ever-lengthening legs and gleaming hair that had straightened and turned to silk under her grandmother's hat, a gray fedora with an alligator hatband. He had seen his daughter.

Lily rose stiffly from the couch and wandered into the kitchen, where she opened the refrigerator, took the bottle from the top shelf, and poured herself a glass of wine that she did not need. But the glass fell; it slipped through her fingers and shattered on the tile floor, cold wine splashing her toes, shards of glass littering the pathway to safety, but she was not so far gone as to walk there barefoot. She stood, instead, exactly where she was, grainy-eyed, drained—Pierre would think her mad if he saw her.

How blind could a woman be, how twisted memory, how deep the shadows if this was all a ruse?

"What has happened?" Yves asked when he arrived that evening, unmistakably primed for *amour* until he caught sight of Lily. She was steaming about Victor, how she found it intolerable if he had rented her house. If he had searched her closets and slept in her bed. If he had seen her daughter's picture.

"I have heard this name all too often in the past two weeks," Yves announced. "I share your indignation, Lily, and what I assume is your sense of trespass." He was vociferous in his condemnation of Victor—until practicality stilled him. Lily witnessed the moment when he realized that an angered woman, flushed and vibrant and, in her agitated state, utterly desirable, would not be easily sidetracked. She watched in amusement as he changed his tactics. Taking her softly by the shoulders and giving them a good shake, he said, "This is preposterous, *non*? This idea that Monsieur Dupré is Victor!"

Thirty-three

*A*dèle asked the next morning when Lily took her swim, "What do you do up there, all the days in that empty house?"

"But it is no longer empty," Lily replied with the flicker of a smile.

"Of course not." Adèle sniffed approvingly, preferring innuendo to the unsolicited soul baring most Americans seemed to favor. "Still," she argued, flicking her chin and pointing upward with her nose, "it is not healthy, all these days without your children. You are too much alone." And Lily found it impossible to explain that she had written the story of an affair she had had, so brief an affair that Adèle would find it amusing. She had come here to France to release the memories caged in her heart, grown wild in their confinement; they were the dark beasts of her dreams and she, both their quarry and their keeper, had been loath to free them. Her writing, conceived as a balm, had become a bloodletting, the words on each page sharp little knives: her daughter, Justine, the sharpest. That story, too, she had written, and she ached to think of Paul and the goodness in that man's heart. He never once expressed his disappointment, his doubts. He never once accused her.

"We'll call her Justine after my mother, shall we?" With those words her cage had been barred, sealing up the lie so that the dark beasts could roam at will, for ten years imprisoned within her.

Now, as always, the dusting, the scrubbing, the sweeping, the sorting—they stood her in good stead. Every surface in the living room was covered with the contents of the corner cupboard. The two ladder-backed mustard yellow chairs that she had always detested looked more tasteful stacked with table linens. The red couch had become the repository for prewar books, musty letters and photographs, and disintegrating cloth-bound albums. The dishes, all cracked or chipped—a few plates from Moustiers, the rest mismatched pottery from Bormes-les-Mimosas—she had lined up on the floor. The long, dark table at which she and her family used to eat when rain was falling on the terrace, or when the wind was blowing, whirling gold dust into their eyes, looked disheveled under its load: stacks of frayed cotton napkins; assorted pairs of rusty scissors; eight faded boxes of cornflakes; Justine Lafond's fedora that her granddaughter, when in France, requisitioned; a cut-glass bowl filled with colored beads, smooth black stones, and a few iridescent feathers; and, in a dusty box, four cloth envelopes for storing napkins.

Lily took out the pouches of hand-stitched linen and laid them on the table. Each was embroidered on its flap with a colorful nosegay of flowers and a name: *Papa* Gérard. *Tante* Giselle. Paul. Justine. A shiver ran up Lily's spine as she pictured the four of them seated at the long table, Monsieur Lafond at one end, Justine on his right, Aunt Giselle on his left, and Paul, the outcast, beside her. The sky darkened as it did now, turned an inky blue gray, clouds heaped on the skyline, great boiling swirls of moisture bearing down on the sea.

Lily imagined Justine slouched in one of the mustard-colored chairs, pouting, opening and closing her napkin holder, prolonging the operation to irritate her brother, whose sandal-clad foot, hidden by the tablecloth, pressed down painfully on her toes. Giselle, across the table, rearranged herself neatly, not wholly at ease, newly arrived from St. Tropez. Perhaps this was their first meal together, the napkin envelopes purchased in celebration so that Giselle would feel a part of the family. Her dark hair, or light, spilled out of a tortoiseshell clip fastened at the top of her head, her laughter brittle as it smacked against Monsieur Lafond's and then Paul's muscled chest, and fell tinkling onto the table.

Justine inserted a spoonful of soup into her mouth and greedily sucked up the creamy liquid. "Little savage," Paul mouthed at her. Monsieur Lafond reached out and tapped Giselle's hand, giving her a bit of advice about these foolish children. He did not mention that Paul had attempted to rape his sister, and that is why he, Gérard Lafond, had beaten his son, and why she, his estranged wife's sister, had been hastily summoned. His stonemason's fingers lingered on the delicate, pearl-smooth skin of her hand. To escape his touch, she dropped her napkin, and, while reaching down to retrieve it, glimpsed her nephew's foot grinding his sister's toes into the tiled floor. A breathy *mon Dieu* escaped her lips, her head still under the table: What had she walked into? A madhouse? She straightened up, unnerved. Justine, seemingly unaware of the mangling her toes were undergoing, lifted her spoon to her mouth with deliberate calm. Monsieur Lafond grabbed the bottle of red wine and summarily refilled their glasses. Giselle felt terror grip her heart as the hand to her left—Paul's hand—gripped her knee. Firmly, he pulled up the peau de soie of her calf-length skirt, which slid smoothly, swishing over her silk stockings. When Monsieur Lafond nodded for Justine to clear the soup bowls, Giselle turned to her nephew, who smiled; nine years her junior, he both intrigued and repelled her. She meant to reprimand him but the peau de soie continued to climb, and she failed to stop it. Already, it was too late. Her napkin lay on the floor, forgotten.

—

Voices raised in song and laughter reached Lily through the open window. Her neighbors were frolicking among the fruit trees at the end of their garden, partway up the hill. They had chosen ferocious weather in which to pluck unripe figs and pelt each other. Christine's voice was shrill; Jacques should remind her how far it carried. His barks of . . . pleasure? protest? were muffled by distant thunder. Lily considered closing the window to provide them with privacy. She considered turning on the standing lamp by the fireplace and another beside the red couch so that she could continue her cleaning without straining her eyes. She did neither. It could have been night; it was that dark, no ships or sailboats visible, the islands on the horizon drowned in a wash of joyless purple. The plane tree leaves looked black against the sky.

For one moment a male voice, swelled in song, resounded in Lily's ears. Jacques was bellowing Puccini, the heart-tearing strains of *Nessun Dorma* swept up by the wind.

Oh, my, she thought and went about her cleaning, although her attention stayed riveted to the unfolding drama. Their voices grew louder, nearer. Were they dashing through the trees toward her darkened house? Were they clothed? Naked? Lightning illuminated the terrace and the cork oaks to the east, but she saw no standing—or fallen—bodies. Instead she heard moans and shouts, more operatic outbursts; a shriek that sounded like a cougar on its kill. She took a seat on the red couch, flopped down to listen. Such joyous and youthful abandon! Christine would never find herself, at fifty-two, in a foreign land, undone by memories. She would have avoided the need for excessive cleaning. She would have pelted her husband with underripe figs and regaled him with tales of her sexual peccadilloes, which would have charmed and enflamed him, sent him nipping at her heels, shedding his trousers as he danced through the orchard, belting out Puccini.

Rain bounced off the flagstones, falling like pebbles, skittering sideways or flung upward on impact, quickly banding together so that the next round of droplets no longer pinged against the rocks but made tiny indentations in the black sheet of standing water. Lily sprinted up the steps to Giselle's garden to take the cushions off the lounge chairs and snatch the laundry from the line. But she arrived too late. The tablecloth, towels, and sheets were sodden.

Hurrying back down the stairs and into the house, she ran a hot bath and imagined the Belgian couple standing in the garden below her, beneath a fig tree, mute with desire and covering each other's faces with kisses. The image of the two of them caught up in an embrace, her lovely cheeks shiny with raindrops, his young arms wrapped around her, made Lily swoon—which is how Yves discovered her half an hour later, swooning in her bathtub. *"Bon Dieu,"* he breathed softly, taking off his cap and unbuckling his belt, as if Venus herself were rising on a clamshell and he, Yves, would be ready to receive her when, dripping, she alighted. Lily stepped out of the tub and straight into his arms, the turgid front of him butting against her. He made no bones about where he was heading, quickly backing her heat-flushed body against the wall, lifting her by the buttocks, and entering her.

"Paul!" she cried out as Yves thrust inside her, the breadth of his chest and shoulders and the impact of his belly a jolt of memory.

"Bon. Comme tu veux . . . ," he managed to groan, a handyman with too great a heart, even in extremis, to suggest that it was Yves Lebrun, not Paul Crisp, who was so rousingly making love to her.

After he left, Lily poked her head out the window, aware of soft nighttime rustlings and chirpings. Raindrops fell on her eyelids from a passing cloud; crickets were busy in the moonlit grasses; gentle music—a Brahms symphony?—added its restful cadence to the slumbering vista. Her neighbors doubtlessly floated in their bed, Jacques directing a slow second movement with a languid finger while Christine lifted, with the warm tip of her tongue, the heartbeat from his neck. There would be an odor and a taste: of sun, green olives, tomatoes, lemons, lavender, and linden . . . "From its leaves, from his kisses, an infusion of slumber, a brew steeped in dreams." Lily remembered writing those words a few nights earlier and was thankful, now, that she had not shared them, transported as she'd been by romantic zeal, by Yves's irresistible neck, redolent of linden. It was he who had murmured as he'd drifted into a doze beside her, "This woman I love . . ."

He loved Giselle?

He loved Lily?

Had she been dreaming?

Was she *still* dreaming, stretched out on her bed, attempting, in a cramped hand, to write all this down? What was it she wanted to believe? That all stories, even sad ones, had happy endings? That Yves loved and would continue to love her? That Giselle, Paul, and Gérard Lafond were merrily conducting a ménage à trois in heaven? That the Belgian couple, in their eighties, would still be pelting each other's bodies with figs and unwinding to Brahms? That Paul Crisp's blood flowed lustily through his daughter's veins? That Monsieur Dupré was a dark-haired Frenchman?

Thirty-four

*E*ver since her neighbors' revels in the garden and the sky's cathartic weeping—which had cast Lily into a reminiscent mood—she had felt light-headed. But she had not been idle. She had carted off the mustard-yellow chairs to the guest room, noting that, with their removal, the living room had taken on a livelier air. It occurred to her that the rest of the furniture had long shared her distaste for a color more attractive spread on ham than on cushions. The wide red couch exuded a nascent cheerfulness. No longer hemmed in by its garish neighbors, it sang its memories of the Crisp family curled up together reading their books with a quilt flung over them; or Paul and Lily wrestling silently in a late-night embrace while Pierre in his small room (and sixteen years later, Justine in hers) dreamed of *tarte tatin* and the red-and-yellow beach balls in Monsieur Bibot's swim shop window.

She had scrubbed the armoire from top to bottom, tacked fresh white paper on the shelves and rubbed lemon oil into the paneled doors, dusted Monsieur Lafond's mummified boxes of cornflakes and lined them up *in memoriam* on the top shelf, and sorted through the napkins, discarding those that were torn or discolored and transferring the rest to a drawer in the kitchen. Justine Lafond's hat she had set on the mantelpiece. The rusted scissors she would take to Madame Bibot, who would claim she had no use for such rubbish, then clean them meticulously and sell them. Lily slipped the napkin holders, like the sloughed casings of departed souls, into a clean cardboard box. She could part with none of the dishes.

For many years now she had regarded this cupboard as a mausoleum, as if the entire Lafond clan, dust-dry as the corn-flakes, were stored inside. She had always avoided it. Paul had always avoided it. "Leave the damned thing closed," he had advised. "God knows if you open it up what will pour out."

The summer before Paul died, when Justine was seven and imagined herself a starlet, smearing on lipstick and mascara and stumbling about in a pair of three-inch-high heels; the summer she drew a picture of Monsieur Dupré with a drooping mustache twirled at the tips, and a fleshy pink lower lip, and she recounted that he was short but not fat, with an inflated belly, perfectly rounded because he ate napoleons with chocolate zig-zags across the icing for breakfast; the summer she drew him again wearing a baggy suit and pointy-toed shoes that were no longer stylish—because he pinched his pennies, she explained to Lily, that was his job, he was a banker—that summer Lily had peeked inside the armoire and a gray fedora with an alligator hatband had tumbled out.

"Isn't this your mother's hat, the one she's wearing in the picture?" she asked Paul.

He bent down and picked up the hat. "Maman told me she found it in the goat shed."

"Maybe Giselle took it up there along with the rope," Lily suggested, as Paul winced and set the fedora back on the shelf.

"Justine will love it," Lily said. And the little girl had. She had badgered her mother into letting her wear it, then swim in it ("*Sois tranquille*, Mom. Take it easy. I'll keep my head up"), then sleep in it, eventually asking, with a wily innocence, why they kept J.L.'s hat in the armoire and not upstairs in their closet. Lily had told her it was happier in with the rest of the relics.

"Right, Mom. With a bunch of dead cornflakes. Yuck."

But tonight the hat, liberated at long last, rested jauntily on the mantelpiece, anticipating Justine's return. Seven days from now she would fling open the car door as she did every summer, so excited that when evening came she would barely be able to eat her supper, and bolt toward the house, the heavy metal key, which Lily would have given her, in her hand. She would turn it in the lock and heave the doors apart, kick off her sandals so that she could slide across the smooth tile floor as if it were an ice skating rink, and then, from pure delight, burst into tears. By the time Lily reached the house, Justine would be wearing her grandmother's hat and twirling in the center of the Persian carpet, or vamping it, her coltish legs and slender brown arms flung wide on the couch. Lily would kiss her daughter's cheeks, moist and salty where the tears had run, and Justine would pull her down beside her on the couch. Then they would cry and laugh and assure each other how long it had taken for a month to pass. Pierre would hang back—balancing on either arm a string bag bulging with fish soup in waxed cartons, melons, tomatoes, a tub of spun honey, cheese, bottled water, and two fresh baguettes—allowing their raucous displays of love to abate before he entered quietly through the French doors, by way of the terrace.

Lily poured herself a single glass of rosé. As of two nights ago she had changed her regimen: She was now on self-rationing. She sat on the edge of the red couch, excited, having pushed aside the stacks of old books and the picture albums, turning over in her hands a thick sheaf of letters damaged by the damp and mostly illegible. Three piqued her interest. They had been preserved in oilcloth wrappers and were addressed in the same sloping hand, the script tall and spidery, to a Mademoiselle G. Godard. *Aunt Giselle.*

Translating from the French, she read:

Monday, the twelfth of October, 1942
Chère Mademoiselle:

I write to you because your nephew Paul and I are lovers. He speaks of you in a manner that wounds me. This preoccupation with you, his aunt, divides us. I implore you to write and tell him that he is a free man. I have eighteen years. You are older and should be wiser, and more understanding. When the war is over, we are going to marry.
As you can see, Paul loves me.

With my gratitude in advance,
Denise Poirier

Sunday, the seventh of February, 1943
Chère Mademoiselle:

I thank you for your kind letter. I showed it to Paul, who arrived last night. This morning he departed. God knows when I will see him again. He says that he no longer thinks of you. His love for you is finished. We will soon have a son whom we will name Paul. If I have a daughter (but Paul tells me that this is forbidden), I will call her Justine. He says that Justine is a pretty name, the name of his sister.

God keep you safe. God keep Paul safe.
Denise Poirier

Sunday, the third of June, 1945
Chère Mademoiselle:

Today it makes a year that Paul is dead. Our daughter Justine did not survive. She died of a fever. I have lied. I wrote that she was a robust baby and that Paul adored her. He could not look at her. He spoke only of you. I think that he carried inside him a

*sickness, this love for his aunt, this forbidden love that has made
me hate him, and hate you. I lied. He was your property, never
mine. It was you, the half of him that was lacking, the emptiness
I saw in his eyes even when we lay together. Alive, and now in
death, he is yours.*

Pray for me.
Denise Poirier

———

Giselle had hanged herself in 1945, on the seventeenth of
June (Lily had looked up the date), two weeks after Denise
Poirier had composed and posted her final letter. Rather than
a missive of love reclaimed, a cause for bittersweet rejoicing, it
must have struck like a blade with a poisoned tip, and killed.
News of Paul's plans to marry, with a son already in the works
and the mother-to-be prattling on about names, had not driven
Giselle up the steps to the goat shed. The report of Paul's death
had not pushed her, rope in hand, through the pillared doorway. Was it the discovery that Paul had always loved her that
had made the setting out of Monsieur Lafond's breakfast every
morning, the pinning up of his laundry to flap in the wind,
the giving in to his thick-knuckled hands and rounded belly
after Sunday dinner (as Yves had suggested), insupportable? She
would have ached for her lover, warm-skinned and devil-born,
blown into a thousand pieces. She would have removed her hat,
the one her niece had left behind, and hooked it over a peg before knotting the rope around her neck, placing a stool beneath
the central rafter, and climbing up on it.

Early the next morning Monsieur Lafond, seated alone at his
end of the table and chafing for his coffee, would have shoved
back his chair and walked with growing agitation to Giselle's
room. He would have rapped curtly on her door and called out,
"Nom de Dieu! Lève-toi!" Was the woman sick? Was she having

her period? *"Giselle. Qu'est-ce qui se passe?"* What was happening? Finally, receiving no answer, he would have thrust open the door to discover the bed empty, the sheet folded tightly over the top of the blanket, the pillows stacked three deep, undented. Shouting her name, his search grown urgent, he would have checked all the rooms in the house before taking the steps to the goat shed three at a time, cursing God, cursing his dead son, cursing the soft-skinned woman who came to him cold and unmoving, a compliant vessel. . . .

It was Gérard Lafond who had cut her down and buried her in the family plot. It was he who, twenty years later, wrote a letter to his daughter in Idaho, asking that when he died, he be laid to rest beside Giselle Godard.

Thirty-five

Families and their secrets, carried into death. Beyond death.
After Paul died Lily had wanted nothing more than
to turn back the years so she could capture in words that held
for him, like hands cupped around a firefly, the incandescent
essence of her love. But she could not, and was caught instead
in a miasma of grief and nostalgia, and since she had foolishly clutched the poisonous secret of Justine's parentage like
a treasure to her heart, she had remorse as well to deal with.
It had not been a healthy mix, and had resulted in Madame
Olivetti—plodding, dependable, and steeled with the requisite
measure of old-fashioned righteousness—being called up from
retirement. Together over the past month, with Yves cheerfully
ministering to both of them, they had fit an assortment of lost
or mislaid and overlooked pieces into the complex puzzle of
Lily's life.

One piece remained.

She was making little progress on the letter she was writing
to Monsieur Dupré, thinking how foolish the subterfuge since
Victor spoke English. What was it she wanted to say? Do you
remember me, Victor? Do you know that you have a daughter,
a child of immeasurable delight and confusion in her mother's
mind? Have you been masquerading as Monsieur Dupré, seques-
tering yourself in my house, avoiding the villagers, lying in my
bed, on the red couch, shuffling through my drawers, opening
the armoire and wondering why, amidst a jumble of crockery,
letters, and picture albums, there are eight dusty boxes of corn-

flakes? Have you been lifting up photographs, noticing—with joy and longing—Justine's transformation into you, her father?

No. Soon she would begin again, this time more simply: a brief greeting, confirmation of the date and time when they would meet—September the first at ten a.m.—a few pleasantries about the weather, the sea, and the state of her driveway. She had only to write, *Cher Monsieur Dupré*—but she let the pen and paper drop onto her lap. Alonso was creeping toward her, stealing across the flagstones, no unmanly peeps as he stalked her shell-pink toenail polish. Would he pounce? Would he sink those stiletto teeth into her flesh, grind her toes between his jaws, before she found her voice and screamed?

He froze instead, and Lily, feeling a stab of hunger, stood up and strolled from the dense shade under the awning into a dazzle of sunlight. She shaded her eyes. The cat cast a cold glance in her direction. She had shattered his advance; it had not been her toes he'd been hunting but a sparrow ill-advisedly pecking in the garden. The bird flitted away, then returned to alight on a clump of lavender, where it warbled joyfully. Alonso, harmless as a topiary cat, held his pose while Lily silently urged the small creature to cling to its branch or take flight. . . . Heedless, it hopped down in a dainty flutter of wings and feet, its fragile heart beating as Alonso streaked forward, launched himself in a flying pounce, and broke its neck.

Lily turned away and walked quickly into the house. Adèle was right, she'd been up here too long: Lily Crisp, a dead bird, and too many memories.

In the kitchen, she put together a lunch of cold fish soup with garlic *pistou* and croutons, vine-ripe tomatoes sliced and sprinkled with olive oil and fresh basil, a glass of white wine, half a baguette, and a wedge of Brie. Then she sat down to eat at the table on the terrace. The wind fidgeted and trembled, a restless companion who worried the pages of the book she was reading. It toyed with her hair, blew gold dust into her soup, the heat having drained from its gusts a more damaging mischief. She welcomed the distraction. She placed a napkin over the cheese; she chewed grit with the tomatoes. Her heart was stirred by revelations, confusion, an infinite number of possibilities.

Then she recalled, without pleasure, the picture albums stacked on the red couch and thought: I'll dust them off this afternoon and replace them in the armoire, below the cornflakes.

⎯⎯

If one climbed for an hour through the oaks above La Pierre Rouge, one could reach the top of the ridge and, breathless from the ascent and the radiant spread of turquoise sea, feel the dry, invigorating sweep of solitude. It was a sight that healed, that reduced, in its immensity, the trivial cares of a blinkered existence, for we are all blinkered in the deep and narrow channels of our lives. Seldom do we pop up for a peek at the greater world, life seething beyond the rim. "With perspective comes forgiveness," Lily's father used to instruct his teenage daughters over Sunday breakfast. Then he would turn to their mother and say (a bit snidely, Lily remembered), "Gladys, dear, what you lack is perspective." He made this pronouncement at other times, in other places: from behind his newspaper on weekday mornings; across a wineglass at the dinner table; through bedroom walls when he thought the girls were sleeping (Gladys Fern's slow burn of resentment fairly heating the plaster). What Lily drew was the only conclusion a young woman could: Her father had a mean streak and her mother excelled at forgiveness.

If so, then surely Lily, their daughter, could forgive herself.

A photograph slipped from between the pages of the album she had been dusting and drifted to the floor, like a feather swirling in the breeze, tipping up an edge as if to say: Take a look. I'm light. I can change your attitude. It had landed face-down on the floor, and when Lily stooped to pick it up and turned it over in her hands, and held it—transfixed—the fish soup she had eaten for lunch rose from her stomach and burst in a sour stream from her mouth. She ran to the kitchen, bent over the sink and retched and retched—garlic, fish, tomatoes, cheese—Oh, Paul, oh, Paul, she called to him, over and over, as she wiped her mouth with the back of her hand, then folded her arms across her breasts and, hugging herself, sank down onto the tiles. She leaned back against the cupboard, still clutching the photograph. She looked again. There was no mistake. . . .

She saw a young woman and a girl in matching white dresses, ruffles, and lace. They frolicked in the sand, their skirts lifted, their bare feet peeking out, the sun-pale sea not far from their toes. White-gloved hands clasped, blurred—perhaps swinging so the camera could not seize and hold them in its eye. They laughed into the sun, into the wind that swept back the dark hair of the woman whose snapping black eyes and wickedly charming upturned lips flirted with the camera.

Justine Lafond? But the clothes predated her.

The young girl's hair, streaming behind her, showed up white and smooth as watered silk. She had pale eyes. A high-bridged nose. High, sharp, handsome cheekbones. A mischievous, cocky, warm, beguiling, laughing mouth. She looked just like Lily's daughter.

But the picture had fallen from Paul's family album. Not Victor's.

Thirty-six

$\mathcal{M}$adame Moreau, seated in the corner of her sun-bright parlor, put on her glasses and squinted at the photograph.

"But of course," she said, "it is Giselle Godard. She is a child here, but there is no mistaking her. You see how she is beautiful?"

Lily had run down the hill from her house, thinking, How we complicate our lives; we take a speck of dust and blow it up into a mountain. Paul knew, or didn't know, but didn't care, and that was what mattered. He had a daughter beyond his dreams, brimming over with life's sweet gifts.... But after sixteen years without conceiving a child and then a creature so unlike them was born—how could she have hoped ... or imagined?

She had run down the hill to the Hotel de la Plage with the photograph clutched in her hand and her hair uncombed, knowing she would create a flurry of tuts and disapproval and affectionate concern when Adèle saw her and questioned, yet again, her mental well-being. Adèle's mother would not care; she had moved beyond such temporal concerns as a neat coiffure and displays of levelheadedness.

Lily had thought: Who can identify this child? And no sooner had she asked the question than she was on her feet and running down the hill toward Madame Moreau, who was eighty-five years old and might not have been born when these two lovely girls danced barefoot in the sand. Yet she held the history of an entire village in the ageless turnings of her mind, and saw into the past with eyes unable to discern her own daughter across the room, but which glimpsed, with absolute clarity, the wondrous accidents that have made us.

Lily blurted out, "I had no idea what Giselle looked like."

Adèle replied, with a slight sideways squint at Lily's mismatched shirt and shorts and lack of a hairdo, "How could you?"

Her mother, with shoulders squared and spine erect, barely touching the back of the armchair, made little chirping sounds as she sucked her teeth and surveyed the picture from atop her long nose, as if her eyes must don skis to schuss down the slope toward a faultless vision. Her skin smelled of gardenias crushed in the hot sun, an odor that conjured Justine Lafond, her cheek approaching Lily's, her bosom heaving with life's unpredictable furies.

"And the woman with the dark hair?" Lily asked.

Adèle tapped her ear with two fingers to let Lily know that her mother had not heard, so Lily spoke up loudly: "Is that Giselle's sister?"

"But certainly!" Madame Moreau cried. "That is Danielle Godard, Justine Lafond's mother. She is young here, married, of course, to Gérard Lafond—but she is not pregnant. That first year she was pregnant. She married him when she was sixteen, a fertile age, *non*?" Behind her spectacles, her black eyes twinkled. "And a husband with stamina! Within nine months she had produced a son—but such a son! God forgive her. Then three years later, a daughter, Justine. So this photo—it must have been taken between the births. But you see ... I wasn't born yet."

"And what about Giselle?" Lily said, but Madame Moreau, oblivious to the question, hurried on with her narrative.

"They were never a match, Monsieur and Madame Lafond. She drove him wild with her flirtations, no shame in that woman, all the men in the village, the baker, the butcher, the greengrocer: she wound them all around her finger. And then, when her daughter was fifteen years old, she ran off with a man who sold corsets. We had a little joke between us, Justine and I. 'I knew a girl who once had a mother who drove off with a man in a truck full of drawers. . . .' Monsieur Lafond was crazed. This was a man who had fallen, like a great lump, in love with his beautiful wife. And there was this handsome son of his lifting all the girls' skirts, including his sister's, and he, Gérard, a moral man to the bones—although not when it came to the bed, I have heard—would have none of that. So he summoned Giselle from St. Tropez to act as Justine's protectress.

"Hah!" She broke into husky chortles of laughter that reminded Lily of Justine Lafond, who used to laugh in just such a way when Lily had asked an impertinent question.

Adèle said to Lily, "*Chérie*, snap out of it. You must stop whatever this is you are doing. We don't see you for days, no visit, no apéritif, no explanations, no *dîner* . . . and then you burst into the hotel with this photograph as if it is burning your fingers. What has happened to my happy friend with her wonderful family?"

"I don't know," Lily responded in a daze. "I don't know, Adèle. But this photo—it could be my daughter."

Madame Moreau shouted to Adèle, who was perched on the arm of her chair, "What does she say?"

"Lily can see a resemblance, Mother—"

"Of course she can," the old woman broke in. "They are exactly alike. It is marvelous, no? How the blood carries the markers of this person who is dead, and *voilà*, in three generations she is born again—this whole delightful being who was once Giselle. I have seen it in my own daughter." She gestured behind her to indicate Adèle, who was standing in front of her. "She looks precisely as my husband's grandmother did. Precisely! One cannot mistake her. But Giselle . . . there were never such eyes and hair, and such legs, on the Lafond side of the family. It is no wonder, is it!" she exclaimed, stabbing a finger at Giselle's picture. "That nephew of hers took her to bed as fast as he could and then, in spite of himself—mad dog that he was—fell in love with her. Ah, such a scene up at the house after Justine married her American and sailed off to that place full of snakes and dry bushes. Her father and Paul alone with Giselle . . . well, you can imagine."

Lily said quietly and to no one in particular, "I did not know who my daughter looked like."

At the corner table, busy with bottles, ice, and a shaker, Adèle had made martinis for all of them. She handed them around.

"To the dead." Madame Moreau raised her glass in a toast. Lily saw that tears had leaked from her eyes and glistened on her powdered cheeks.

"To Paul, your husband," said Adèle.

"To my husband," Lily said, and dropped her glass on the carpet and began to weep as she had not wept when the officer stood in the doorway and Justine, almost eight then, asked if he had come for her mother's birthday party. He was dead, Paul was dead, Justine's father by blood and love and a Mexican dawn when he had planted the seed of his own immortality.

Adèle put down her drink, walked over to her friend, and held her against her breast for a very long time.

Before Lily's tears were spent, Madame Moreau finished her martini, took off her glasses, and closed her eyes.

Thirty-seven

The relief, solitary and appalling, overwhelmed her.

She sat. For three days she simply sat. In her bed. On the red couch. On a straight-backed chair at the long table. A somber sky and the patter of raindrops, like a troop of Alonsos scuttling across the roof, seemed to sanction her sitting.

In the evenings Yves held her and tried to relieve, with the soft comfort of words, the bitter ache in her heart. But she stared blankly into his eyes. Who was there to ask? Had Paul known? Surely he must have. But why, then, had he never said, "It's amazing, *non?* She looks just like Giselle."

Who was there to ask but the dead?

For three days Lily sat and mutely gazed through a shivering scrim of rain toward the sea.

Then the telephone rang and she decided to answer it, her life unfolding, swinging into the current and out of the eddy that had held her circling, like a hapless twig with no self-propulsion. One can sit forever and go mad, she thought as she eased herself off the red couch and strolled to the window, noting that a burst of windy sunshine had displaced the rain. She reached for the receiver, not quickly, a languid drooping of the wrist, the hand, to pick it up: smooth and boneless fingers, a head tipsy with deliverance. *"Allo? Allo?"* Her voice sang out shrilly, foolishly, and she began to laugh, to protest to whoever it was on the other end of the line—for no one had spoken—that she was sorry. *"Je suis desolée—"*

"Mother, what the hell is going on?" Pierre interrupted.

"Oh, my dear, I had no idea . . ."

She could not stop laughing.

"Look, Mother," he said, at a loss for how to handle her. Retreat into brusqueness signaled his confusion. "We're arriving on Tuesday. You know the flight? Will you be there?"

"Of course I'll be there," she exclaimed. "How's Justine? Excited? Intransigent?"

"Impossible."

"Good."

"She's all yours," he said.

I know. I know!

He said—shaking his head, she could see him, with his lips turned up in a reluctant smile, for his love for his sister was immense, unassailable—"I don't know where she came from, Mother. We cannot be related."

Lily answered him quietly, careful not to shout her joy, "Believe me, Pierre. You are."

Thirty-eight

And so they came, her children, and for three weeks the hefty stack of her memoirs lay hidden in the closet and Yves kept his distance. While Lily gave herself over to the long-awaited visit, Madame Olivetti dozed beneath her cashmere shawl. Lily imagined her dreaming of Yves, his maestro's touch and exquisite ease of lubrication, the way he had rolled her platen and gripped her bony flanks and lifted her and tipped her over, as if she were a lightweight newer model, molded of stardust and plastic. Madame Olivetti awoke once when Pierre typed a letter to Sara, a rather stilted love note, Lily suspected, compared to the graphic sexual mischief to which the type-writer had become accustomed. "Where's your laptop?" Pierre shouted at his mother. "Why are you typing on this old dino-saur? It takes forever. I keep making mistakes!"

One night Justine grabbed Madame Olivetti's shawl, wrapped it around her shoulders, and vamped, "Like Greta Garbo, Mom. D'ya ever hear of her?" on the foot of Lily's bed.

"You might put that back," Lily suggested mildly.

"No way. I think I'll keep it," drawled her daughter, playing the coquette, the shawl pulled up to cover her face until only her eyes were exposed.

"You might put it back now," Lily said again, quietly. "It keeps the dust out of the typewriter."

Surprised at the band of steel threading the affectionate tones of her mother's voice, Justine replaced the shawl without further protest. "You need to darn it, the shawl," was all she said.

And the tender balance between mother and daughter slightly shifted, without notice or fanfare.

Pierre was distracted during most of his visit, mooning over Sara and awash in hormones, monopolizing the phone. Attempting to cope with the sexual fulminations and brusqueness of her love-struck son, Lily was reminded again of love's intoxicating dance, each dip and twirl freshly discovered, each musical note—be it Puccini belted into the teeth of a storm or Yves's imaginary orchestra—vital in its magic. So she humored her son, and drank in the daily wonder of her daughter's face tipped up for a kiss, her voice bright and clear as an Idaho summer morning. "Hi, Mom. Sleep well? You look beautiful today," Justine tossed off briskly at breakfast, as if she was a grown-up now, before reverting the next instant to the petulant whine of childhood. "Can I take it back this time? Please? J.L.'s hat?"

"But it lives here, honey"—Lily's standard dismissal.

"Maybe it would like a trip to America," Justine suggested, not without a hint of preadolescent exasperation.

"The cornflakes will get lonely. We discussed it, remember?"

"Oh, screw the cornflakes."

"Justine! Where do you hear such language?"

"I'm sorry, Mom, okay? I get the message. But this is the thing, I love that hat. We can buy the cornflakes another hat, something more modern, bring them up-to-date. Before Daddy died you said I could keep it, but now you forgot. That's not fair."

"Honey, life isn't always fair."

Justine kept silent, wisely, while Lily recalled that this was a nine-year-old to whom she was speaking. In her daughter's mind, Lily had broken her word. Yet, she was reluctant to spirit the fedora out of the house, out of France, this last witness to Justine Lafond's youth, to Gérard Lafond's Sunday passion. To Giselle's hanging.

"Please, Mom," Justine pleaded in a small voice, no unreasonable request: simply an old hat that could stand a good cleaning.

Lily said, "We'll see."

⎯

She gave Justine the hat. In the end the good mother relented, although in the rush of leave-taking Justine had forgotten the hat on the mantelpiece. She had already phoned twice, from Idaho, to remind her mother. Feeling extraneous, useful only as the bearer of a hat, Lily glanced ruefully out the window to where her neighbors had appeared on the terrace below her. Alonso, looking chagrined, strained against a slender leash in Christine's left hand.

"Qu'est-ce qu'il a fait?" What has he done? Lily called down to her.

Christine tilted her chin upward and announced, with a warbling note of distress in her voice, "This naughty cat has made his breakfast on the last of Monsieur Léon's pet canaries."

"Are you certain Alonso was to blame?" Lily shouted as she hurried down the stairs to the plane tree beneath which they were standing: Jacques in a pressed white linen shirt and trousers, Christine in a sundress of some shimmering fabric that looked painted upon her shimmering skin.

Christine shrugged her shoulders, smooth and golden as a spill of molasses. *"Pauvre chat,"* she lamented, "it was the yellow feathers caught in his mouth that condemned him."

Jacques, the assiduous tender of eggplants and peppers, handed Lily a small oval basket filled with figs. "These look delicious," she said. "How kind you are."

"But you are a neighbor that one must treasure," he enthused. "We appreciate our good fortune. Around the corner, Monsieur Léon with his dreadful camping ground and his plumbing that stinks—"

"And his dreadful canaries!" Christine chimed in.

"And the mayor, with his damnable golf course! One values fine neighbors such as you, Lily. So calm, and everything so clean and well-ordered."

Lily thought with a sinking heart, How uninteresting and predictable, and middle-aged, he has made me sound.

"Your renter arrives when?" Christine inquired while administering a tug to Alonso's leash as he squatted, puppylike, to do his business in the flower bed.

"Tomorrow," Lily answered her. "You have met him?"

"Never. He arrives each year in September when we have already left for Brussels. Our paths do not cross, but Adèle has told me that he keeps to himself, an invisible man. She cannot say for certain that she has ever seen him."

Lily gave a short laugh. "Finally I shall meet him, my reclusive renter."

"Bonne chance!" Jacques said. Good luck!

"Bon voyage à vous," Lily wished them in return.

As they left, arm in arm, casting a final wave in Lily's direction, Alonso delivered a parting meow so plaintive that Lily considered rushing after them, wresting the leash from Christine's hand, and giving her comrade of so many hot, soul-wrenching afternoons his freedom. But, having found the strength to step back from the gross mismanagement of her own life, she could certainly step back from the reversal in fortunes of this killer cat, no matter how exquisite his sensibilities.

"Au revoir, Alonso," she called after him. May Monsieur Léon's canary rest well in your belly! We make our choices and, alas for you, alas for Lily Crisp, we must accept responsibility.

With a light heart, she ran up the steps to Giselle's garden. The sea had darkened, as if a giant's hand had swept across it and cast its shadow, although the sky held but a single cloud.

The cork oaks pulled their parched leaves closer, like knotted caps; no autumnal breeze cooled their ash-green foliage. No coastal wind blew in her direction the dusty sweet scent of sun-scorched bark. Seated on a lounge chair, her skirt pulled high across her thighs, she cut the moist flesh of a fig into petals, and sucked it from its skin. She was loath to release the summer's memories, for how could she be certain that Christine would ever again wave a long-fingered hand in her direction as Lily trudged, salt-sticky from a swim in the sea, up the hill? How could she be certain that Jacques would bend over his peppers, his knotty brown legs tensed beneath brief cotton shorts, his mouth twisted in profound disapproval as the thwack of golf balls wafted down the slopes on the wind? How could she be certain that Alonso would survive the winter, not be taken in the jaws of a large Belgian dog and crunched, a high-protein meal for a hungry canine (just as a pet canary had served as breakfast for a hungry cat)? How could she be certain that she would return to this garden where the traces of a love built on longing and persistence—on Giselle's surrender—still glinted like gold dust in the sunshine?

⸺

Yves came to her that evening, their last evening together, bringing with him *clafouti aux myrtilles* that his mother had made especially for Lily.

"Why this change of heart?" Lily asked with a mixture of surprise and amusement.

"These mothers," he grumbled. "As they age, they get craftier and wiser."

"Oh," she said. "Do we?"

They lay naked on her bed, the swarthy forest of the Maures spread below them like a mounded sheet of green velvet, the sea as mesmerizing in its movements as the flames of a fire, leaping and brooding. As always the play of light and shadow on the water worked as a relaxant on Lily's mind, washed clarity through it. She rolled toward Yves, curling into his body.

"You were dreaming when I came here," he told her.

"I was sleeping."

"You were smiling."

"I was dreaming of Paul humming Mozart in China."

"Humming Mozart?"

"Yes." She ran her fingers through his hair and touched her lips to his. "Do you think you can release someone, Yves, without ever letting go?"

"Your husband?"

"Yes."

"I am sure of it."

"So am I. Now I am sure. It just takes time."

"Why China?" he asked.

"I don't know," she sighed. "Maybe that's why I was smiling."

Calm. *Du calme.* Where had it come from, this beneficent calm? From Yves's loving? Had he gentled the pain of Paul's loss right out of her? Had his spectral orchestra seduced her back to health? The strings weeping for her, the woodwinds taking over the pathos, the brass cheering, the percussion announcing the arrival and departure of death on his pale horse, the hiss and rattle of bones. Had Yves with his toolbox of possibilities *tap-tapped* on her skeleton, vibrated her muscles, warmed the stiffness in her ligaments, lubricated her tender workings and set her adrift on this quiet music? This calm?

"Tell me, are you done now, Lily?" he said. "Now that your children are gone and you are leaving in the morning, have you finished your remembering?"

"Yes."

"Do you feel much better?"

"I feel empty and full at the same time."

"This is not a bad way to feel."

"No," she conceded. "I don't want to bore you, Yves. Tell me your plans. Have you made plans?" she asked and nodded, smiling, as if he had already told her.

"I will send you cases of pâté de foie gras from the Perigord," he choked out over the rising lump in his throat. She patted his cheek to hide her confusion and the depth of her affection, recalling Victor's speech about love being a stolen season, how it was damn sweet while you were living it. With Yves, yes, it had been sweet. But Victor had been mistaken, for love remained, unaltered, regardless of separation, be that parting as sudden and final as Paul's heart that stopped beating, or Yves springing nimbly up from the bed.

He began to dress.

"So you're off then?" she asked.

"Yes."

"And your mother?"

He pulled on his trousers, held them open, gave a little hop to settle his shirttails, and zipped up his fly. He buckled his belt and bent down to pull on his socks and boots. He laced the boots up carefully. Then he cleared his throat and said, "I am taking her with me."

"After all your tough talk . . . ?"

"After all my tough talk."

He swept the unruly lock of hair from his forehead and put on his cap and then spun around, like a stolid soldier overcome by sentiment—he had finished with his mending—and marched onto the porch and down the steps to the terrace, where he turned only once, not to wave but look back at the old house.

Lily watched the space grow empty where Yves had turned and looked.

Late that same night, when the sky arched over La Pierre
Rouge like a black satin canopy studded with diamonds, Lily
knelt on the hearth in the living room. She touched a match
to a nest of newspapers crumpled beneath a lattice of kindling,
which flared up, lighting thin strips of pine and oak logs hard
and heavy as metal. The fire cast crackling shadows and licks of
orange light across the rough stone walls. She was in no hurry.
She tossed handfuls of paper into the fireplace and watched the
pages curl up and char and burn. She poured herself a glass of
white wine and sipped it at intervals. She took a seat on the
red couch beside Madame Olivetti, carried downstairs for the
occasion, and looked into the fire. Every now and then, when
the flames had consumed one portion of her life, she fed them
another. If she had been asked to describe the scene, admittedly
Gothic—the stone-walled room, no light beyond tongues of
flame licking up memories as if they were sweet sap and honey,
a barefoot woman dressed in a sarong knotted across her breasts
and an old woolen cardigan, and a typewriter regally ensconced
on a red cushion as if she were a queen invited to a bonfire—
Lily would have mentioned Light. Lighter. Lightness. None of
which were in evidence that night (discounting the firelight and
the stars), except to Lily and perhaps, if inanimate objects have
something approaching a soul, to Madame Olivetti.

Thirty-nine

The alarm clock sounded: flute and strings in a Haydn concerto. Lily rolled out of bed, stretched, pulled on shorts and a T-shirt, laced up her running shoes, and set off down the hill as if today were a day like any other; as if at ten o'clock a spit-shined Peugeot, Victor at the wheel, would not jerk in low gear up the rutted road; as if at noon, she would not slip into the driver's seat of her rental car and leave behind her the old stone house that had been her sanctuary.

Her legs carried her alongside the oleanders blooming brighter now that the army of tourists had swung north toward new battles; past the steam-clouded light in the baker's window; past the hairdresser's shop that in mid-October would close for the season—at no great loss to Adèle, who had once patronized the woman and wound up with hair "sheared like grass on a putting green," she had told Lily. She jogged by the faded towels and sorry beach balls—tail end of the stock—in Monsieur Bibot's swim shop window. Madame Bibot had gone to Hyères to live with her mother. "But not forever," she had confided in Adèle. "I only give him the opportunity to cook dinner for himself. At his age he will soon discover that sex is not as filling as a good potage. And then he will miss me."

Smooth and summer-warmed, the sea invited Lily in for a good-bye dip. She told it she would swim later, after she had run the length of the near-empty beach where so many voices had dinned and children had built their castles, and breasts had been bared. Admittedly, she was not as carefree as Adèle might have supposed had she seen her lope by. But it was not her friend who swept the clay tiles on this fine first-of-September morning. Mathilde, a hotel maid, broad-shouldered and aggressive, though sluggish at this hour and dawdling with her broom, slowly circled the terrace as Lily's thoughts circled Victor.

What was it she felt? So little in the end. A tweak of curiosity, for he had been a most ardent and elegant lover. A tremendous weight lifted. He had been a bit player in Paul's life, as he would have been in hers, except for Justine. That was the beginning and the end of the story. What remained were ashes of the finest sort; blow softly and they would vanish.

Lily swung onto the sidewalk midway down the beach and sprinted back to the Hotel de la Plage for a quick swim, then a dash homeward. Time grew short; she had yet to finish her packing. As she climbed the steep hill past Monsieur Léon's campground, she mourned for Alonso and the bright dead canary. The crowds had thinned, caravans no longer choked the field, Monsiuer Léon would have empty pockets next Friday at the disco.

At the corner where she stepped from pavement to dirt and into a pothole, Lily glanced up at the Belgians' house: lime-green shutters fastened against prowlers and winter storms, pink walls shiny as the lip of a conch shell in sunlight, the striped awning dismantled and carried inside, where Lily imagined it rolled up and wrapped in sheets on the red tile floor. The garden bloomed on. An old woman down the road would harvest the vegetables and share them with her granddaughter.

Returned to her house, Lily made a hurried breakfast of figs and yogurt, took a quick shower, slapped together her toilette, and pulled a knee-length shift of salmon-colored linen over her head. The dress neatly capped her shoulders, revealed a provocative swell of breast, and flowed pertly over her hips. She looked clean and crisp. "Crisp?" Paul would have queried with a grin. "No pun intended?"

She finished off her outfit with a pair of three-inch-high heels, just for the hell of it.

Fifteen minutes later, at ten o'clock on the dot, the hum of an engine pulling steadily up the potholed driveway carried in through the bedroom window.

———

A mustache arced handsomely over his upper lip. He cut a relaxed figure, dressed in black jeans and a pressed blue shirt open at the neck, a cashmere sweater tied over his shoulders. He wore sandals, without socks. His hair, worn long and flecked with silver, was casually tucked behind his ears. He slammed the door of his Peugeot behind him and strolled toward Lily, smiling widely with the easy welcome of an old friend. There was a sparkle in his eyes, and the jaunty mustache.

He was not Victor.

"Bonjour, Madame. Enchanté de faire votre connaissance. Enfin."

"Monsieur Dupré. It's nice to meet you," Lily said, smoothing the shock from her voice. She spoke to him in English.

He smiled, and might have gone on to explain himself fully but for Lily offering him—prematurely in the course of their meeting, but she was clearly at a loss, tongue-tied in the aftermath of his not being Victor—a cup of tea or coffee or a glass of lemonade. "It's a long way to come," she insisted.

But he waved aside her offer and tendered his condolences. "Only this past June did I learn of your husband's death. You didn't write, no one told me. The moment I heard the news I telephoned your house in Idaho and spoke with—"

"My daughter," Lily interjected with a small grin. "In English. Why did you—"

"Write in French?" he countered in English, looking equally amused. "Because I *am* French. To write in one's own language is so much easier. But I admit," he conceded, "it *was* a long drive. Would a cognac be possible?"

"Mais oui," she said and walked into the living room and poured one for him—one for herself—and then led him onto the terrace, where he eyed the two lounge chairs spaced widely apart. With a polite cough, he pulled his chair closer, to a conversational distance, and seated himself sideways on the edge of the cushion. Lily reclined on her chaise, feet up. The minutes ticked by. They sipped their cognacs. The sparkle in his eyes invaded his smile as they talked about their lives with a growing ease. After a while Lily was glad to be wearing daytime décolleté and hooker's heels.

She did not ask him about the panties under the red couch, or in the lavender.

An hour passed quickly, and she realized, with regret, that soon she must be on her way. There were last-minute details, instructions—

"This will be my tenth visit to your house," he interrupted politely. "I need few instructions."

"Of course not," she responded as he rose to his feet, reached over and pulled her upright, lifted her hand to his lips, and kissed it. She was his, for life. She would not tell him, if he asked, that Pierre had requested the house in September. She heard herself say, "September is your month, Monsieur Dupré, as long as you wish to come here."

"Ah, Madame," he said. "*Merci.* You are so kind. This is something about which I had planned to speak, but the cognac . . . and the sun and the garden . . . our meeting. I have been so enchanted, I forgot some news of great importance. Next year at this time I am going to marry."

"Marry!"

"Perhaps you suspected?"

"Not at all. I'm surprised." Intrigued as pieces of the puzzle seemed to fall into place, she asked, "Is she Spanish?"

"I understand," he said at once, with a delighted smile. "My trip to Spain, to Alicante? So unexpected?"

"Exactly."

"No. Renée is Parisian. You see, I work all the time, she complains of course, who would not? So I decided to surprise her with a romantic trip to Spain."

"I would never have thought . . ." They were standing face-to-face, too close for a comfortable dialogue. As if aware of her discomfort, Monsieur Dupré took one long step backward.

"One does not expect such spontaneity from a banker. Is that it? And from you, Madame, what does one expect?"

Lily smiled broadly. "No surprises."

"I doubt this. You have surprised me."

"How?"

"From the photographs, I had no idea of your beauty."

Waving away his compliment, Lily reverted to their previous topic. "Was she here? Was your fiancée here? A few years ago I found—"

He interrupted her. "I am so sorry, I apologize. I did not want to upset you. It is I, a bachelor, a quiet man, to whom you entrust your house, not to lovers. I thought . . . we keep to ourselves, we do not dine locally, no one will know."

"It's fine," she told him. "It's not a problem."

"Unfortunately it is, for Renée. She would prefer Spain, she has told me, in September."

"Spain? Why Spain?"

"There's a harshness to the country that appeals to her nature. It puts you on alert, she says. Even the food puts you on alert. I too enjoy it. I have a friend there. . . ." And at this he smiled. He could see that Lily was stunned by his disclosures, and so he said very quietly, very gently, in French, as though he had not intended to let this slip, *"Je crois que vous le connaissez. Il s'appelle Victor."* I believe that you know him. His name is Victor.

Forty

Lily stood frozen, as Alonso stood frozen when he had spied, out of the corner of his eye, the twitch of a mouse's tail or a bird's wing.

Monsieur Dupré said, "I have more to confess. . . ."

But Lily held up her hands, open-palmed, and said with a touch of asperity, "Why didn't you tell me you knew Victor?"

"I will explain it all, Madame. If you please, sit down. I will be quick." He resumed his seat, as did Lily. She gave him her full attention. "Once again," he said, with a note of rueful apology in his voice, "I must beg your understanding. Victor and I have been friends for many years, since we studied together at the Sorbonne in Paris. In those early days we were two young men eager for adventure. We climbed, we hiked, we kayaked—we were always going somewhere. Over the years we never lost touch, and still, when we meet, we speak frankly. Your brief friendship, Madame—it meant a lot to Victor. This is my inter-pretation, not his, you understand? But due to circumstances neither of you had foreseen, you separated without . . . an ac-ceptable closure."

"It was acceptable to me," Lily said quietly.

"*Oui. D'accord.* Of course," he assured her. "But we have little time before you leave and I must tell you now, Madame, that it was Victor who noticed your advertisement in the *International Herald Tribune*, which he reads every day. La Pierre Rouge, the Red Stone—this is not a common name for a house, there can-not be many. He remembered the story you had told him and so he telephoned me. 'Philippe,' he said, 'I have found your September getaway. You must write to this address.' I did. I wrote to you in Idaho, which I searched for on the map—it is famous, is it not, for its potatoes? You replied with such promptness, in such excellent French, I was thrilled with my good fortune."

She gave a curt nod. "Has he been here? Has he stayed in this house?"

"Victor?"

"Yes."

"Jamais."

"Never? You are certain?"

He answered quite forcefully, "I will tell you this. Victor may have a weak spot for the ladies but he is not without integrity."

And Lily laughed. She laughed long and heartily, tipping back her head and looking up into a sky so clear and blue it could have been Idaho—Paul's sky—and releasing with her laughter all the misconceptions and doubts and the unnecessary dither she had worked herself into. With Monsieur Léon's campground at the foot of the hill, there must be plenty of tall blond Germans walking up her road.

An expression of amusement crinkled the corners of Monsieur Dupré's eyes as he remarked, "I have made you laugh. Renée does not laugh in such a way. With such openness."

"That's probably a relief to both of you," Lily said, with a wry grin. "Does she come every year?"

"She has joined me here a number of times, but I have grown attached to my days and nights alone in this house . . . with your family, whom I follow through the gallery of pictures always changing on your desk. I feel protective, you understand. For the past two years I have come here without her, with a tall stack of books and bathing trunks instead. She labors to understand me but it is simple. I have lived alone for so long, I enjoy my solitude."

"As do I."

He dipped his head in recognition. "Please, call me Philippe."

Lily said, laughing, "I'm not sure that will be possible."

He smiled warmly, then glanced at his watch and rose to his feet, leaning over to pull her from her chair—not an easy task, levering up a woman wearing three-inch heels. She flicked off her shoes. He said as he whisked her upright, "Victor has sent you a message."

Not until she was standing barefooted and solidly planted on the flagstones did she ask, "What is the message?"

"He said to tell you that he has not forgotten, he owes you three days in the hot sun. Three days on the beach. You are welcome to collect them at any time, anywhere. . . ." He broke off, stepped forward, and kissed her on both cheeks. "I do not mean to presume," he said, "but it is warm and sunny and quite romantic, Renée and I found—in Denia."

Epilogue

*L*ily no longer lived on the ranch in Idaho, where Pierre and Sara had been filling the rooms of the log château with strapping, rambunctious children. Nine months after her son's September wedding—a year after Monsieur Dupré had canceled his marriage for unspecified reasons—Lily's first grandchild was born. Jane had Sara's squat build, her clear gray eyes and raven hair, but the Lafond nose; that particular French gene proved unquenchable. When two years later a second daughter, Giselle, was born with wisps of pale hair and blue eyes, there was much laughter but no cause for speculation. Pierre never questioned what blond-haired, blue-eyed milkman his wife had slept with.

Twice a year, when Justine was on school holiday, she and her mother flew from France to visit Pierre and his growing family. Fourteen years old and as tall as Lily, Justine was as self-possessed and outspoken as had been her namesake, her grandmother. She delighted in her young nieces, entertaining them for hours with puppet plays and costume dramas. But she awaited, with impatience, the birth of a nephew. "Chances are it'll be another girl," Sara told her.

But Justine did not waver. "It'll be a boy," she insisted. "I just know it. But what will you name him?"

"If it's a boy we'll call him Paul," Sara said gently, "after your father."

Often Justine, wearing her battered gray fedora, accompanied her mother to the base of the tall cliffs where they had scattered

Paul's ashes. As evening drew on, the rocks turned green-gold in the sunset glow and the sky was swept with glitter. Squinting up at the cliffs, drenched in yellow light, mother and daughter sat side by side on a wide, flat rock that jutted out from the sagebrush. They told each other stories, mostly about Paul. Invariably Lily's laughter called forth a mixed bag of memories, while Justine's husky giggle suggested that she knew far more than a young girl should, as if Justine Lafond, unable in this instance to pass on her nose, had passed on her chuckle.

Lily found this whimsical evidence of life's continuum deeply comforting.

Lily did not take Victor up on his offer, although she wrote to him, and from time to time received an answer. He was kept busy by his work, he explained, and a burdensome number of amorous entanglements. One July when he was passing through France, he paid her a visit. His skin was toasted brown as a Spaniard's, his pale hair pulled back in a ponytail. He wore wrinkled shorts and a wrinkled shirt—"So you'd recognize me," he informed her, grinning.

But that insouciant edge, that irreverent spark that had first attracted her, had lost its singular magic. Victor, too, seemed content with friendship, even relieved when she made no mention of love or commitment or intimate memories. They laughed over Justine, who said to Victor, "So—are you Mom's old boyfriend?"

"Would that I were," he replied, ruffling her short blond hair as he and Lily exchanged a smile.

It was in Victor's small house in Denia—his shed, he called it—that Lily typed the postscript to her story, for old time's sake on Madame Olivetti. Through the open window she watched as sunlight poured into the transparent sea and inked its waters a pale turquoise. Justine buried Victor, limb by limb, in the wet sand. He lay motionless, eyes closed, smiling serenely, while inside the house Philippe Dupré, sun-warmed from the beach, snuck up behind Lily and planted a kiss that tickled on the back of her neck. "*Rien ne soulage comme un aveu sincère.* A frank confession is good for the soul," he whispered in her ear.

Once a year Philippe brought up the subject of marriage, and once a year, reconsidering his offer, Lily graciously declined it. "Why don't you just marry the guy?" Justine urged her mother in ill-concealed bouts of frustration. What chance was there of finding more than one man in the world who would consent to being served, and devour with such lavish delight, napoleons for breakfast?

Pierre said, "You get that cowboy to make an honest woman of you, Mother."

Still, on certain nights, although she slept in Philippe's arms, she dreamed that she was digging toward China, and if she dug deep enough and long enough she would find Paul alive, wearing blue pajamas and humming Mozart in Beijing. So she said to her children, as their father had once said to her, long ago, over the telephone, when she had asked him to marry her, "Whoa there, Macduff. What's the hurry?"

She heard nothing from Yves, although one summer a case of pâté de foie gras arrived on her doorstep. The stamps were French, but there was no return address and the postmark was illegible. After that, she took to driving past his house on a more frequent basis, opting for the sea route—she told herself it was more scenic, and Justine enjoyed her horrific daily viewing of topless bathers with their breasts "just out there flapping in the breeze, for the whole *world* to see! My *God*, Mom!" The windows were shuttered, the steps up to the front door denuded of earthenware pots and scarlet geraniums. The house had a look of abandonment, as if no one had lived there for centuries.

"It's odd," Lily told Adèle. "It's so lifeless and empty."

Adèle raised an inquiring eyebrow, but as was her wont

showed little interest—although this was not a large village, and Yves and his mother were not strangers to their neighbors.

But from that time onward, twelve jars of pâté de foie gras notwithstanding, Lily could not get the notion out of her head—Antonio's black hair, Paul's intractable waistline, his zest in bed, the Lafond nose, a mother who kept her son afloat with her imaginative cookery—had she made Yves up? Adèle's amusement was edged with quiet horror when Lily asked (admittedly after a second martini) if Yves had ever existed.

It was Madame Moreau, ninety years old and still enjoying her cocktails, who trumpeted the answer through the walls, down the hallway, and into the guests' lounge of the Hotel de la Plage. "That summer we watched the smile grow back on your face. And your roof does not leak. It is mended."

Photo by Bill Vanderbilt

Annie Vanderbilt graduated from Radcliffe College and has been a Peace Corps volunteer in India, a leader of wilderness programs for high school students, a co-owner of a ski touring company in Idaho, and a round-the-world bicyclist. Her writing has been published in several magazines. She lives with her husband on an island in Florida and in the mountains of Idaho.

The Secret Papers of Madame Olivetti

Annie Vanderbilt

This Conversation Guide is intended to enrich the
individual reading experience, as well as encourage us
to explore these topics together—because books,
and life, are meant for sharing.

A CONVERSATION
WITH ANNIE VANDERBILT

Q. This is your first novel. What inspired it in particular and why did you wait to write your first novel in, let us say, the second half of your life rather than the first?

A. Actually, I wrote my first novel twenty-five years ago. In 1983, just after I finished it (or thought I had finished it—in retrospect, it was a first draft and needed many rewrites or a quick trip to the shredder), I fell off a cliff. That accident stopped my writing life cold; all my creative energies went toward healing my foot and being able to walk again. Unfortunately (or fortunately), the only copy of the manuscript burned up along with our house in 2005, so I won't be doing any of those revisions.

I then wrote a book, as yet unpublished, about bicycling through Japan with my husband, Bill, interweaving our adventures on wheels with the tale of my fall from the cliff, my survival and recovery. A good friend and freelance editor worked with me on this book and it was through her critical eye and heart-stopping honesty (she never hesitated to write *Yuck, Trite, You can do better*, or *This makes me swoon*) that I honed my skills. When I was fifty-one (one year younger than Lily), I finished the Japan book and immediately began writing *The Secret Papers of Madame Olivetti*.

It took ten years. I was leading a three-part life at the time and trying to achieve some sort of balance. I was writing a novel because Lily Crisp just popped out on the page one day, and then Paul and Victor and finally Yves and all the others, and it gave me such pleasure to tell their story and spend time with them. During those same years my sister and I were care-giving an elderly aunt and my parents and seeing them, one after the other, into death. And finally, I was trying to keep some fun and spice in my marriage by joining my husband, Bill, on some of the backcountry and overseas adventures we have always enjoyed together. So I would be partway through a draft of the book and then there would be a health-care crisis with my mother or a monthlong expedition to some mountain in Bolivia or jungle river in Honduras. By the time I returned I would pick up the thread of plot and characters and find that I had changed, that I had new insights from my adventures or caregiving, so the book changed, too. It was never a smooth, clean reentry; I moved backward before I could move forward again. All this took time, none of which I regret, because when you write a novel in your fifties, you have more perspective on life (you hope) and can let the vo-luptuous side of living and loving take center stage.

Q. What did you hope to achieve in writing The Secret Papers of Madame Olivetti?

A. When I began working on this book, I wanted to take the readers' senses and immerse them in the landscapes in which the story takes place: lakeside Wisconsin; a French village on the Côte d'Azur; the rain forest in Chiapas, Mexico; the stark Idaho hills. I saw the scenes, smelled them, and felt them, and then tried to paint those sensations in words. Within this framework I envisaged a plot that was densely layered, moving fluidly between past and present, so that a delicious soup of intrigue, lushness, passion, disaster, humor, and quirkiness would enhance the background flavors of my settings. Long-term married love, romantic love, sexual love, parental and sibling love, the loss of a loved one—all these interest me and went into the mix. I created Lily Crisp, a strong and yet vulnerable woman who would wind her way through this often messy labyrinth of love and death and emerge, in her own imperfect way, with a clearer understanding of the fragility and resilience of human nature.

Q. As you mentioned, the novel has several distinct settings. Are you as well traveled as your knowledge of all these places would suggest? Do you have a personal connection to any of these places?

A. Bill and I started going on adventures from the day we were married. We began in the Peace Corps in India in 1968, then backpacked to Everest Base Camp in Nepal in 1972 and managed after that to sandwich wilderness and overseas adventures into our lives for the next thirty-five years.

I have a personal connection to all the places about which I write. I grew up in Wisconsin and spent my summers in a rustic two-room pine cabin that belonged to my aunt. Every day I swam across the lake towing the canoe behind me so no motorboats would run me down. And yes, our neighbor scattered her husband's ashes in the lake and my sister and I would snorkel the shoreline in a state of titillation and horror. I've lived in Idaho for the past twenty-five years and know the dry sagebrush hills and open-sky landscape from hiking and biking the trails and back roads and waking up every morning to that clear, high-altitude sunshine. As for France, my husband and I have bicycled across the south of France three times and, in 1980, lived for three months in an old stone house overlooking the sea. The village and the warm waters of the Mediterranean lay below us, through the cork oaks. Finally, Mexico. We spent two winters living and working in Chiapas, in San Cristóbal de las Casas. Every month or so we would drive to the rain forest and camp beside the hut of a Lacandón friend. Often we have walked to the *cascada*, slipped through the sheet of water, and stood with our backs against the cool rock wall where Victor and Lily exchange their first kiss. These are my experiences. But in *The Secret Papers of Madame Olivetti* most of the specifics and all of the characters and what happens in these locations are imaginary. I had great fodder for the mill and loved dragging aromas, landscapes, birdcalls—you name it, I dragged it—out of my memory.

Q. The typewriter on which Lily writes her memoirs becomes a sort of character in the novel, and in fact the novel is titled after her. What inspired Madame Olivetti?

A. When I wrote my first book (the one that burned up in the house fire), I typed part of it on an Olivetti Lettera 32 Portable that my mother sent to the house in France where I was writing at the time. It was laborious work, lots of thunk-ing and clicking of the keys, lots of mistakes, lots of cut and paste. But I became quite attached not only to the slow pro-cess of creating on a typewriter but to the machine itself. It had character and tooth. I lost my Olivetti in the fire, but it was alive and well and sleeping in the closet all those years of working on this book.

Q. *Why is the cat Alonso in the story?*

A. Alonso mirrors Lily. Both are sensual creatures who enjoy their meals. Both fiercely guard their independence but love deeply. Both relish their solitude but welcome company on a selective basis. Both wander off and misbehave but have gentle, loyal hearts. Plus—any woman who can have a close and satisfying relationship with a cat and a typewriter is the kind of woman I would want to know and write about.

Q. *I found Lily Crisp to be a complex and fascinating woman—and one of the sexiest female protagonists I've come across in some time. She is very much a physical being, completely comfortable in her own skin. There are also times when she seems fearless—willing to commit herself wholeheartedly to relationships with men she loves, even when she hasn't known them for very long. What about her particularly interested you—or is she based on you?*

A. I certainly don't have Lily's bizarre way of dealing with loss through self-violence of one sort or another, nor do I see my life as a muddle. I would have told Paul the truth and risked losing him rather than hold it all inside. Lily keeps her secrets. I wear my heart on my sleeve. But both of us savor good food, believe in passion and romance in life, love to travel, and can laugh at ourselves.

I wanted to write about a woman who was comfortable with her sexuality, a naturally erotic but not neurotic being, who could love deeply and was a good mother and wife, sister and daughter, but who had a quirky, off-the-cuff, solitary side to her. I love the complexities and contradictions in people: hence, Lily's combination of fearlessness and vulnerability, her ability to jump into experience, sexual or otherwise, and then take responsibility for her misbehaviors and misjudgments. I was interested in a woman who is earthy and grounded but who makes mistakes and at times is her own worst enemy. Yet with her lusty sense of humor, her recognition of her own inadequacies without whining about them, and her ability to forgive both others and herself, she always manages to get back on keel and sail onward.

Q. In her early fifties, two years after her husband's death, Lily is taking some time to reassess her life. In your experience, do most women go through a period of reassessment at some point in their lives?

A. I think that most women, as well as most men, go through periods of reassessment in their lives. Many of us require time alone to do this, although most of us don't have the luxury of retiring to France with our typewriters (and a sexy, empathetic handyman) for five weeks. Especially in our fifties, when the future is still uphill but the downhill stretch is alarmingly visible—not over but on the horizon—many of my friends and I have felt the need to step back and gain perspective on our lives and priorities. Sometimes the only way we can chart where we're headed, or might choose to head, is to take a look at where we've been, as Lily does in typing out her memories and recounting them to Yves. It's so easy to zip along in life and suddenly, since time moves exponentially faster with age, you're not fifty but seventy and you haven't stopped once to ask, Who the hell am I, and is this what I want to be doing? Do I still want to drag out the same old whips and beat myself up because I made some mistake or misspoke? Do I still want to keep my pleaser tag lit up in neon and hanging around my neck? Do I still want to say no, no, instead of ripping off my clothes and diving naked into the water?

Q. I'm curious about your reading habits. Do you find the time to read? Have you ever been part of a book club or reading group? Is there a list of books that you feel have particularly influenced your life or helped shape you as a writer?

A. I have always read voraciously. For me, reading is one of life's great pleasures, along with fine dark chocolate devoured on a daily basis and walking on a beach or in the mountains or even down the street and back. I have been in the same book club, called Qui Legit, for the past fifteen years. We read books that "have stood the test of time," including classics as well as recent novels. We allow gossip with soup before the discussion begins but then try to keep to the book. Since we have no leader, we each try to read critically and guide the discussion into interesting channels. Over the years we have bonded in a very special way through discussing books. We now have a shared memory of 180 books we have read and talked about.

The books that have resonated for me are *The Lover* by Marguerite Duras, because of the lush, atmospheric landscape laced with the eroticism of the love affair; *The Leopard* by G. di Lampedusa, because of the painterly sensual quality of his writing; *The English Patient* by Michael Ondaatje, because of the remarkable sense of place, both in the ruined villa and the desert, and the intensity and poignancy of the love stories; and *Kalimantaan* by C. S. Godshalk, because of the humid, dripping, heated sensuous jungle atmosphere and the strange turnings of love.

Sound familiar?

QUESTIONS
FOR DISCUSSION

1. If each of our lives is a train on which we are riding and we are looking out the window at events as they pass by, we sometimes get stuck on the same window. Lily says to Paul when she suggests they move to Idaho, "Don't you think it's time the train moved on? For both of us?" In choosing to spend a summer in France and type out her memories, Lily has recognized that she is stuck on the window of grief and remorse. Discovering that Paul is Justine's biological father obviously helps her to become "unstuck." But what other experiences and discoveries help her to move on? How does Lily mend herself?

2. Lily is at ease with her own sexuality, evidenced in her movements, in her appreciation of the bread and produce of the village, in her love of the sea, in her love affair with Yves, which is short term and, thus, light on the soul. Her life has been largely defined by her physical/sensual responses. Do you feel any kinship with Lily in this regard? What traits do all of Lily's men share? What separates Paul from the rest? Do you value or fantasize about any or all of these traits in a partner? What does Lily's choice of men say about Lily? Do

you think that her sexuality is her undoing, or does it add to her strength and ability to roll with the punches?

3. Lily is very interested in the women in her family, and in her husband's family, who have come before her. Why do you think the author has put Lily in the context of several generations of women's romantic and sexual lives?

4. When Lily drives off in Paul's truck to work through her disappointment after he has reneged on her birthday trip to Rome, Lily says to herself, "Welcome to the Club of Disappointment, and then count your blessings." What does she mean by this? Is this a realistic and helpful concept for getting through the difficult times in any close relationship? Did it resonate in any way with your own experience of working through disappointment?

5. How does a woman forgive a sister who has married the man she loves, basically stealing him away from under her own sister's nose? Many siblings would harbor resentments for the rest of their lives over such a betrayal. How does Lily manage to release her anger, forgive Phila, and continue loving her sister? Could you do the same?

6. Why does Paul choose not to confront Lily about her affair with Victor? Does he accept equal responsibility for the breakdown in their marriage? Does he recognize the severity and the consequences of that breakdown? What traits does Paul possess that allow him to deal with what he suspects or knows about Lily's infidelity and Justine's parentage?

7. Why doesn't Lily tell Paul the truth about Victor and share her doubts about who fathered Justine? Clearly she has not moved through her guilt, although, after Justine's birth, her family life and marriage are deeply satisfying. Would telling Paul the truth have been a healthier way to deal with the situation? Would you have told Paul what happened? Do you think he wanted to be told?

8. What is the glue that holds Lily and Paul together despite their obvious differences? How do their interests and personalities complement each other so that the marriage works? What insights does this provide into long-term relationships?

9. The author moves back and forth between present and past. What are some of the devices she uses to make these shifts in time flow smoothly? How does she ground the novel in the present, in a village in France, so that when Lily returns from her memories you know she is back in La Pierre Rouge? Which characters in the village, be they inanimate, animal, or human, did you most enjoy?

10. Is Yves simply a mender of broken roof tiles and hearts, or does he play a larger role in Lily's story?

11. Annie Vanderbilt's writing has been called evocative and lyrical. Are there specific sentences or passages in the book that drew you into an exotic setting, be it a landscape, a meal, or a romantic encounter, so that you could see and smell, touch and feel Lily's surroundings and experiences? Are there lyrical passages that beg to be read out loud?

12. Often what you remember after reading a novel is not the details but the universal truths and revelations that relate to your own life. What are the themes in this novel that resonate for you? Are there specific passages that, when you read them, made you pause and think, I've been there, or, That is so true?

13. In Qui Legit, the book club to which the author belongs, she has fallen into the role of reading the last sentence or paragraph of the chosen novel out loud and giving her opinion on why she thinks it's a good ending or a fizzle, a fabulous or a weak last line. If she is not at the meeting, one of the other Qui Legit members reads the last sentence and then they discuss what Annie would have said about the ending. What do you think about the ending and the last sentence of this novel?